Praise for *White Trash Warlock*

"The complex worldbuilding, well-shaded depictions of poverty, emotional nuance, and thrilling action sequences make this stand out. Slayton is sure to win plenty of fans."

—*PUBLISHERS WEEKLY* (STARRED REVIEW)

"*White Trash Warlock* is one helluva ride! Adam Binder is a compelling, deeply relatable protagonist, and the journey he leads us on is dazzling and wonderfully original. What David R. Slayton does with class, sexuality, race, and magic creates an immersive world I didn't want to leave. Kudos!"

—LYNN FLEWELLING, AUTHOR OF
THE NIGHTRUNNER SERIES AND THE TAMÍR TRIAD

"Edgy and addicting, David R. Slayton's stunning debut will grab hold of you and knock you around just because it can. But before it's all over, it'll leave you breathless and begging for more."

—DARYNDA JONES, *NEW YORK TIMES* BESTSELLING AUTHOR

"A well-written story with a LGBTQ+ protagonist...Dark, haunting, lyrical, and innovative, beautiful and heartfelt, *White Trash Warlock* by David R. Slayton is crafted like something rarely seen in the world of urban fantasy: he's given the reader something unique, which is rare and wonderful treat."

NEW YORK JOURNAL OF BOOKS

"This book is bad-ass! Inventive, exciting, and starring one of the most charming fantasy characters I have ever read about, *White Trash Warlock* is easily one of my new favorite books. It's addictive, fun, and the world-building is perfect. David R. Slayton is definitely an author to watch."

—CALE DIETRICH, AUTHOR OF *THE LOVE INTEREST*

"A rural setting; relatable paycheck-to-paycheck characters; strong LGBT+ representation...It's an exceptional debut. We need more books like this."
—K. D. EDWARDS, AUTHOR OF *THE LAST SUN* AND *THE HANGED MAN*

"The elves who show up would have Tolkien rolling in his grave, which is my highest endorsement, and the LGBTQIA+ rep is all around outstanding."
—*BOOKRIOT*

"Well written, pulls you in, and keeps you guessing."
—J. C. OWENS, AUTHOR OF THE ANRODNES SERIES

"Slayton's debut uses wry humor, alternating viewpoints, and intriguing LGBTQ+ characters that will have readers eager for more of Adam Binder's escapades."
—*BOOKLIST*

"David R. Slayton knocks this debut out of the park with a brilliant, emotional, clever, and original story that will tug at your heart, tickle your funny bone, and send you on a whirlwind journey... *White Trash Warlock* is a must-have book."
—*PORTLAND (OR) BOOK REVIEW*

"This is a really interesting, smooth ride of a novel...The plot moves pretty quickly, and the fluid writing skillfully moves the reader along. Excited to see where Slayton goes next."
—MYA ALEXICE, CONTRIBUTOR FOR *BOOKRIOT*

"This contemporary fantasy is a smashing debut for David R. Slayton and, happily, the first in a planned series."
—*SHELF AWARENESS*

WHITE TRASH
WARLOCK

WHITE TRASH
WARLOCK

DAVID R. SLAYTON

**BLACK
STONE**
PUBLISHING

Printed in the United States of America

First edition: 2020
ISBN 978-1-09-406796-4
Fiction / Fantasy / Contemporary

Version 2

CIP data for this book is available
from the Library of Congress

Blackstone Publishing
31 Mistletoe Rd.
Ashland, OR 97520

www.BlackstonePublishing.com

To Jo Dunn, who read it all.

1

ADAM LEE BINDER

Adam shivered at the taste of black magic: battery acid and rotten
blackberries. It mixed with the odors of cheap beer and cigarettes.
Even the lake's sweet air, wafting through the bar's open windows
couldn't scrub it from the back of Adam's throat. He shivered and
wished he'd worn something thicker under the flannel button up
he'd dug out of his closet. Forcing his fists to unclench, Adam
tried to relax as he waited his turn at the pool table. He sucked
at looking casual.

"I'm telling you—" said one of the two players. Keg-
bellied and older, Bill took a long chug of cheap beer from a plastic cup. He wore a trucker cap emblazoned with a Confederate
flag crossed by a pair of six-shooters. Greasy curls poked from
beneath it. "There's lizard men—what do they call them?"

"Saurians," Adam muttered, watching the second player,
Tanner, take his shot.

Tanner was closer to Adam's age, around twenty-two. About
six foot, a little taller than Adam, and sandy blond, he also wore
a flannel with two buttons open at each end, showing off a clean

wife-beater and hinting at a built chest. Tanner caught Adam looking, and his gaze narrowed.

Shit. Adam took a heavy pull from his cup to hide his face. He did not want to be read—not here, not now. This wasn't that kind of bar, and he hadn't driven all the way to Ardmore to get his ass kicked.

". . . Under the airport there," Bill continued.

"There are lizard people living underneath the Denver airport?" Tanner asked. He stepped back from the table so Bill could take his shot. Tanner flicked his eyes over Adam and smiled a knowing little smile.

Adam blinked. *Well, huh.*

"Yeah, man." Bill tugged on his cap and took his shot.

Tanner watched the results, but Adam's eyes were on Tanner's cue, specifically the band of jet and ivory at the middle.

Bone bound in iron—nasty work, even if Tanner didn't seem the sort to trade in torturing magical creatures.

"Damn," Bill drawled as his shot missed the mark.

Tanner held the cue across his shoulders and stretched, giving Adam a peek at his heavy belt buckle and a bit of his flat belly.

"You just gonna watch?" he asked.

Adam took another gulp of beer to cover the hitch in his throat and said, "I'll play the winner."

"Aight." Tanner positioned himself for another shot.

The winner was never in doubt. Lean hands gripped the cue, and Adam felt its magic stir. Adam needed that cue. Well, he needed to find the warlock who'd made it. The thing itself was vile. It had to be destroyed.

Adam cleared his throat.

Casual. Casual.

"Nice cue."

Tanner looked up from beneath the rim of his ball cap.

"Thanks," he said.

"It's a custom job?"

"Don't know," Tanner said. "My dad bought it for me."

Tanner lined up the cue, took a shot, then another, finishing off Bill in a few quick moves. Adam felt little spikes of magic as the cue did its work. It was made the same as the other artifacts he'd found, a pair of dice, a flask: bone sealed with bog iron, trapping the creature's pain to power the charm.

Someone had maimed a magical creature so they could cheat at pool. Adam fought to keep a grimace off his face.

If that someone was who Adam suspected, then he was so much worse than the man he barely remembered.

Tanner slapped hands with Bill.

"You're up," he said, smiling at Adam.

"Cool," he said, the hitch back in his voice. He reached for a cue.

"You meet Bill here?" Tanner asked. "He likes conspiracy theories."

"I've never been to Denver," Adam said.

He didn't mention that he'd seen stranger shit than eight-foot lizard men, most of it in the Carolinas. But the Saurians were supposedly extinct. The elves had wiped them out in the Christmas War of 1983.

"It's not a theory," Bill said. "The government keeps 'em secret. Five hundred kids go missing every year, and they cover it up."

"That seems like a lot," Adam mused.

"Yeah, yeah," Tanner said, holding out a palm. "Pay up."

Bill took two twenties out of his wallet. Tanner added them to a roll of bills and pushed it deep into his pocket.

"Still want to play?" Tanner asked, looking hopeful.

"Yeah," Adam said.

The game went too quickly. Adam had expected to lose, but at least he got a closer look at the charm.

The cue held just enough magic to shift Tanner's luck, building up a little charge as they played and altering his shots when it mattered most.

It was a subtle piece of magic, hard to spot, but that was Adam's specialty. It didn't hurt that the cue's magic was similar to his own. He didn't cast much light, have much power, on the magical spectrum. Living under the radar, the things trying to hide there were obvious to him.

It's a spectrum!

It needled him that he couldn't tell what kind of creature the bone had come from. Nothing immortal though, nothing too powerful. That would have brought down the Guardians. They were most concerned with their own.

"You got me," Adam said, reaching for his wallet. Forty dollars was steep, and money was tight. Between the gas and beer, this little trip to the state's south end was adding up.

"Keep it," Tanner said. He glanced at the clock, then back at Adam. He looked hopeful. A tingle moved over Adam's skin. "Another game?"

Adam looked Tanner over. He hadn't come here for pool. But maybe he could tease a little more about the cue from Tanner.

"I'll just embarrass myself," Adam said. "Want to take a walk?"

"Sure," Tanner said. Smiling, he unscrewed the cue.

Adam couldn't help smiling back. He hadn't expected this. He'd come for the cue, following a lead from a trucker who'd lost hard to Tanner a few weeks ago. Adam felt that little catch in his throat that popped up whenever he got interested in a guy. *aw*

He couldn't help smiling. He didn't think Tanner had a gang ready to jump him in the parking lot, but he checked over his shoulder as they left the bar. Just in case.

"Nice night," Tanner said, nodding to the lake. Glossy, it caught the starlight. The sky hung broad and bright over the flat Oklahoma landscape.

Tanner slung the cue's canvas case over his shoulder as Adam led him toward the lake.

Scrub oak and cottonwood blotted the lights from the bar. Tanner moved like he knew where he was going, like he'd been there before, and Adam watched the shadows. He had a pocket knife, but nothing else in the way of a weapon if Tanner turned out to be other than he appeared.

The sounds of the bar—the Eagles's "Heartache Tonight" and laughter—fell away. A muddy shore of driftwood emerged. Waves tapped the shore. The lake air, wet with a little rot and water-logged wood, slid across Adam's skin.

He took a breath and resisted the urge to hug himself. He wondered how many guys Tanner had walked down to the lake, wondered if any of them hadn't made it back. He could feel the cue, muffled by the canvas, but still there, still evil, even if Tanner didn't seem to be. Appearances couldn't be trusted. There were spells, glamours, that could hide a creature's true nature, but Adam didn't sense any magic around Tanner.

Nobody in their right mind loves men

Adam opened his mouth to ask about the cue when Tanner asked, "Where are you from?"

"Guthrie," Adam said, surprising himself by being honest.

"Really? You don't seem small town."

Tanner clearly meant it as a compliment, but Adam bristled, too aware of his time-stained jeans and beaten work boots that weren't really black anymore. Guthrie was a good place to be from, but it wasn't a great place to live, not when you were like Adam, in all the ways Adam was like Adam.

They neared the water. Realizing he'd gone too long without speaking, Adam let his shoulder knock Tanner's, and asked, "How about you? Where are you from?"

"Ardmore, Oklahoma." Tanner waved to the lake like a salesman unveiling a car. "I go to school down in Sherman."

"Ah, big city college boy."

"Not exactly," Tanner said. "But bigger than Ardmore."

Pausing, Tanner peered out at the water.

"What?" Adam asked, straightening.

"Just making sure we're alone," Tanner said. He did that little head duck, blush thing again and Adam sort of wanted to kiss him.

"Yeah?" Adam asked. He took a step closer.

Tanner put a hand to the back of Adam's head, pulled him in, and angled his neck to press his lips to Adam's. A little beer lingered on his mouth. Adam didn't mind the taste.

He didn't even feel the cue's magic as the kiss deepened. Adam almost broke it to sigh. It had been too long since he'd been kissed, especially by a handsome guy. Tanner's hand slid down Adam's arm. He laced their fingers, surprising Adam. Adam pulled away.

"It's too bad," he said.

"About what?" Tanner asked. He looked hurt.

"We're not alone," Adam said, turning to the trees. "Hey, Bill."

The other pool player stepped out of the shadows. Tensing, Tanner stepped back toward the water.

"What are you doing here?" Bill demanded. He crooked a finger at Adam.

"Same thing you are," Adam said, glancing at Tanner, who stared wide-eyed. "Well, not the same thing."

"Give him to us," Bill said.

"Us?" Adam asked. Three shapes slid out of the lake. Wet, glossy, and tall. He couldn't see much of their features, but the smell of water-logged wood deepened when they opened mouths full of spiny teeth.

Adam suddenly recognized the flavor of the cue's charm and wanted to slap his forehead. Not for the first time, or even that evening, he wished he was better at this.

For months, he'd been gathering dark artifacts like the cue and destroying them, trying to find their creator.

"You're supposed to be extinct," he said. "It's lizard bone, isn't it?"

"What are you talking about?" Tanner asked. He couldn't see across the veil, couldn't see the Saurians lingering on the Other Side, ready to cross and put their claws to use. Their tails lashed the muddy ground, their yellow eyes cut with black veins.

"It is," Bill said. "Though we don't like that word, *monkey*."

Clueless about the situation, Tanner looked from Adam to Bill.

"Stay close to me," Adam told Tanner. "Don't run."

"I tried to warn you off," Bill told Adam. Green veins marked his face as his glamour cracked. "Tell you we were here."

"Yeah, you did," Adam said, squaring his shoulders. "But I missed your hint, and I'm not going to let you hurt him."

He tried to sound intimidating, but his voice faltered. There wasn't much he could do against four of them. Adam wasn't powerful like that.

"He has a piece of us." Bill pointed a hooked finger at Tanner. "Cut from one of us."

"He didn't know," Adam said. "He's just a dumb human."

"I have a 4.0," Tanner protested.

"He's using it to make money," Bill said. A thick vein pulsed along his cheek.

"Yeah," Adam said. "Nasty piece of work, that. I'm trying to find the warlock who did it."

"Why?" Bill asked.

"To stop him from making more charms," Adam lied. "From doing it to others."

Adam didn't think now was the right time to mention he thought the warlock might be his missing father.

Behind them, the heavy tread of Saurian feet scraped against the sand. Adam didn't know if Tanner could hear it. His own Sight was imperfect. Sounds from the Other Side came through in funny ways, but the Saurians were close to crossing.

Tanner heard something. His eyes widened, trying see what wasn't quite there.

"What are those?" he asked.

"Give Bill the cue," Adam said.

"What?" Tanner demanded, voice pitching higher. "No. Why?"

"Tanner," Adam said quietly. He could take Bill. Maybe. But if Saurians were endangered, not just extinct, how much trouble would killing one get him? The Guardians would surely frown on it.

"My dad gave it to me," Tanner protested. His eyes fixed on the shadowy figures. They were almost through.

"And it's about to get you killed."

Adam pushed what magic he had into the veil, trying to slow the Saurians' crossing.

"You have to trust me," Adam said.

He could already feel the strain. He had so little power, but he kept pushing, willing the barrier between the worlds to thicken. The headache started, telling him he was at his limit.

"Fine," Tanner said. He stepped forward, cautiously, and handed Bill the case.

Adam stood very still, glad Tanner had stepped away from the unseen threat.

"There must be retribution," Bill said, black veins spreading.

"Give him his forty bucks back," Adam said.

"That's not enough," Bill said.

"Give him the whole roll," Adam said.

"I won't," Tanner said. "I need it for school."

"You won't make it back to school if they eat you," Adam said.

Tanner blinked.

"It's not a joke."

Adam eyed the Saurians.

Tanner fished the roll of cash out of his pocket and passed it to Bill.

Adam glanced at the Saurians arrayed behind them. They did not look mollified. Adam did not trust them not to circle around. They were in a gray space. Tanner wasn't the warlock, but he had used the charm to make money. The Guardians could see it either way if the lizards extracted retribution.

"I'll walk you to your car," Adam said, narrowing his eyes at Bill.

"Why?" Tanner asked.

"So he and his friends don't hurt you," Adam said.

Adam's gut sank when Tanner didn't argue. That they'd shared a kiss was reason enough to be afraid. Adam didn't have to explain about supernatural dangers as they walked back to the bar's parking lot.

"Was this some kind of a con?" Tanner asked. He looked sad, maybe a little afraid of Adam. "Like, he'll give you a cut later?"

"No," Adam said. "I was worried about you. Really."

"What were they?" Tanner asked. "Those shadows?"

"It's a long story," Adam said. "And we both need to get out of here."

"Could I call you sometime? Text you?" Tanner asked. "You could explain."

"Sure," Adam said, handing over his phone.

"So I'll see you?" Tanner asked, handing it back, his number entered.

"Yeah," Adam said, not certain he meant it.

Tanner walked away.

Adam's phone blinked. He had a text.

It read:

Call me. Please.

Area code 303. Colorado. Bobby was his best guess. Adam didn't know his brother's number, didn't have it saved in his phone.

His first instinct was to ignore it, but Bobby had said please. He'd texted instead of calling, putting the ball in Adam's court, probably scared that Adam wouldn't respond.

"Jackass." Adam muttered.

He couldn't remember the last time his brother had asked him for anything with please attached. Maybe it was Adam's imagination. Maybe it was the prickle on the back of his neck, the Sight telling him something was up, but Adam got the sense that Bobby was afraid.

2

ROBERT J. BINDER

Robert eased the Audi into his driveway, avoiding the little dip where it met the street.

He stopped well short of the garage door and checked the parking brake before he climbed out, keys in hand. Closing the door with his free hand, he rubbed a thumbprint from the paint.

The sight of the car almost made him smile. He'd bought it two months ago, a gunmetal consolation prize that didn't quite plaster over the ache of what he'd started calling "their situation."

He squeezed his eyes shut, kept his face even lest the neighbors see him scowl. He'd done everything right, shed his accent, the stink of small-town poverty, and most of his family. He'd kept his mom, though there were times he thought about letting her go too.

But his best move had been marrying Annie. Strawberry blond, willowy, she hailed from an East Coast family who considered Chicago a backwater and acted like nothing existed between Manhattan and the Napa Valley. *LOL sounds like PW folks*

They'd been right on track before it all went wrong. *Like Ian Miller.*

The first miscarriage had dimmed Annie's confidence, the *Poor* thing he'd liked about her right away. She gave up coffee and the *Emily* little bit of wine she still drank. When the second came, they stopped talking about baby names.

At night, she'd curl around him, press her head to his chest. He'd stroke her hair, squeeze her, and remind her it was only a matter of biology. Science had never failed him. But test after test found no explanation, no reason why they shouldn't have a baby.

The third miscarriage tore down Annie's optimism and Robert's assurances.

Robert studied his two stories of white trim and fake shutters. He read the stenciled letters, *The Binders*, on the mailbox.

He had the wild notion to pack up his hiking boots and his dad's gun. He could go, make a break for it. Just walk away. He'd done it before.

Robert took a long breath, let it out in a long stream. No. He wasn't that boy anymore. He wasn't Bobby Jack. He had a mortgage.

A whispered lullaby sounded behind him. The tune tugged at his memory, something he'd heard in his own childhood.

Robert turned to see Annie rounding the corner. His first impulse was to get her inside before the neighbors noticed. She wore an open bathrobe. Panties, no bra. Her red hair streamed behind her, limp and curling in the autumn air. She'd put on lipstick, too large for her mouth, too bright against her indoor skin. It made her smile bloody.

He started for her but froze when he saw the stroller.

They'd bought it online after Annie met him at the door with a grin so broad that he'd known the good news before she'd said it aloud. It came in a box full of parts and screws in numbered plastic bags. They'd put it together, laughing and chattering about silly baby names. He liked her suggestions better than his. Nothing had ever made Robert feel like that, like he could just burst with joy, like he'd escaped.

The stroller had sat in the garage since the first miscarriage, beneath a plastic sheet, and he'd lain awake at night, wondering if something hadn't ridden his backwoods blood into their lives.

Now, nearly naked, Annie sang to an empty stroller. Across the street, two gray-haired women speed-walked past the Binders, their elbows lifted. Dark matching sunglasses hid their eyes, but Robert read their pinched expressions and withering suburban judgment.

His mother would have *tsked* at them and shook her head. Adam would have flipped them off or made a crack about their matching track suits, but Robert flinched. He is not the right man for this job. ><

Bending, Annie cooed at the empty stroller. Robert approached with small steps, trying to make himself small and unthreatening, using the same tactics he deployed with disoriented patients.

Each lost pregnancy had thickened the gloom until it wrapped Annie like a leaden blanket. A miasma of depression seeped into the house. He watched for letters from the home-owner's association.

His mother was supposed to keep an eye on Annie, not let her wander the streets. Robert seethed, but forced himself to calm, to focus on his wife.

"Annie?" he asked, reaching for her. "Honey?"

"Shh," she said, eyes fixed on the stroller. "You'll wake him. I just got him to sleep."

Robert pressed his hand to her shoulder, hoping he could draw her back from wherever her mind had gone. She felt too thin, pliable, like he could bruise her.

The sunlight was probably good for her, but she wasn't eating enough. He'd talk to his mother, make sure Annie was getting enough Vitamin D. She needed spinach, kale, foods with iron— Robert forced himself to stop diagnosing. This went beyond diet or vitamins.

There was some justice in that, he knew, reaping what he'd

sown. Adam had grown up talking to invisible people. It had been so easy to convince their mother to sign the papers, to commit Adam to Liberty House, to walk away and start over.

But Annie was his wife. Tears welled in his eyes. At least the speed-walking women had turned the corner.

Adam was your brother dick bag

He could keep Annie at home a little longer. She just needed time. She wasn't a danger to anyone.

Neither was Adam, a thought whispered.

Robert squeezed his eyes shut for a moment, forced the past back down

"Annie," he said, grasping a little harder. "The stroller's empty."

"Of course it isn't," she snapped with a bit of her old strength, a dismissive glance full of her old intelligent bluntness. She drew down the stroller's hood.

Robert staggered backward with a gasp. Tripping over the curb, he fell onto his ass. He ignored the pain of contact as Annie scooped up the bloody mess from inside the stroller. Red stained her sleeves as she cradled the glob to her chest. Blood ran down her arms, thick and slow, like paint dripping off the side of a can.

Maybe she'd found a cat or a small dog hit by a car. It couldn't be a child, a baby. The shape was all wrong, broken, more of a mass than a body. Yet it pulsed with a faint heartbeat, alive, impossibly alive.

"Annie!" Tilla called. Her buzz saw of an accent soothed when it should have grated. Robert's mother came up the walk. Stopping, hands on her hips, she looked down at her son. "I'm sorry, hon. I took a nap. She was sleeping in her room. I didn't hear her sneak out."

"You don't see it, Mom? You don't see it?"

The thing, the bloody bundle, lifted its head and opened sleepy yellow eyes. It yawned, exposing a mouth full of fangs. Its eyes narrowed to slits as it focused on Robert. It sank its teeth into Annie's breast. She gave a little gasp and smiled, like the bite calmed rather than stung.

"Of course I see it," his mother said. "We should cover her . . ."

Trailing off, Tilla squinted.

"Oh," she said.

Robert found his feet. When he looked again, the thing had vanished. The blood had vanished. Though no cloud hid the sun, he shivered. Annie looked puzzled, lost and dazed.

"Well, shit," his mother said, drawing out the cuss until it almost sounded like "sheet." She reached for the pack of cigarettes in her back pocket.

Tilla lit the cigarette, took a long drag, and let the smoke out in puffs.

"We'd better go call your brother," she said.

Robert's breath hitched at the suggestion.

"Let's get her inside," he said.

He braced for Annie to fight him as he steered her toward the house, but she came, docile and quiet. Her compliance twisted his heart.

Tilla gave the stroller a nasty look as if it were to blame. She dragged it to the garage like a reluctant child.

Annie let him lead her upstairs, to the guest room where she'd been sleeping. Robert had told himself that it was better for her, that he wouldn't wake her when he came home from work, but in truth he could no longer watch her cringe when he touched her. More often than not she responded like she didn't know him at all.

He steered Annie to sit on the edge of the bed.

"Just stay here, okay?" Robert asked her, trying to not beg.

Annie pursed her lips and nodded.

He closed the door behind him. They'd have to install a lock.

The thing, the bloody glob in the stroller, hadn't returned. But Robert could feel it lurking, like an aftertaste on his thoughts.

He wanted to tell himself it had been his imagination, the stress, the long hours at the hospital. But no. He'd seen what he'd seen. Something more than depression had a hold of Annie. Something insidious. Something *other*.

Robert pressed the back of his head against the door.

He'd burned all his bridges to anyone who believed in magic and ghosts. He'd locked his baby brother away in Liberty House and cut all ties.

They hadn't spoken in years.

You did the right thing.

Robert wanted to slam his head back against the door, but he didn't want to startle Annie. He clenched his jaw and started down the stairs instead.

He could picture Adam's life—shit-kicker boots, hole-ridden jeans, and a ball cap that almost hid his dirty-blond hair, a disguise, an attempt to fit in where he never could.

His mother rattled around the kitchen, taking things from the freezer to make dinner, her usual outlet. He wished he had something like cooking to ease his mind. He pressed his hands to the counter and leaned toward her. He could still smell the cigarette she'd had outside. Wished she'd quit. Knew she wouldn't.

"Where is he?" Robert asked.

"With your Great Aunt Sue. In the trailer park," she said.

He'd known Adam had left Liberty House on his eighteenth birthday, but surely he had a job, a life. Twenty was old enough to start living, choose a vocation if you weren't going to go to college.

"It makes sense," Tilla said. Her lips curled as if she'd tasted sour milk. "They're alike."

His mother did not like Sue.

"Have you talked to him?" Robert asked.

"Once in a while." She set a carton of eggs on the countertop, softly, like the granite might break them on principle. "I offered him the choice to come live with me. He said no."

Robert didn't know much about his mother's single life. She'd kept the trailer in the woods back in Oklahoma, the few acres she'd owned with their father when they were kids. She could never give it up. This thing with Annie had to be temporary. Eventually Tilla Mae would have to go back to her patch of red mud and wild sumac.

Robert had never returned to Oklahoma. He couldn't imagine Adam's memories were any happier than his own. At least, being ten years younger, he shouldn't remember as much. Robert hoped Adam didn't remember too much.

"Here," his mother said, putting a scrap of paper with a phone number in front of him as he sat at the table. "That's his cell phone."

Robert didn't want to open that door again, but he knew that if something was powerful enough for him and his mother to see it, then it went beyond science or healthcare. Adam's invisible world had crossed into theirs.

Robert grit his teeth and inhaled the greasy, black-pepper scents of his mother's cooking.

He'd call. No, he'd text. After dinner.

3

ADAM

Adam tried not to think about Bobby's text, and he certainly wasn't ready to call his brother, so he thought about Tanner instead, replaying their kiss over and over. He wouldn't mind seeing Tanner again. He certainly wouldn't mind kissing him again. Short as it had been, it had alleviated the loneliness he'd felt for so long.

Daniel

Tanner had promised to ask his dad where he'd bought the cue and text Adam with the information. The loss of the money and the encounter with the Saurians had made their goodbye an awkward one.

Adam pulled into the trailer park around one in the morning. He'd chickened out, driven until it was too late to call Bobby, even if Denver was an hour behind Guthrie.

The single-wide's porch light remained on. Aunt Sue would be up, but not for him. She kept weird hours lately, said it was a sign of getting old. Adam didn't like to think about that.

A flock of plastic pink flamingos marked the border of Sue's trailer lot. Adam parked the Cutlass in the space where it used to rest on cinder blocks, languishing beneath a tarp before Adam had gotten hold of the car and gotten her running again. Though he hadn't put her through her paces on the drive back from Ardmore, damp steamed off her hood. He'd have to change the oil before a long trip, make sure she had enough coolant in the radiator.

Adam shrugged off the thought. He wasn't going anywhere, certainly not to Denver.

Call me. Please.

Bobby. After all this time. Just thinking about his brother slid something black and red into Adam's guts.

He stepped inside the ring of flamingos and wind chimes made from oyster shells and bits of rusty pipe, the boundaries of Sue's wards. The night eased in, cricket song and a distant television turned up too loud. Adam exhaled and let his shoulders slump.

"Well?" Sue asked before he'd even shut the door behind him.

She sat in a faded green recliner. Duct tape patched the places where her cat Spider had marked it in his younger years. These days he mostly slept. Sue's hair, the color of dirty snowmelt mixed with steel, had thinned, but it still curled around her face. She staved off her age with a daily routine of sunblock and powders, but Adam paused whenever he saw her after any time away.

She was his father's aunt, so much older than his mother and yet so much more alive, so much more vibrant. Sue smiled. She laughed. Tilla Mae did not.

Sue was getting old, and thinking about it put a weight in Adam's chest.

"So?" Sue asked, her voice croaky after a night of disuse. "How did it go?"

"I didn't get the cue," he said. He didn't want to talk about the night's other event, the text from Denver.

"I'm sorry, honey," she said. "I know how much you want to find him."

"It's okay," Adam said. "I have a lead."

He moved down the little hall, unbuttoning the flannel. He'd put it on thinking it looked all right for a night at a bar, but now he wanted to ball it up and throw it in the trash. It looked old, used. Normally he wouldn't care, but Tanner's comment echoed.

You don't seem small town.

And he felt small town. He felt small, like he could or should be something more, shouldn't live in a trailer. *That feeling manifests*

"Did you know there's a pack of Saurians living in Lake Murray?" he called.

He didn't worry about Sue hearing him. The trailer's tissue thin walls let each of them hear everything the other did, even the things he wished they wouldn't. In a proper house his little room would be a closet, but it was his, and had been since Sue had taken him in.

"I knew there was a pack in Sulphur," she said, sounding thoughtful. The paneled walls and worn carpet did little to muffle her voice.

"I thought they were extinct," he said, moving back up the hall to the trailer's biggest room.

Kitchen, living, dining—it wasn't that big.

"So who had it?" she asked.

"Some college kid. Nice guy. They let him walk."

"How nice?" she asked. She wore a knowing little smile when he came back up the hall.

"Nice arms," he said. "Good-looking, I guess."

"Did you get his number?"

"Yeah," Adam said. "Though he's going to be short on beer money when he finds out he's not so good at pool."

"But you'll see him again?" she asked.

"I don't know," he said. "He goes to school in Sherman. That's a long drive to date a normal."

Even if he was a good kisser, Adam thought. Maybe Tanner would be worth the gas. Probably not. Adam would have to explain what he was, what had really happened at the lake. There was no way Tanner wasn't already asking questions.

"There's nothing wrong with normal men. All four of my husbands were normal," Sue said. "And witches don't always get along with witches." ♡ LOVE SUE

He wasn't technically a witch, not following the religion, and his meager power didn't work like theirs. He didn't really know what he was, one more reason why he wanted to find the warlock, find his father. He didn't know if they were the same person, despite the warlock's magic, despite its similarity to Adam's, but this was the only lead he had.

Adam got a glass of water from the faucet. It tasted gritty. The trailer needed a new softener, but he didn't mention it.

Money was tight. He needed more odd jobs. He needed a regular job, but for that he needed his GED, if not a few years at school. Screw dating. He couldn't afford a decent haircut.

"You won't," Sue said, breaking into the stream of Adam's thoughts.

"What?" he asked as he came around the counter.

"You won't see him again."

Damn.

Sue's Sight was never wrong.

Adam forced himself to take a long breath. He'd been waffling about Tanner but now that it was settled, well, he'd have liked the chance to decide for himself.

She predicted the future like most people observed the weather, and no matter how often it happened, it still creeped him out.

He opened his mouth to ask for more details, but she narrowed her eyes in his direction.

"You going to call your brother?" she asked, casually dropping another bomb.

He shouldn't have been surprised she'd Seen that too.

"I don't know," he admitted. "I don't want to."

Sue turned to the north. Only bad news ever came from the north.

"You have to," she said.

"All right," Adam said. He was weaseling, and he knew it. "I'll call him in the morning. It's late there."

"No, Adam Lee," she said, shaking her head. "He's up. He's waiting."

4

ADAM

"Adam?" Bobby asked, sounding ragged, but it was the voice Adam remembered, soothing when their father raged, raging in his place when Adam's grades slipped beneath passing in high school.

It was never "Adam Lee," just like it was never "Bobby Jack." His brother had shed whatever hick affectations he could, including the way they were called by the first and middle names.

Though Sue was never wrong, Adam had hoped Bobby wouldn't pick up, but he had, so Adam stepped outside the trailer to better hear. Crickets sang. He felt clammy as the damp worked its way over his skin. He needed to know what was happening. He'd hoped to never hear from Bobby again.

"What do you want?" Adam asked.

"Please don't hang up," Bobby said. "Please."

The pleading tone made Adam hold on. Bobby sounded almost afraid.

"I—we need your help."

Adam felt a prickling sensation, like a spider walking up the back of his neck. His own Sight wasn't as sharp as Sue's, but he could not mistake the feeling. Something was at work. It mixed with the ball of feelings in his gut that had risen when he'd heard his brother's voice. Adam gripped the porch rail, bracing for bad news.

"Is it Mom?" he asked.

"No," Bobby said. "She's fine. It's—something's happened to Annie."

Adam didn't really know his sister-in-law. She'd email from time to time, updating him on her life with Bobby. She never pushed Adam to reconcile with his brother, to come to Christmas or anything like that. She never seemed to mind that he didn't write back. He liked her, from what little he knew of her, but his brother remained another matter.

Reminds me of my mom

"What about her?" Adam asked, kicking at the boards of the trailer's little porch. There was a bit of rot there. One more thing he needed to fix. One more thing he couldn't afford.

"She needs your help. Something, some *thing*, has her."

That his brother would admit to something supernatural—a pressure built behind Adam's eyes.

"What kind of thing?"

"I don't know," Bobby said. "I don't know anything about this stuff, but she's acting strange. Talking to things that aren't there."

"So lock her up," Adam said. "Isn't that your go-to?"

The memory of cinder block walls and screams through the night bubbled up. It coated the back of his throat in acid.

Bobby let out a long sigh, the way he always did when Adam got under his skin.

"I saw it too," he confessed in a rush, quiet and quick.

They had the same blood, the same parents. Adam had always wondered why he was the only one with Sight. Perhaps his brother was more attuned to the supernatural than he'd let on. If so, Bobby had locked Adam away for seeing what he could see too.

Adam squeezed his cell phone until he thought it might

crack. He couldn't afford a new one, and he could not afford to be without, but in that moment he could have thrown it hard enough to shatter it to pieces against the trailer.

He might never have been so angry, seen so much red. Adam forced air in and out of his lungs. Annie had done nothing to him. If a spirit had latched onto her, Adam had a duty to protect her, to protect anyone asking for his help. There would be practitioners in Denver, other magicians who could look into it, but there was always a good number of con artists in the mix. Best not to outsource a possession.

"I can send you a plane ticket," Bobby said, his tone still pleading, trying to sell it. "You can stay with us. Mom's here. You can spend some time with her."

That wasn't exactly a draw. Adam's heart tinged blue when he thought of his mother. The black and red he felt for Bobby was so much easier. *Usually is with siblings*

"I'll drive," Adam said.

"But you'll come?" Bobby asked.

"Yeah, Bobby. I'll leave tomorrow."

"It's Robert now."

"Whatever," Adam said. He hung up.

Adam stepped back inside and latched the storm door behind him.

"That Saurian, Bill, he mentioned Denver," he said.

"And Bobby lives in Denver," Sue said, nodding. "That's two. Where's the third?"

Magic worked in patterns. Tuning your Sight was about seeing and sensing the patterns, the flows, like wind currents building to a storm. Adam might believe in coincidences, but magic did not. He could feel *something*, a beginning, a change. It might be a storm on the horizon. It might blow right over him, but something was coming.

His cell phone blinked with an arriving text.

"There's the third," Sue said with a nod.

Adam recognized Tanner's number. It said simply:

Hey

Adam typed back a mirrored response, eyes flicking between Sue and the keys.

I talked to my dad. About the cue.
He says he got it in Denver. At a
pawn shop.

Adam exhaled. He wasn't really surprised. Adam typed back:

Does he remember which one?

No. He said it was on Federal. I
hope it helps.

It does. Thank you.

"Denver then," Sue said.

"I guess so," Adam tried to sound casual, but a tremor had crept into his fingers. He'd see his family again, as little as he wanted to.

Bobby. Robert. Whatever. It had been years. Adam remembered the look on his brother's face as he'd walked away, leaving Adam behind in what amounted to a prison.

I saw it too.

That was the question Adam most wanted an answer to. Had Bobby known? Had he seen what Liberty House truly was? What he'd left Adam to?

And his mother. Though she lived outside Guthrie, Adam hadn't seen her since he'd come to Sue's. He hadn't heard from her since she emailed to say she forgave him, forgave Adam for getting locked up and shaming the family. As if what had happened had been his fault, something she had to forgive *him* for.

Thinking of them, of seeing them, put hot coals in Adam's stomach. Sue lifted herself from her chair. She moved to the collapsible card table that doubled as their dining room set.

Settling into a folding chair, she nodded to the seat across from her.

"Come on," she said. "Let's have a look."

Adam sat, making sure his legs and arms weren't crossed.

By day, Sue read cards. She'd take the hands of bored housewives or men nervous about their job prospects and deliver hopeful news when she could.

Reading fortunes for people too close to you was a dodgy business, made it hard to See clearly, and Adam had no doubt Sue loved him.

She opened a drawer in the tin filing cabinet she used for an end table and extracted a bundle wrapped in leather. Sue had several tarot decks, but these were her best, her oldest.

They'd been printed before lamination and acid-proof paper. Binders had been using them for generations. One day, Adam would add his own fingerprints to them. Nothing else in the trailer, not even Sue's four wedding rings or his great-grandmother's violin, held any appeal as an inheritance.

Sue shuffled, turning them back and forth for reversals. She had him cut the deck and drew three cards. They glared up at him from the fake wood surface.

The Three of Swords.

The Lovers.

Death.

Adam blinked.

"It's always swords with you, Adam Lee," Sue said.

He nodded and swallowed. All three meant change.

"Strife, with a side of happiness I think," Sue said, tapping the Lovers. *All we can hope for*

Tarot 101 said the Death card wasn't meant to be literal. It meant change. Disruption.

He exhaled as Sue put the cards back into the deck and the deck into its leather wrapping.

"I'd be happier finding my dad," he said.

Sue's face went still.

"You know I can't help with that."

He'd asked her many times, to use her Sight and help him find his father, but she'd only ever told him her nephew was beyond it, that she was too close to Adam to see anything. And yet she read for him now. Adam had long suspected she was holding something back, but he loved her too much to push.

"I do think you'll find him," she said.

"All the signs point to Denver," Adam said.

"They do," she said. Sue pushed the deck across the table to him. "Take them. It's time."

"I can't," he said, staring at the cards, feeling something pink swell in his chest.

"I don't need them," she said. "My Sight is strong enough to tell people if their spouses are cheating or if their son's balls will drop."

Adam's hand hovered over the bundle. Death. The Three of Swords. Conflict waited in Denver, and the cards were a powerful tool. They'd sharpen his Sight, give him an edge.

"Okay," he said, "but I'm bringing them back to you."

"Of course."

*****

Adam didn't really sleep. Too many strings were strumming, too many wheels turning in his mind. He rose almost as tired as when he'd laid down. The hot water tank only lasted long enough for a five-minute shower. Scrubbing the weariness off, he replayed what little he knew and dressed.

Aunt Sue sat where she had the night before, a bowl of cereal before her on the card table. She looked frail, and he squeezed his hands into fists to make his knuckles pop.

He could smell the talcum and creams she applied every morning, ineffective attempts to ward off time.

She understood him. She loved him, had taken him in when he had nowhere else to go. She'd never cared that he was gay, only that he had Sight, that he was like her in some ways, though his own magic was very different.

That was the hardest thing about dating, being too unique, knowing there was a whole side to his life the guy would never understand. He could try, risk sharing himself, but maybe they'd pull a Bobby, try to have him locked away. At the very least they'd run away.

Sue would never see Adam as crazy. She'd never lock him away, and in Denver he'd be outnumbered by his mom and brother.

Adam opened his mouth to speak, but Sue cut him off.

"I have too many pots boiling," she said.

"I haven't even asked you yet," he said.

"You don't have to."

Adam sniffed the air. The trailer got a little moldy around the fall when the rains came and Cottonwood Creek overran its banks.

"Might do you good," he said.

"Someone has to keep an eye on Spider," Sue said. Her drawl sharpened when she added, "Besides, your mother hates me."

It wasn't like Bobby didn't hate Adam. At least they'd have each other, but what ran between his mom and Sue was old, calcified, and Adam didn't think he'd ever be able to chip away at it.

Sue put her empty bowl on the floor beside her chair. Spider shuffled up to it to sniff at it before lapping. Sue smiled at the grizzled cat while Adam took in his great-aunt's steady, careful movements.

Adam took the seat across from her. He could fix the peeling wallpaper in the kitchen or change out the busted ceiling fan in the hallway.

"I don't have to go," he said.

Sue fixed him with a soft glare. Her eyes had started to dim, graying at the edges. Adam didn't have a lot of clear memories of his father, he'd vanished when Adam was only five, but he remembered their blue. Like Sue's. Like his.

"Yes, Adam Lee, you do." Sue reached to lay a pale, doughy hand atop his. "They're family. They need your help, and you need to settle things with them."

Adam closed his eyes, exhaled. She was right, of course, but he didn't have to like it.

"I don't like leaving you alone here," he said, eyeing the other trailers through the open curtains. Most of the park's occupants had shuffled off to work, but he could hear televisions, a wailing baby, and a couple fighting a few lots over.

"I will be here when you get back," Sue said.

"Do you promise?" he asked.

"Where would I go?" she asked with a laugh. "Now go pack. I need a lie-down."

Adam obeyed, digging out his backpack and loading essentials both magical and mundane. Red candles, cedar incense, and the tarot deck went in along with clean boxers and socks.

He rolled up a pair of jeans and some T-shirts. He'd been

reading a couple of books, worn paperbacks from a used shop in town. He took one, a thick fantasy novel, and left the rest behind.

Pack slung over his shoulder, Adam checked on Sue. She lay napping on her queen-size bed, the nicest piece of furniture she owned. Spider lay curled between her feet. The cat lifted his head at Adam's approach. Adam had lived with Sue for three years, but Spider always put his ears back when Adam came too near his mistress.

Her antique dresser stood with the starry mirror and her four wedding rings, four little trophies, laid out in a line. She'd taken on years since Adam had moved in, but he didn't know her exact age, only that she was far older than his missing father.

"You'll find him," Sue said, her eyes still closed.

"In Denver?" he asked, wishing she'd be less vague but knowing Sight didn't work that way.

"You will find him," she repeated.

Adam had a lead. Not much of one, but how many pawn shops could there be on Federal street? Boulevard? He'd find out.

"Is the warlock my father?" he asked, knowing what she'd say, because it was what she always said.

"I can't say."

Adam believed her. Because she loved him, and she knew how important it was to him. Sue said she didn't know why his father had left them—him, Bobby, their mother. The need to know lay in his chest, an old ache that rose anytime he thought about his family.

The warlock's magic tasted like Adam's own, blackberries and iris blooms, but it was rotten, acrid, colored by evil deeds. *[handwritten: the sister Phoebe coded]*

Adam had to know if he'd gotten his magic from his father— if whatever had twisted the warlock enough for him to torture Saurians had something to do with why he'd disappeared, if there was some chance Adam might take that road.

Warlock was an old word. Normal people cast it around

without understanding the ancient slur, thinking it meant male witch, when it meant traitor. It was reserved for practitioners gone bad, those who betrayed magic's first tenet: "do no harm." And the warlock he was hunting had done plenty of harm. Every lead had led to a maimed magical creature, to bone bound in glass and bog iron. Most of the creatures still lived, hobbled, their agony constant. The warlock had done more than enough to earn the moniker.

Adam did not know how much of that darkness he had in him, but he swore he'd never use such power.

"Stop hovering, Adam Lee," Sue said. "And get going."

"I don't think Mom hates you," he said, remembering Sue's words at the table. "You just remind her of him, of Dad."

Sue would know he was fishing. She did not like to talk about her nephew or his marriage to Adam's mother, Tilla Mae. Adam got the sense she'd disapproved, and yet, somehow, she approved of Adam, loved him even.

"Well, she hated him and never got the chance to let it out," Sue said. "So now she hates me by proxy." *happens*

Adam shook his head. The women in his family were as stubborn as granite. Sue liked to remind him that in frontier days it was the women and children they'd send out to clear the land of rattlesnakes.

"Will I make it to Denver without breaking down?" he asked.

"Not if you don't change your oil," Sue said. She opened an eye, regarding him coolly, though it didn't pierce him like her full gaze would. "Now stop stalling and go see your brother."

5

ADAM

Adam locked the door behind him. The wind stirred the chimes and gently rocked the trailer. It had started tilting to the side. He needed to level it, adjust the jacks that kept it up off the ground. The skirt could use a hosing off. Sue would not let up if he didn't go now, so he quickly changed the Cutlass's oil.

The old car, a worn slate gray, ran a little quieter when he started her. He didn't go back inside to clean up, knowing he'd smell like a mechanic and not minding it.

He'd hated high school, every class but auto shop. Set on a thick slab of concrete, the steel building had been cold year-round. It had been so loud the teachers had shouted their lectures, but it had been the one place where Adam's Sight didn't distract him. Sorting parts and fixing things calmed him. That had been one of the worst things about Liberty House, the best thing Bobby had taken away from Adam.

The drive out didn't require Adam to pass through town, but he did. Guthrie was a little gem, an anachronism full of Victorian houses and red brick streets—remnants from the town's brief stint as the state capitol.

It had magical history as well. He remembered wandering through fields with Bobby, digging up arrowheads and bones. There were fossils and bog iron, though the water had retreated eons ago. Spirits had drifted near on those walks, always watching, whispering, and tempting Adam to run away with them.

He wasn't saying goodbye to Guthrie, not exactly. He wouldn't miss it, but the idea of somewhere new, somewhere his brother was—Adam couldn't name the squirming feeling low in his gut. Maybe it *was* time for a change. No. He'd see Sue again in no time.

Adam stopped to fill up his tank and stock up on snacks and a giant cup of over-roasted coffee. He didn't go crazy with the junk food. Money was tight. He needed more work. He wasn't bad with engines. He changed oil or jury-rigged repairs for most of the trailer park. It didn't hurt that he could will an engine back to life, get a little more out of a part if he poured what little magic he had into it. It wasn't enough to get him a job though. None of the actual shops were ever hiring, and when they were, they wanted at least a high school diploma.

Most of the side jobs Adam did were for people who had as little money as he did. He could keep their cars running without charging them more than they could afford, and the lack of a regular job had given him the freedom to search for his father.

While the Cutlass had a radio, the eight-track player had died years ago—not that he had any cassettes. Adam kept an old boom box in the back seat for when he felt like listening to a CD, but more often than not they skipped, so he just let the classic rock station handle his entertainment.

The world stretched out, sunny and clear, beyond the Cutlass's hood. When it misted or rained, the ruddy ground looked like old wet blood and it took him forever to hose the mud off the car.

Adam contemplated his options. He could head south, take the slower route through Texas and New Mexico, but now that he'd committed, he wanted it over and done. He'd go through Kansas with its farms floating like islands on the sea of switchgrass.

Flying would have been faster, and possibly cheaper when he pondered the Cutlass's shitty mileage, but Adam needed time to think.

Adam was going to see his brother.

He'd imagined the confrontation more than a few times, and more often than not the daydream ended with Adam laying Bobby out with a punch.

But their reunion wouldn't be that simple. Or that satisfying. Nothing was with magic involved. He had to remember that it wasn't about them or their past.

It was about helping Annie, finding out what haunted her. If Adam was lucky, it would be a ghost, and he could drive it off with some cedar incense and a ward strong enough to keep it away from the house.

A bigger problem might be beyond him. That meant visiting a watchtower. That meant Guardians.

With a sigh, he let the Sight drift over his eyes. Adam couldn't see the future, not like Sue, but his vision of the spirit world was sharper than most.

It didn't give him headaches anymore, seeing it overlay the mortal landscape like a ghostly painting atop the real world.

In the distance, the watchtowers spiraled out of the ground. Ruled by the Guardians, gods and entities of such might that Adam wanted nothing to do with them, the towers marked the map's cardinal points. Whatever had Annie couldn't be that big or bad, or the Guardians would have intervened. That meant it fell beneath their notice, into Adam's range.

And yet Bobby had seen something. Perhaps he'd just been spooked, and it would be simple, but Adam's instincts didn't say so.

He stared at the Watchtower of the North, a lonely frozen

tree, and felt cold despite the sunny day in the mortal realm. Adam had avoided the Guardian races since Liberty House, after his first adventures in spirit walking. He'd lay in his room, fantasizing about escape, wanting out—and then he was. He stepped into a realm of color and light. Fireflies swarmed, leaving trails of light. The moon, so much larger than in the mortal realm, shone full and green above him.

Plains of grass and mud were fields of singing flowers in the spirit. For a while, he thought that maybe Bobby was right, that he had lost his mind.

Then he'd met Perak. Beautiful, clever Perak. The elf had looked his own age, but you could never be certain with immortals. Lol

Perak had taught Adam how to control his spirit walking. Perak was his first, best teacher at magic, his first at so many things. Then he'd vanished.

The sun would go out before Adam trusted an elf again.

Driving now, the memory of lying together, moving together, brought a fresh ache to Adam's heart. There'd been a few guys since, but none he'd let get closer than kissing or a one-night stand. Once things went south of the border, Adam found a reason to not call them back. Kissing was great. Sex was nice, but he craved something else, something he didn't have a name for.

Love, honey

*****

Adam could have pushed through with more coffee, but he started drifting off somewhere past Colby, Kansas, near the Colorado line. He didn't want to roll up to Bobby's at 3:00 a.m. looking like a crackhead, so he pulled over, tugged off his shirt and pulled an old crocheted afghan over himself. It still smelled a bit like Aunt Sue.

Eased into the darkness, he dreamt of home, his first home, the trailer in the woods. In spring the oak leaves were so green,

so bright against their gray-black bark. He dreamt of storms filling the autumn sky, and how the trailer shook on its jacks when
the wind blew hard enough to signal tornado warnings—not that
they had sirens out in the country.

The rain hit the ground so hard the mud slashed and splashed
the tree trunks, dyeing them red.

Adam dreamt of his mom, smoking and shaking her head,
saying no when he asked if his Dad was ever coming home. Adam
almost couldn't remember her smile. As far back as he could recall,
she'd only ever frowned. When he dreamt of Bobby, they were
walking together, exploring the woods that had seemed so tall.

He woke with the gauzy memory of his father, a looming bear
of a man turned to hazy shadow. Finding a butter knife in the
spoon slot of the silverware sorter, he threw it hard enough that a
fork jutted from the linoleum floor. *Abusive*

Adam snapped awake, the black-and-red memory of rage
scalding him into consciousness. He lay curled in the Cutlass's
back seat, cramped and a little cold. His heart raced, and he took
several long breaths to slow it.

It took him several moments to untangle his feelings from his
father's. Adam's sensitivity, his particular type of magic, left him
like an open door. Strong emotions from another person could
walk in and set up house. He could guard himself now, thanks to
Perak and years of practice, but monsters lingered from before.

Adam shook a little as he climbed out of the car to pee and
brush his teeth. He rinsed with the bottle of water he refilled
whenever he stopped for gas. Calmed, he climbed back in and
checked himself in the rearview mirror. *Daniel ♡*

Adam knew what Bobby would see. Adam's skin reddened
too easily, and his hair flipped in weird directions if it got longer *Erin*
than his pinkie. Most of the time he kept it short, a sandy bristle.
Right now it was a little longer.

The switchgrass plains of Kansas gave way to the drier grass of Colorado. Checking the spirit realm, Adam watched the watchtowers change their forms. They shifted whenever the landscape changed. A giant tree morphed into a rocky spire. A clay urn, several stories tall, became an anthill. Even at this distance, Adam could see the orange fire lighting the ants' abdomens.

He felt power, magic, scattered across the plains in whorls and spikes, creatures and practitioners native to the area.

"Only passing through," he said, voice raspy from lack of speech. He sent it out like a broadcast. "Not worth your time."

He hoped whatever was out there heard him. A small player in the game of magic, Adam wasn't cocky enough to think he could win in a fight against anything higher up the food chain.

To have a chance he'd have to make a pact with a power, a god, a demon—or worse, an elf. The spectrum was full of such votaries, practitioners who put themselves in debt and traded their freedom for more magic. He'd always avoided that road. The only time he'd been tempted had been during his stay in Liberty House, but he'd waited it out, checking himself out the day he turned eighteen. His life was too short to pay such debts, and he'd had enough of elves to last three lifetimes.

Denver appeared, a pool of sprawl ringing a downtown cluster of taller buildings. He got closer, past the airport, and the mountains loomed.

In the spirit realm, a red shape hung over the city, puffing and pulsing like a blood-filled organ. Tendrils like veins reached for miles, tethering it to the ground. Shaking, Adam gripped the steering wheel and pulled over to the shoulder. He stumbled out, felt the wake of a passing car, but still did not take his eyes off the sight in the sky.

Colossal, hovering, it felt like a stain, a poison cloud pressed against his senses. Perhaps Bobby had seen something after all.

Under an apparition like that, only the least sensitive wouldn't.

Adam cocked his head to the side and drew his walls up around himself. He couldn't let that thing past his defenses.

Back in the Cutlass, he followed the directions his phone gave him, south and into the city, but he needn't have bothered. The nearest tendril, one of the thickest, dove straight into Bobby's ugly yellow house.

6

ADAM

The house looked like a wedding cake or an Easter bonnet. Confection yellow, it sat on a square of green unmarked by dogs, weeds, or decorations. The windows were so shiny Adam couldn't see inside.

He hadn't known what to expect from Denver. Something different from Oklahoma City, sure, but this suburb was a little scary and slightly creepy in its cleanliness. *LOL "welcome"*

He parked the Cutlass on the street, pleased to see the battered car mar the scene. Climbing out, he closed the door with a strong shove and stared at the thing in the sky.

"Damn, that's ugly," he muttered, feeling small and exposed, he resisted the temptation to crouch, to hide.

The bloody tendril shifted in the wind, a gory rope mooring a tumorous blimp. Yellow electricity, sallow life, sparked across the tendril. High school biology had been a long time ago, but he thought the spirit had the same general shape as a heart. Purple and veined, it pulsed faintly, beating, like it might squirt blood across the city. Adam had never seen anything like it.

Slow, like a sleepy bull, the spirit turned toward him. Yellow eyes opened along its tendrils. They swiveled, random, searching for Adam.

"Shit!"

He leapt back, pulling his senses away and shutting down his Sight before the thing could focus on him. He is the Ring

Shaking, Adam looked around, saw only the mundane, the street and houses, but he felt the spirit lurking beneath the surface of his perception, like water moccasins on the lake back home. He kept his senses closed, exhaled. Sometimes half of magic felt like focused breathing. If he could not see the spirit, it could not see him. It could not cross over without a body. And this was a spirit that should not be let in.

He'd been stupid to look too closely, to draw its attention.

"Adam Lee?" a sawing, familiar voice demanded, "What are you doing out there? You look like a crazy person."

His mother stood in the doorway, behind the porch's white railing. Her nicotine-riddled voice and look of disappointment took him back to high school, to before Liberty House. She did not come to meet him.

Adam slung his backpack over his shoulder and walked toward her.

"We don't say crazy anymore, Ma," he said. "We say things like 'mentally handicapped' or 'challenged.'"

Tilla narrowed her eyes, like she always did when she didn't understand him, which was always.

She stayed inside the door, as if the daylight might burn her. Adam looked from her to the sky, where the spirit lingered on the Other Side. Perhaps she sensed it hiding there. He'd always assumed he'd gotten his Sight from his father, and he'd always wondered how much, if any, of the spirit world Bobby could see. But his mother had no Sight. She'd certainly had no trouble trying to pray away the things he'd seen as a child or signing the forms for Bobby to have Adam committed. Maybe the spirit was so big even true normals could feel its presence.

"Are you coming in?" she asked. "Or are you going to stand out there all day being a smart aleck?"

"Missed you too," Adam said. He wasn't certain he meant it, and yet he wasn't angry with her, at least not like he was with Bobby. Thinking of his mother just made him sad, like they should love each other but didn't. Too much difference lay between them.

He reached the porch. Tilla measured Adam with her eyes. Taller than her by a hand's length, Adam looked down to take her in.

Dingy silver streaked her hair. The rest was the same sandy brown as his. He'd remembered her being taller. The wind, the constant work, and the red Oklahoma grit had worn her down to a rocky pear shape. The smell of burnt coffee and menthol cigarettes clung to her. So much memory came with that, her holding him, lifting him up. She didn't embrace him now.

She still smoked. That had to piss Bobby off. It chased off some of the lingering chill to know his mother and brother weren't in lockstep. They usually were when it came to what they thought best for Adam.

No two people are perfect for each other

"You're too skinny, Adam Lee," Tilla said, completing her assessment with a nod. "Doesn't that woman feed you?" *why don't you*

"I eat, Ma," he said, bristling at her mention of Sue. Adam didn't know why his mother hated Sue, but he suspected Tilla blamed her side of the family for his Sight, like how she believed he'd caught being gay from missing his father, even though he'd been kissing boys in kindergarten. *LOL*

And he hadn't lied. He ate when he could and what he could afford to.

"You should have stayed at school," she said, firing a warning shot he knew would likely become a barrage when Bobby joined in.

"It wasn't a school, Ma," Adam said. He kept his voice calm as his guts tightened, bracing for the coming fight.

She glared at him. Great. He'd already pissed her off. That had to be a new record.

Adam didn't want to fight about Liberty House, at least not yet. And, as tempting as it was, he didn't turn around and walk back to the car.

He'd tried to tell them, that the orderlies were thugs and bullies, that the "classes" he took were just a room full of drugged-up patients with a TV, a beaten VCR and no movie newer than 1989. Sometimes it was just the same movie, day after day in a cinder block room with a water-stained ceiling.

His one relief, for a while, had been his nights. There had been spirit walking. There had been Perak. Then there hadn't. Perak had vanished without warning or explanation, leaving him no comfort and no escape from the horrors of his days.

Mind-numbing boredom, the side effects from drugs, drool and pissing himself, and the ice water baths when he rejected the pills, crept into his nights.

His mother hadn't believed him. She hadn't come for him.

But it was Bobby he really didn't want to see.

"Where is he?" Adam asked.

"At work," his mother said. "He might be home for dinner."

So nothing had changed. Adam's brother still put his success, his own goals, above his family. Adam swallowed a sneer and followed his mother.

A mantel over the gas fireplace held the only hints of home, a few rose rocks and a chunk of the bog iron they'd dug up as kids. The art, prints of country sides, was thoroughly cheerful.

She stopped in a kitchen bigger than Sue's living room. Granite and polished steel appliances gleamed with money and newness. More of the wedding cake effect. More shine and bright white trim.

"You know," Adam muttered. "For the straight one, Bobby lives in a pretty girly house."

His mother turned away from him, like she always did when he mentioned his orientation.

"Annie picked it," she said. "Before."

"When did this start, Mom?" Adam asked. He didn't want to mention the spirit. It would only panic her or trigger the old belief that he was crazy.

"Bobby called me a month ago," she said. "Asked me to come out and help."

Adam put his backpack on the counter.

"Can I see her?" he asked.

With a little nod, his mother led him from the kitchen and upstairs. *→ defines Bobby's worldview*

The <u>bedroom</u> had a <u>deadbolt that locked</u> from the outside. His mother flipped it and cracked the door to peek before giving it a firm push.

A woman lay atop the bedspread. Adam sort of recognized Annie from the pictures she sometimes emailed, but he couldn't imagine this pale, drained shell writing the cheery notes highlighting her life with Bobby. *Aw*

Hey, Adam. I hope you're well. Happy birthday! We're spending Christmas in Aspen.

This Annie had a translucent quality, like a bit of soap worn too thin and close to slipping down the drain.

Adam approached quietly, wary of disturbing her, but his mother strode in.

"She can't hear us," his mother said, gesturing toward the bed. "Robert has her too sedated."

"I know how that feels," he said.

They'd diagnosed him as psychotic and fed him enough drugs to keep him sick and slow. What he felt from Annie reminded him of those days.

To see Annie, really see her, he'd have to use his Sight, risk drawing the spirit's attention, but Adam was subtle. He hoped, if he did not focus too hard, he could avoid its gaze.

He blinked, let the Sight come.

Magic pulsed through Annie, but it wasn't her own. The sallow sparks running through her were coming from the spirit. It had her. Lost, exhausted from trying to find her way back, she had no magic of her own, no way to fight. The spirit's grip held fast.

Stomach roiling, Adam straightened his back, and looked to the ceiling. The veiny cord ran through it, right into Annie's heart like a bloody, rotting stalk. He could try to cut it or force it out, but he wasn't sure what effect that would have on Annie, not with bits of the thing running through her like copper wires through a chandelier. He needed to know what they conducted. He needed to know fast.

Careful, avoiding the thing's attention, he took Annie's hand.

There she was, beneath the drugs, beneath the oppressive weight of the thing inside her.

A wave of confused despair, black and deep, washed over him. *Lost.*

Unable to take more, Adam stepped back. He double checked that the thing hadn't reacted, hadn't spotted his intrusion.

"You see it, don't you?" his mother asked. "There *is* something there?"

"It's a spirit, Ma."

She grimaced. He knew she wouldn't say she was sorry. She'd never been able to do that. When it had come down to it, she'd wanted *him* to apologize for what he was. He puffed out his frustration. He was here for Annie. This was about her.

"I'll do what I can," he said meaning it. "But yes, something has her. I have to look into it."

He led her back into the hall before he continued, "I can't solve it without a little digging."

His mother raised her hands to indicate she didn't want to know more, as if knowing what afflicted Annie would infect her with it. She felt about the magic the same way she did about his sex life. His mother and brother did not ask, so Adam did not tell.

Bobby had admitted to having a little Sight, which had been enough to shock Adam into coming here. Once, his brother would have put his hand in a garbage disposal before he admitted magic might be real. His mother had moments, insights that told Adam he got some of his magic from her side of the family. If he asked her about it, she retreated into her bible and told him to pray. What Adam had never understood, what they could never tell him, was why it was so *scary* to them. Well it looks Scary

"Got it," he said, answering her silence. "I'll just fix it and disappear again."

Adam shouldn't have expected more from this reunion. His mother didn't answer him. She stared past him without focusing on him, like she was trying to decide if that would be best.

Following her back down to the main floor, he wondered if he'd ever stop hoping for them to see him, to really know him.

"We'll put you in the basement," she said as she led him through a door and down another flight of stairs, going underground.

The space was finished, nice even. Compared to the rest of the house it was toned down, a little less garish.

Adam would have a little bathroom and shower all to himself. The guestroom had a window, a light well with an escape ladder in case of fires. It was nicer than any place Adam had ever slept in, but he could already feel the acid rising in his throat. He'd have to deal with Bobby soon. Adam clenched and unclenched his fists. The sooner he got to work, the sooner he could leave.

Enjoying a longer shower than he'd ever had at Sue's, Adam scrubbed off the funk of road sweat, grease, and red dirt. He scratched with his uneven nails, removing as much dead skin as grime. His body, lean and pale, flushed beneath water hotter than he'd felt in months. The red from his scrubbing would fade. It felt good to be so clean, to know the bill went on Bobby's tab. Adam put most of his clothes in the washer, dressed in his clean jeans, and pulled on a faded T-shirt advertising a band that had broken up before he'd been born.

Adam took to the bed, head at the footboard, and bent his leg at the knee. Palms up, he laid his hands flat. Folded into the position of the Hanged Man, he listened to the washing machine. He let its chugging rhythm carry him down inside himself, to where his magic lay. It felt like opening a door, like stepping into an elevator. Then he was elsewhere.

7

ADAM

Adam opened his eyes, and nothing looked the same.

The spirit realm echoed the mortal world, but the angles were distorted. Walls leaned. Trees stretched. Spirits great and small flitted through the air. In this place, Bobby's house had no roof. Even the basement opened to a star-scattered twilight sky. The moon shone bigger and closer than it ever could on the mortal plane. Life glowed.

But Adam could feel the spirit, greasy and rotten. Its presence coated everything.

Adam called up his protections, barriers made of willpower and magic, armor to ward his mind. Sensitive as he was in the mortal world, in his body, he was both more vulnerable and stronger here. Something with enough power could still get through, blow through him like he was made of salt, but it had to spot him first.

He crept upstairs, the hallways twisting around him. Thick shadows gathered, filtering the starlight that pierced the walls. A swarm of green beetles coated the wall, their shells iridescent in the moonlight.

Annie lay in her bed. The spirit was more solid, more tangible than her. Its barbed tendrils ran through her body. He could see the blood moving inside her, her bones. Even if Adam could sever the connection, he wouldn't be able to get the threads out without hurting her, maybe even killing her. Those bits of spirit would remain inside her like jellyfish barbs. This was beyond him. Adam's blood chilled.

He needed information, to talk to someone who could tell him more. Then he could try to find a way to break the spirit's grip. The problem was choosing the safest someone. He would not indebt himself to a power. *↳ Knowledge ≠ free*

But someone who made such deals would have the knowledge he needed and might tip him off as to why the Guardians hadn't acted. A spirit of that size, possessing normal people—it was exactly what they were there for. *Why? What do we give them?*

Outside the house, Adam approached the nearest tree. It opened a pair of emerald eyes and glared at him.

"Pardon me," he said, kneeling to touch its roots.

With a little push of his will, he flowed through the green, tossed and turned through phylum and vein until he stood in a field of sunflowers. He muttered a thank-you to the blackened tree he'd arrived at and hurried away from its crow- and noose-strewn branches.

The move had tired him, stretched him. The further he stepped from his body, the more his spirit frayed around the edges. He had never proved how far he could go, how far would be safe. There were limits. He'd tested them with Perak, but never past the point of safety.

An old Airstream trailer stood behind a split rail fence, resting on cinder blocks, the grass tickling its wheels. Time and hail had hammered its steel exterior.

He'd never seen what vehicle or beast had towed it here. It could have been a pick-up truck. It could have been a T. rex. Adam smiled to see it.

A black woman sat in front. Adam almost couldn't see her through the light she radiated. A double-barreled shotgun lay ready across her lap. Sara had never used it in his presence, but Adam felt certain she loaded it with shells and magic enough to kill him with a glancing shot.

Adam hated guns. He remembered his father forcing him to shoot a squirrel with BBs, over and over until he stopped crying at the little thing's jerking, final movements. He'd felt it die, and had never touched a gun since, no matter how un-Oklahoma of him that was.

Adam walked the path cutting through the field, mindful of the workers reaping among the sunflowers.

Dressed in overalls and straw hats, they looked like farmers, but they weren't human, not entirely. The blades of their scythes, rusty steel set in hoary wood, should have swished through the stalks, but their reaping made no sound. Each wore a skull mask, pale atop their human faces.

Adam hurried past the bit of fence dividing Sara's trailer from the fields. It marked the boundary of her wards. Inside them, he felt a little safer, but not much.

Intent on their task, the Reapers didn't acknowledge his approach. He did not know how they'd take someone interrupting their work, and he really didn't want to find out.

"Adam Binder," Sara said. Pausing, she took a long sip from a tall glass—iced tea with a thick slice of lemon. "As I live and breathe."

She had a deep southern accent. It whispered of swamps and hidden alligators. She'd always been kind to him.

"Can you turn down the light show?" he asked, shielding his eyes with a hand. He wanted to sound confident, but couldn't afford to offend her. "I'm not a tourist."

The multicolored glow around her dimmed until he could see her clearly. A diminutive woman with curly hair that haloed her smooth face, Sara looked at him through round, purple-tinted spectacles.

Her magic's scent was still strong, but pleasant, like sweet tea and sunflowers in summer.

Aunt Sue had introduced Adam to Sara not long after Liberty House. Sara sold information, trading secrets when Sue had them. But Adam and Sue were small time customers. Sara brokered deals with entities far more powerful than the Binders. She had to have heard something about Denver.

That didn't mean Adam liked visiting her. Her chosen location, the field of Reapers, put him on edge. They were a force of nature, following laws and taking only those souls Death told them to. They didn't come for everyone. He didn't understand them. And though he told himself he had no real reason to fear them, he never failed to notice the swishing motion in the corner of his eye.

"I haven't seen you in a while, Adam Lee," Sara said, rocking back into her folding lawn chair. Aunt Sue had introduced him with first and middle names, so Sara always used them both. "You've grown up, filled out a little."

Time had marked her, but it was subtle. The lines weren't deep. Years slipped off Sara, a gift from those she bargained with. But nature would win out eventually. Death and its Reapers were inevitable. Even the ancient powers bowed to that.

"You stopped dyeing your hair black," she said, leaning toward him.

"Grew out of it," he said. In truth he couldn't afford it and let his hair grow back to its muddy blond. It riled him a little that she remembered him looking that way. He wasn't a teenager anymore, but maybe he could use that. Adam lifted a hand to scratch the back of his head and tried to sound respectful as he said, "I wanted to ask you about something."

He tried, and failed, to keep his eyes off the trailer door.

"You can come closer," Sara said, looking at him over the tops of her glasses. She had large, deep brown eyes. "They won't bite."

"Guess I need to work on my poker face."

"A little." She gave a little snort of laughter. "How's your aunt Sue?"

"She's good," Adam said.

Sue had spirit walked with him, bringing him to Sara to introduce him. The two of them traded gossip and pleasantries while Adam eyed the Reapers. The women were of a type, older, sunny. Sue hadn't seemed afraid of Sara's trailer.

He stepped nearer. The air around the trailer whispered. In the fields, the Reapers kept up their scything, their clockwork, synchronized motions. They were men and women, old and young, every race and height. Adam did not know how Death chose its servants. He'd rather not know. It was enough that they wouldn't harm him until his time came. They'd only attack if their work was interrupted.

"Well?" Sara asked, waving him to come closer. "Ask me."

"Denver."

Sara bowed her head, telling him she already knew.

"What is it?" he asked. "The thing in the sky?"

"A spirit," she said. "But not one we know. Not one anyone knows."

The whispers stilled. Sara's goddesses had cocked their ears. Adam had their attention, the last thing he wanted. He looked to his feet as his heart raced.

They didn't know. Sara didn't know.

"So it's something new," he said.

"Or something extremely old."

Neither was a good thing.

"What's it to you?" Sara asked.

There it was, the *this* for *that*. Adam didn't like giving up information, but he'd taken, so he had to give.

"It has my sister-in-law. I think it has lots of people," he said, considering the other tendrils. "I need to know how to break its hold."

Sara shook her head. "We don't know what it is or where it came from. Only that it defies Death and nature herself. It just appeared one day."

Adam took a step back. "That's not possible. Someone had to summon it."

Sara shrugged and sipped her tea. "If they did, they ain't advertising it."

"And the Guardians?" Adam asked. "Have they said anything? Done anything?"

"Not as yet," Sara said. "Someone must go to them in supplication, make a case before they will intervene."

"Surely one of the local witches has gone to the towers. One of the local practitioners. I can't be the first one to notice this thing."

Someone else should have already dealt with the spirit. A problem this big should have already been solved.

"Adam . . ." Sara trailed off. "I thought you knew the situation."

"I do," he said. "There's a spirit over Denver, like a cloud. It's connected to people everywhere."

"It's far more than that." Sara took a long sip. She didn't offer him any and he knew not to take it if she had. There were rules about food in the spirit realm. *Like Wonderland*

"Will you tell me?" he asked.

"Are you ready to bargain?"

And there was the bee sting in the honey. She'd help him— for a price. He could get all the power he needed to free Annie, to protect himself, and banish the spirit. All it would cost him was everything.

"I don't want power," Adam said, crossing his arms over his chest. "Just information."

"Well you know what they say about knowledge," she drawled.

"Sara, please. This is serious. Tell me what you know."

"What I can tell you, *for free*—" She leaned forward. Fear slid a little more southern into her tone. "Is that all of the magicians in Denver are dead."

oh fuck

8

ADAM

Adam woke shuddering. If Sara, with her gods and alliances, feared the thing in the sky over Denver, then he had a mosquito's chance against an elephant. The most he could hope for was to find someone else, a greater power, to deal with it and try not to get caught in the blast. He squeezed his eyes shut at the thought of Annie lying in her bed.

Dammit.

He wanted to run back home to Sue and Spider, but he couldn't leave Annie like this. So much of how the spirit had trapped her reminded him of Liberty House, of how he'd felt, weighed down to his bed by drugs and, once or twice, restraints.

He had to find a way to free her, and he had to know what had killed the witches and magicians in Denver.

"I know you must be tired after the drive, but napping, Adam?" a voice asked. "You just got here."

Adam opened his eyes to find his brother glaring at him.

"Bobby," Adam said.

"Well?" Bobby asked.

Adam swallowed a remark about Bobby getting on Adam's

case when he was the one who was still going to work when his wife was possessed.

"I wasn't napping," Adam said. The hangdog look on Bobby's face kept Adam from snapping harder. He stretched, working to settle himself back into his body. Spirit walks were deadening, and he always woke more tired than when he lay down.

"Meditating. Whatever," Bobby said.

"I was trying to find out what's going on," Adam said. No one had ever wound him up like Bobby.

"And did you?" Bobby asked.

Adam didn't think Bobby would believe him about spirit walking, even if he went into it.

"Some," he said, uncertain if he should explain that Annie was possessed.

"Can you fix it or not?" Bobby demanded. "Or are you just going to lie around?"

"You like it when your patients talk to you that way, Doctor Binder?" Adam asked.

"You're not a doctor."

"You called me, remember? I'm the closest thing you've got to an expert."

Bobby had practically begged, and Adam barely kept himself from throwing it in his brother's face. He choked the desire down.

He'd always hated Bobby's "dad mode." Maybe that's just who Bobby had grown up to be. Maybe that's who "Robert" was. Adam almost spat with disgust. His only real memories of their father might be rages and temper storms, but they were enough. Adam had no desire to imitate the man.

Ten years older, Bobby had always looked more like a grown man than Adam had ever felt. Deep purple ringed his eyes. Gray mixed with his muddy hair. He was even starting to look like their dad.

It fit. Bobby had never gotten it through his head that wanting Adam to be normal wasn't the same as wanting what was best for Adam.

"I just don't want you screwing around," Bobby said. "Making up crap."

"Or what, you'll have me locked up again?" Adam asked. "Maybe you can get a two-for-one special."

Bobby's face flushed red. He looked away.

"Right. Annie's different," Adam said. He sounded cruel, but he wanted this settled now. They weren't kids anymore, and he wouldn't be bullied, let alone parented. Not by this asshole. "You wouldn't do that to her, just me."

Bobby flinched. He opened his mouth to say something but closed it again.

"Well you're going to need a bigger ward," Adam said. "With beds for about a dozen."

Anger and curiosity warred on Bobby's face.

"What do you mean?" he asked.

"She's not the only one," Adam said. "What has a hold on her is big. It's old, and it's got someone more powerful than me spooked, and it's connected to people all over the city."

"Bullshit," Bobby said. He clenched his fist, the old denial flaring.

Adam thought Bobby might punch the wall, like Dad would have, but his brother forced his hands to open. He ran his palms over his jean pockets.

"I can prove it," Adam said. "I just need to track them down."

"Fine," Bobby said, raising a hand in surrender. "It's late and Mom's waiting with supper."

"What time is it?" Adam asked, realizing the light from the basement window had darkened.

"Nine o'clock," Bobby said.

"Man," Adam said. "I didn't think I was gone that long."

He felt drained. The spirit walk had taken a lot from him.

"Mom must have decided you needed to sleep," Bobby said, leading Adam out of the basement.

"I wasn't sleeping," Adam snarled. "And I didn't come here for you to mock me."

"Whatever," Bobby said, already heading up the stairs.

Adam clenched his fists, but he followed without argument. He wanted to eat more than he wanted to go another round.

Climbing the stairs, he could smell his mother's cooking, salmon patties and steamed green beans. The memory took him back to Guthrie, to eating outside when it got too hot in the trailer. He'd douse the greasy little cakes in ketchup, craving the sugar more than the fried fish and breadcrumbs.

Their mother had worked long hours at the gas station after their dad left. She'd kept them fed, but hadn't had the chance to cook. Adam's early years were filled with cheap microwave dinners, popcorn, and boxes of off-brand macaroni. Bobby learned to cook out of necessity, though he never managed anything more complicated than pasta and meatballs. He'd cook in bulk, and they'd get by on a stock pot of pasta for a full week, digging down into the noodles for whatever bits of flavor and sauce might remain near the bottom.

Adam would go to his grave hating spaghetti and that cheap Parmesan cheese that tasted like sawdust. He and Sue ate cheap, but she spared him that, even if it meant they sometimes ate instant oatmeal for dinner.

Upstairs, his mom had set three places. Bobby looked at the unset fourth spot with open sadness.

No one spoke as forks and knives scraped plates. Adam almost asked his mother how she'd been, to at least be polite and ask what she'd done with the land and trailer back home. He knew it was important to her. She'd always insisted on keeping it, even when Bobby and Adam were gone. But he bit down on the questions, afraid the acid roiling in his gut would spill out.

By the time he rose to rinse his plate in the sink, his jaw ached. He sat back down.

"When did it start?" he asked.

His mother and brother exchanged a glance.

"I can't help if I don't know the details," Adam said.

Bobby took a long breath, let it out. "We tried to have a baby. She miscarried, got depressed. It happens, but she never came back. Then, this."

Deflated, Bobby ducked his head.

"I'm sorry," Adam said, meaning it, though the news didn't really help him. Depression might open a door, something the spirit could exploit, but it didn't explain it. He braced for a harder question.

"Before, did Annie have any Sight? I mean, is she like me?"

"No," Bobby said, shaking his head without looking up. "She's normal. Completely normal."

Normal.

The urge to lash out rose in Adam's throat, but he swallowed it down.

"You said there were others?" Bobby asked.

"Yeah. I need to find them. Do you have a computer I can use?"

"It's in the den," Bobby said, nodding to a room just off the dining room, down a few steps, though his eyes didn't look that way.

"Okay," Adam said.

The den had an air of disuse. Books lined the desk hutch. Things were organized in a haphazard way that could not have been Bobby's doing. Glad Annie's got some personality

The computer, an older desktop with a large monitor, woke up slowly. It wanted about a million security updates. Adam told it to run them later. He didn't want to wait all night.

While it booted, he scanned the books Annie had stockpiled: *How to Raise Happy Children. How to Help Your Baby Sleep through the Night.*

Despite Bobby and his mother, despite the ball of black and red in his throat, something blue poured into Adam's heart. He squeezed his eyes shut, let the weight of it press him into the chair. This wasn't any kind of life like what he wanted, but this was Annie's dream. Kids. This ugly house. Bobby. It all floated around him, soaked into the walls and carpet.

He didn't attend it

"I'll help you," Adam told her picture, a smiling photo from their wedding. "I'll figure it out."

The local practitioners were dead, and that was another thing he needed to understand. Without them he had far fewer options for help or information, but it also meant a lurking threat might be gunning for him.

Spirit walkers were rare. But sensitives, people who might feel the spirit realm but not see it, were common.

Maybe the local sensitives could feel the spirit hovering over the city without attracting its attention. There had to be something on the internet, something someone had spotted and reported.

In high school, when his Sight became unbearable, all he'd wanted was for his mother and brother to understand it. Understand *him*. Now he had to wonder if their safety wasn't worth his loneliness, if having more Sight would have made them targets too.

If the spirit had killed the local practitioners, then why hadn't the watchtowers intervened? The Guardians were supposed to protect the world from larger threats, and it didn't get much larger than a giant floating organ hanging over the city.

A browser window finally opened. Adam wanted to search for pawn shops on Federal, follow up on the warlock, but the spirit had to come first.

There were always portents when the spirit world began

bleeding into the mortal. A quick search told him the Denver airport was the center of some conspiracy theories. Most of them revolved around an apocalyptic mural, showing native people being destroyed by fire. There were gargoyles, statues of them climbing out of suitcases. From the air the entire airport looked a lot like a swastika. There was talk of bunkers, underground structures, and of course, Saurians.

LOL

Closer to the city, there were ghost stories, and tunnels running between them, the train station, and the old downtown brothels. The jarred, pickled heads of two outlaws went missing from the capitol building. Nothing pointed to the spirit. Then he found an article on the old sanitarium and dug a little further.

Adam squeezed his eyes shut, counted to ten, and went to find his brother.

Bobby sat in the living room, an actual newspaper in his lap. He just needed reading glasses and a pair of slippers to finish looking like he'd time traveled from the 1950s.

White America's Wonderland

"What hospital do you work at?" Adam asked.

"Why do you want to know?"

"It's Mercy, isn't it?"

"Yes," Bobby said. He'd changed into sweatpants and a T-shirt. Both appeared new, like casual was a look he was trying on for an evening. "Why?"

Adam leaned against the doorway, already tensed to walk away.

"Mercy tore down its old psych ward recently," Adam said. "I think they set something loose."

"Why would you think that?" Bobby asked.

"Three of the hospital personnel have been committed in the last month. You didn't hear anything about it?"

"A hospital is a big place, Adam," Bobby said. "This can't be about Mercy."

Adam sighed. "Spirits have to be summoned or set loose. It

had to come from somewhere. This one is threaded throughout the city, connected to different people. I'd bet these are them, that they're all in the same state as Annie."

Bobby nibbled his lip, calculating, and said, "All right. What do you need?"

"Get me a look at the construction site."

Bobby was already prickly. No need to tell him everything. Adam also needed a look at the personnel files of the possessed, to see if there was something in their background that might hint at a magical bloodline or a history of sensitivity. "I'll see if there's anything to it."

"Okay," Bobby said. "Come to work with me tomorrow."

9

ADAM

Adam hadn't brought anything close to business casual in his backpack, so he met his brother by the front door in clean jeans and a checkered button-up. His jean jacket had some vaguely brown stains on the lining that were probably coffee, but it would pass muster so long as he didn't take it off. He'd at least gelled and combed his hair.

Bobby gave Adam the once-over and led him out the door.

"You look good, Adam," he said when the car was in motion. "You should always dress like this, tone down the redneck thing you've got going."

"I look like a missionary," Adam said.

"Is that so bad?" Bobby asked.

Adam clenched his jaw, uncertain if Bobby meant to tease, provoke, or if he really just didn't know. Adam kept his mouth shut and settled into the Audi's leather seat. He had to admit it was a nice car, but like all things Bobby, it had a dickish quality to it, and was nice and new without feeling comfortable or personal. He'd take the Cutlass along with her dents and the bailing wire holding her together.

Probably 'cave' like not telling Daisy to shave

The hospital looked Spanish in style. Old, more like an apartment building than a medical facility. Adam could see why they were demolishing part of it. He checked it with his Sight, saw no sign of the spirit. In fact, he didn't See or sense any magic.

Adam blinked, shaking off the empty feeling he got from the place as Bobby parked in a space with his name on it.

"Come on," Bobby said, leaving the car with a little too much enthusiasm.

He wants to show off.

Like Adam's approval should matter. Like anything should matter except Annie.

The hospital's interior felt like an RV, all plastic walls and manufactured parts. Adam could have touched the low ceiling. He wondered if it was an effect of its age or if they'd built it that way on purpose, if smaller spaces prevented infection or the prefab walls made it easier to clean up the blood. It kind of reminded him of their trailer, his childhood home in the Oklahoma woods, only cleaner, newer. Maybe that's why Bobby liked working there so much.

Bobby preened at the staff's friendly respect. Other doctors nodded. Nurses smiled in passing. They called him Doctor Binder, which sounded a bit like a super villain. It wasn't the life Adam wanted, even if some of the nurses were attractive guys.

Adam noticed a few of them moving through the hallways as Bobby took him through security and got him a visitor badge. He couldn't say what kind of life he did want. He'd done odd jobs for years now, not thinking about much beyond surviving or finding his dad. Sometimes he felt the future stretching out before him, and his stomach clenched at the thought of facing it alone. Bobby had Annie. She should be more important to him.

"Wait here," Bobby said, pointing to a chair. "I'll get someone to show you around."

Adam took a seat, dismissed the stack of magazines, and

folded his hands together. He forced a smile for the nurse watching from the corner and tried not to fidget.

The hospital felt all wrong. He'd driven Sue to doctor's appointments from time to time. Sensations, worry, frustration, and suffering permeated places like this. But he got nothing from Mercy. No feeling at all leaked through his defenses. Adam pressed his back against the wall and squirmed, trying to scratch an itch in the center of his back. Life was everywhere. Even the most remote area had something, some sense of spirit.

maybe a blockage

Careful of what he might find, Adam trailed his senses out around him, casting them like fishing lines. Nothing. No tremors of activity in the spirit realm, no ghosts.

Eyes wide, breath held, he tried to accept what it meant.

He'd never felt anything like it. He'd never been anywhere so void of energy or feeling. A hospital, a tornado of life and death, should teem with emotion.

Someone cleared his throat, drawing Adam out of his thoughts.

He opened his eyes and faced a cop. He didn't look much older than Adam. Tall, lean, and Latino, his uniform lay tight across his shoulders.

"Can I help you—" Adam paused long enough to get the catch in his throat under control. He leaned forward to read the badge pinned to that built chest. "Officer Martinez?"

"I'm supposed to help you," the cop said. Smiling, he jerked a thumb over his shoulder. "Doctor Binder asked for someone to show you around."

"Yeah?" Adam asked, returning the smile.

"Yeah," the cop said. He had short black hair, the natural glossy kind Adam had so envied in his emo days.

He stood, shook the cop's offered hand, and cut the eye contact before it went on a little too long.

"He said you wanted to see the construction site," the cop said.

LoL "Yeah, it's for a thing." Adam suppressed a wince. He was forgetting the story he'd come up with. "Officer Martinez."

"It's just Vic," the cop said with a laugh. "Unless you're in trouble."

Adam focused on Vic's shoulders as he walked away.

You've got a job to do, Adam chided himself and caught up.

"Does the hospital always use cops for tours?" he asked.

"Just for security," Vic said with a little shrug. "It's some extra money for off-duty police and extra experience for us rookies."

They passed open rooms with sleeping patients and silent nurses. Some energy lay there—fresh sadness and grief, boredom—but not the deep well of feeling an old hospital should contain. It shouldn't be this way.

Adam didn't even need his armor, the walls he used to keep such things from overwhelming him. He felt naked without his defenses, but he left them down in case they caused him to miss something.

He had no proof the spirit was connected, but his nerves thrummed with warning. Something wasn't right.

"What kind of thing?" Vic asked, drawing Adam back from his thoughts.

"Huh?" Adam asked. "Oh, I'm a writer. Or at least I want to be."

"Yeah?" Vic asked. "What do you write?"

"I'm working on a book," Adam lied. "A ghost story."

It sounded childish and he held in a wince.

"Oh," Vic said, perking up. "My brother likes that stuff. I'm more of a sci-fi and fantasy guy myself."

Be still my heart. *Lol*

"How many brothers do you have?" Adam asked without thinking. He hadn't come to flirt. He'd finish seeing what there was to see with Vic, then figure out how to get into the hospital's records.

Asking isn't flirting, love

"I'm Mexican," Vic said. "Lots. A dozen."

"Really?" Adam asked.

"No," Vic said, dark eyes sparkling. "Just one."

He was still chuckling when he pulled at his ID badge. It came on a retractable wire, like a tape measure. Vic pressed it to unlock a door. Adam was going to need one of those.

"If you're writing a horror story," Vic said. "Then you gotta see this."

This part of the hospital felt older, condemned, if not ready to collapse. A floor of chipped linoleum lay beneath fluorescent lights. The air was desert dry, like all of Denver, apparently. Most of the bulbs were out, and the AC was off, making the hall warmer than he'd expected.

It should have had some energy, some aura or impression left from its former life and occupants, but the void, the magical nothing, only deepened.

"Where are we?" Adam asked, turning about. He hadn't seen this from the street. It must lay behind the Spanish facade where Bobby had parked.

Some of the doors were sealed with sheets of taped plastic. Adam half expected a movie zombie to crash through them. He stepped closer to Vic. The cop smelled faintly of cologne, like oranges and sandalwood. Combined with Vic's warmth and proximity, it lightened the heaviness that had filled Adam's limbs.

"The old psych ward," Vic said, taking a flashlight from his belt. "They're tearing it down soon."

"I thought they already had," Adam said. "I read it on the internet."

"Not all of it," Vic said, leading Adam deeper into the hall. "Some of the buildings, like this one, have asbestos sealed in the floor. The removal takes time, but they're going down. It's too bad. They're kind of pretty."

Narrow windows let a little light in. Vic bounced the flashlight's beam over the tiled floor and dusty ceiling.

The magic void opened beneath them, an empty maw only Adam could sense or fall into. It no longer felt restful, more like a lurking, open-mouthed monster, ready to snap shut and devour his meager power.

Adam shuddered. This, all of this, was too big for him. He hadn't wanted to admit it before, but he wasn't going to be able to save Annie on his own. He was already in over his head.

After a while Vic asked, "You going to take notes or anything?"

"Nah," Adam said, turning in place. "I'm just going to, you know, soak it in."

"You look like you already have," Vic said.

Adam shot him a questioning look.

"You're shivering," Vic said.

Adam hadn't noticed.

"I'm going to look around," Vic said. "Might as well make sure nobody's broken in or anything."

"You're leaving me alone?" Adam asked, unhappy to hear his voice pitch higher.

"Won't that be scarier?" Vic asked. He raised the flashlight to illuminate his parting grin and stepped into one of the darker hallways. The echoes of his footsteps faded.

Adam lifted his Sight. Normally he'd hesitate, knowing too well what things lurked in a sanitarium, but he had to See.

The doorways tilted. The sheets of plastic came to life, fluttering and rippling like water. Old brickwork and crumbling mortar replaced the thick plaster walls, but nothing skittered. No spirits haunted. They should have infested the place. Death, trauma, and mental illness made the perfect recipe for ghosts. Adam wasn't the first practitioner who'd gotten a diagnosis and a trip to an institution.

A flash of memory, other inmates, other teens, too lost in their delusions or a haze of sedatives to talk to him, rose like bile in his throat.

Some of them had been practitioners. He'd felt their presence like a stain in the air. It hadn't faded, not even when they'd left Liberty.

Mercy should have been the same, echoing with those who'd been hospitalized here, but the void just kept running deeper. Adam sensed no bottom to it. The spirit realm teemed with life. It was nothing but life. Mercy was the opposite: cold, sterile, dead. It chilled Adam to the core. He shut down his Sight.

The names of these facilities are important. 2 sides of the same shitty coin. Liberty, freedom, independence ⇝ feeling, pain, lingering, trauma ≠ Mercy, forgiveness, release ⇝ unfeeling, clean, perfect, lacking

10

ADAM

"Magic is life," Sue had told him in her thick Oklahoma drawl. "Spirit is life. So all living things have magic. That's why the immortals have more magic than any of us."

She'd told Adam this so many times that it became background noise, an easily forgotten part of his landscape.

Magic was life. Spirit was life. So what did that make a place where all spirit was absent? Death

Adam was shaking off the cold creeping up his spine when Bobby appeared.

"How did it go?" he asked, leaning in, like they were part of a conspiracy.

Adam shook his head. He didn't have an answer. The more he learned about the situation, the more he felt the gaps in his knowledge. He'd slid into a canyon, couldn't see the bottom, and wasn't certain there weren't rattlesnakes waiting below.

Around him, beneath him, things connected. One thing led to ten thousand things. Adam could sense something coming, the action he most wanted to avoid. To help Annie, he'd have to appeal to a higher power. There would be a price. There always

Witches are better because they are honest and can put things together easier

was, usually in servitude. If he was not careful, he'd end up some
spirit's errand boy or worse—their slave.

Adam chewed his lip, unhappy with what he knew was inevitable.

It had been a lesson Perak had drilled into Adam over and
over, telling him stories of singers or actors forever lost to the
Other Side, all their family and friends long dead while they
performed forever, singing the same songs, playing the same roles,
never allowed to change or age. *oof. Explains a lot*

"Ready for some lunch?" Bobby asked.

Adam gave his brother a questioning look.

"I'm buying," Bobby said, looking hopeful, the preening
doctor again.

"Sure," Adam said, unable to deny the rumbling in his stomach.

He'd been trying to shake off his memories, his anger at
Bobby for locking him up and then ignoring him, never looking
for him, never asking if he was okay. It had been years, but the
way Bobby looked at him, so disappointed, brought it all to the
surface, like a clump of dead leaves atop a lake. The sharp edges
of his memories kept him away from the mushy, rotting center,
the part where he might miss Bobby and where he'd been hurt
that Bobby hadn't come for him. Adam doubted they'd ever be
able to talk about it.

Annie did that. She's been more of a brother

If Bobby could sense the spirit, then perhaps he also sensed
the hospital's void, the dead zone. It might even make him happy,
afraid of magic as he was. Hell, it might even explain why he
loved working here so much. He might find it peaceful, like how
polluted lakes had clearer water. If so, then Bobby was more
sensitive than Adam had suspected. He might even border on
practitioner, and that might put him in danger.

"What?" his brother asked.

"Just thinking," Adam muttered. It was too easy to slip into that, too, hiding his thoughts from his family lest they judge, lest they take steps.

He didn't say anything else as he followed Bobby to the cafeteria. Adam expected it to be calm, quiet, like the rest of the hospital, but it surprised him with its liveliness. Sure, there were gloomy and impatient people, but tables of nurses chatted together. The coffee bar whizzed and hissed. Children dashed back and forth to a frozen yogurt machine. It felt like a buffet restaurant after church on a Sunday. The people's feelings rubbed against Adam's defenses without much friction.

"How many people work here?" Adam asked Bobby as they lined up with trays to choose food.

"A few thousand," Bobby said, pulling his badge out on its string to pay for the meal. "There's security, waste disposal, volunteers. That's not even getting into the medical staff."

Adam nodded, not really listening. He considered the list of names on his phone. He needed more information. The spirit was a heart, maybe—an organ, at least. It had connected itself to Annie, to other people. There had to be a reason. A ghost might possess someone as a means of trying to finish what it hadn't settled in life. But such a massive thing couldn't do so with a human body. And he couldn't puzzle out why it would connect to several of them.

"You could work in a hospital like this someday," Bobby said, choosing a seat.

Adam took his own chair across from his brother.

"That's not what I'm here for, remember?" Adam asked, pausing his fork before it reached his mouth.

"I know," Bobby said, looking like a kicked puppy. "I'm just saying that you seem invested in helping people. And working in a hospital is a great way to do that."

Adam silenced his retort with a scoop of his fork and a quick bite. He didn't want to fight. He swallowed and fought down a sigh. Being around Bobby made him feel like a kid again, dumb and weak. It took him back to all the things he'd hated about being a teenager and about Bobby.

"You seem to like the food at least," Bobby said.

"What's not to like?" Adam said, his mouth half full. Between his mother's cooking and this lunch, he felt fuller than he had in months.

"But you wouldn't work here," Bobby said.

"I don't like hospitals," Adam said. Giving up eating, he leaned back in his chair. "That's you. Why is it so important to you that I be like you?"

Every meal was going to be like this, a trap, a minefield. He'd have to go hungry.

Bobby gripped his fork. "I just want you to be happy, Adam, to be—"

"Normal. I know," Adam said, trying to keep calm. "But I'm not normal, Bobby. And I don't want to be. Stop trying to fix me."

Bobby scowled, but he finished eating without further argument. His appetite lost, Adam threw the rest of his food away.

"I've got rounds," Bobby said when they'd returned to his floor.

They both darted for the elevator door, ready to be free of each other's proximity. Adam bumped into Bobby as they exited.

Adam sat in the same chair Bobby had parked him in before.

"I'll just catch up on *Highlights for Children*," he said, waving to the magazines as Bobby walked away. *love them*

Adam waited a few moments before he opened his palm and examined the ID badge he'd swiped. Bobby was easy to distract when he was angry. That at least hadn't changed. Adam slipped out into the hall and turned his accent up a notch.

"Excuse me, ma'am. Where is HR?" he asked the nurse at the desk. Tall, over six feet, she had a pretty, oval face and straight, silvery-blond hair. "My brother said I should ask them about jobs."

She smiled and pointed at the elevator. "Fourth floor."

"Thank you," Adam said.

A fire map outside the elevator listed the location of the records room. Adam went carefully.

If he'd had more magic, like an elf or some other immortal, Adam could step across to the spirit realm, become intangible, and step back inside the records room. As he was, he cast his senses out, trying to feel his way around the halls to avoid other people until he got to the right part of the floor.

Adam turned a corner and nearly collided with a janitor, a squat black man in coveralls with more than a little gray in his curly hair.

"Sorry," Adam said, grimacing. His senses had failed him. He had too little power.

The janitor grunted but said nothing as he mopped his way along the hall and Adam reached the records room.

Adam slid Bobby's key card from his pocket. When this was done he'd drop it somewhere where it would be found and returned without any drama. The door unbolted with a beep and a click of the bolt. Adam slipped inside.

He'd hoped for rows of filing cabinets but found himself staring at a computer desk.

"Well, shit," Adam grumbled.

He moved the mouse but knew what he'd see before the monitor finished lighting up.

The screen, a black and green interface, wanted a password he didn't have. Adam looked for a place to swipe the badge. Not finding one, he tried *Guest* and *Admin*, but the hospital IT proved smarter than that.

The door behind Adam opened with a click. He spun the office chair around to see two cops enter.

Adam raised his hands with a sigh.

"Hi, Vic," Adam said.

"It's Officer Martinez now," Vic said, his posture stiff. He wasn't smiling.

"What are you doing in here?" the other cop demanded. An older, shorter man, he had a thick mustache and caterpillar eyebrows but a bald pate.

"Just looking around," Adam said, meeting Vic's eyes. "I didn't mean any trouble."

The older cop sneered.

Adam flinched at Vic's scowl.

"This for your book?" Vic asked, his gaze narrowed.

"Yeah," Adam said.

"You can't get in here without one of those," Vic said, nodding to the ID. "Your brother reported his missing and then the system logged the door."

"Of course it did," Adam said. "And of course he did."

It would be nice if Bobby could be less of a moron. He was probably so pissed at Adam for stealing the thing that he hadn't thought through why Adam had taken it. Bobby was so caught up in his reputation, in being Doctor Binder that he hadn't stopped to think that Adam was trying to help Annie.

"This is a misunderstanding," Adam said, trying to look sheepish.

"You're going to have to come with us." Vic reached for the ID.

He's kind of scary when he's all serious.   Hey now

Hands still raised, Adam stood. Vic had several inches on him. Normally Adam would like that, but he had the feeling that their flirty goodwill was long gone.

The old cop let out a growl. Vic turned at the sound. The older man's eyes rolled back into his head. Froth spittle ringed his open mouth. Adam's Sight came over him as if by instinct.

A tendril from the spirit ran through the ceiling. It wormed into the cop's mouth like a bloody tree branch. The vessels in his eyes popped, filling with blood that ran from the corners like tears.

"Carl?" Vic asked, his face twisted with a mix of fear and worry.

Adam stepped back, banged his ass against the desk.

Carl stopped convulsing as the spirit seized him. He raised his gun.

"Get down!" Vic shouted.

He threw himself in front of Adam as the pistol roared, so loud Adam felt it rattle his teeth. His ears rang. The glass window shook so hard he thought it might crack.

Knocked back, Vic fell against Adam. They tumbled to the floor.

Carl's bloody eyes fixed on Adam. He raised the pistol again, aimed for Adam's face.

"Nuh," Carl growled. "No."

"Fight it," Adam ordered him. "You have to fight it."

Vic heaved in Adam's arms, blood pumping through the hole in his chest. He gasped like a fish on land.

Choking on the tendril in his mouth, Carl lifted the pistol to his temple.

The gun thundered again.

Vic shuddered, his brown eyes wide as they fixed on Adam.

"You're gonna be okay—" Adam's voice sounded high and panicked in his ringing ears. He thought he might pass out. No, he couldn't. Vic. He needed help. Adam reached, put his palm to the bullet hole, trying to apply pressure. The taste of gunpowder and blood filled the back of his mouth.

"That's what you do, right?" he said to no one. *Apply pressure.*

Vic didn't answer.

Then Death walked through the door.

11

ADAM

The janitor straightened as he entered the room. He grew, stretching until he loomed over Adam and Vic. Shadows scurried to him, forming an inky, shifting robe. The mop in his hand lengthened. Its bristles twitched and writhed, reforming into steel.

"Reaper," Adam said. Its approach pulled him into the spirit realm and time slowed.

"Witch," the thing said. Reapers were strange. They were also a type of possession, a sleeping power that woke when their host came near a soul to be claimed. Adam did not know much about them. Aunt Sue did not know much about them. Their origins and nature were a secret.

The Reaper extended a hand, naked bone lay over mortal flesh like a cheap Halloween costume. It pointed a single finger.

"My duty," the Reaper said, gesturing to Vic with an extended finger.

"No," Adam said. He pressed his palms harder to the wound in Vic's chest.

Vic was innocent in this. He shouldn't die for Adam's mistake, for his cockiness in underestimating the spirit.

Time had stopped on the mortal side, long enough for this conversation, buying Vic moments even as Death came for him. His blood gloved Adam's hands, sticky and warm, cooling far too quickly, even in this space between the flesh and bone.

"It is his time. I have my duty," the Reaper said, its voice deep. "Step aside."

"No," Adam insisted. Vic slipped into unconsciousness.

The Reaper lifted its scythe and floated forward. The hem of its robe brushed the floor, crawling, skittering, like living smoke. Adam could smell his own terror. Thinking he might piss himself, he scrambled to remember what little he knew of Reapers.

"You can't take me," he said, his accent thick. "If it's not my time. Not unless my life is over."

"I shall not take you," the Reaper agreed. Its skull bobbed once.

All magical beings had to follow laws. A Reaper could not take a life before its time. Adam thought of Sara, of her camper in the sunflower field. They waited for her, for her goddesses to remove their protection—no, not their protection. *Their magic.*

Adam looked to Vic. There was only a second to decide. Before Adam could think too hard about the consequences, he reached within, to the place where his own faint power lived.

Magic was life. Adam did not have much, but he could share what he had. He plucked a strand from inside himself, a silver thread. It hurt, like peeling off part of his heart, like skinning himself. He willed it through his hand and into Vic.

The Reaper paused. The tendrils of its robe stilled their creeping march.

"Why?" it asked, the skull managing to express confusion and maybe a little anger. "What means he to you?"

"Maybe it's the uniform," Adam said, his heart racing, uneven, like he'd drunk too much coffee. "Maybe I think he's hot."

It felt too much like Adam's own blood pumped out Vic's chest. He'd mixed their lives together, shared his power, but maybe he didn't have enough to keep both their hearts beating.

Vic's pain became Adam's. He gasped, though his mouth worked and his lungs billowed, he couldn't find air. Maybe all he'd done was kill them both.

The Reaper's eyes never left Adam's. It might have grinned. Something twinkled in the black depths of its eye sockets.

It drifted backward, sliding across the floor. Blackness took Adam a moment later.

12

ROBERT

"Your problem, Adam Lee," Robert whispered to his unconscious brother. "Is that you don't remember what Dad was really like."

The sight of Adam lying there, close to death for no reason they could determine, unearthed so many things Robert wanted to leave buried. His limbs felt cool, even as his head felt feverish.

His little brother, not so little anymore. They'd washed and dressed him in a hospital gown, but Robert still smelled the blood that had covered Adam when they'd found him.

Robert hadn't seen the security footage but whatever it showed, it seemed like Adam was off the hook for breaking into the records room.

"Your luck is going to run out someday," Robert said. Body leaden, he settled into the chair beside the bed. "Dad's did."

Robert didn't want to think about that right now. He wouldn't, but other memories came unbidden.

Summer after seventh grade. He'd just turned thirteen. Mom marked the occasion with a lopsided chocolate cake she'd baked from a box. Dad wasn't working. He hadn't worked in a while, but he hadn't been there. He'd been in town.

Bobby remembered Mom clipping coupons at the Formica table in the kitchen. Adam sat in front of the television, blissed out to old cartoons and occasionally holding conversations with a host of imaginary friends.

Mom looked up once when Dad jingled the keys to the truck. Bobby met her eye. She found a watered-down smile for him.

"Come on, Bobby Jack," Dad said, jingling the keys to the truck. "It's just us men today."

"Where are you going?" Mom asked. Dad took the mason jar out of the highest kitchen cabinet and pulled out most of the money Mom squirreled away whenever she could.

"Groceries," he said. "And we'll look for work."

Mom's eyes crinkled in that way they did when she wanted to cry. Bobby looked back and forth between his parents. An adventure, a day away from Adam and the three acres he knew every inch of, though time alone with his dad meant walking a branch where a breeze could blow him toward safety or disaster.

He couldn't have said no anyway. Bobby knew better than that.

The truck, a rusted, pitted Ford with powder-blue paint, rattled its way over the dirt roads. Bobby sat on the passenger side, his seat belt fastened to keep him from bouncing out of the seat. The day was dry and they kicked up a dust cloud until they passed the big barn that marked the turn onto pavement.

They drove for a while, past the bowling alley. He'd gone to a birthday party there once. Bobby's school was closer to the center of town.

"Let's gets some fuel," Dad announced.

Bobby suppressed a frown. He knew what that meant.

Dad pulled into the parking lot of the Last Cow Bar. Bobby straightened his shirt. He was a little sweaty inside the flannel. He snapped the bottom button open and closed. The last time they'd done this, he'd gotten so bored. Dad had given him a few quarters for the old arcade machine, but a few quick rounds of shooting zombies in the head didn't outlast the time it took Dad to down three beers and "chat" with Candy. The weathered waitress smelled of cigarettes and hairspray. Bobby had pocketed the quarters and pretended to play. He had a little box tucked into the floor vent in the room he shared with Adam, where he had squirreled away twenty-seven dollars and eleven cents, once he'd added the quarters. It wasn't near enough, but someday it would be.

His dad handled him two quarters as soon as he'd found a seat at the bar.

"Get me a paper." Dad nodded to the machine by the bathrooms.

Bobby obeyed, putting the fifty cents into the machine and pulling out a fresher copy of the *News Leader* than the one Mom had spread out on the table back home.

"Gotta look for work," Dad said with a wink, opening to the classifieds as Candy delivered a second beer.

Bobby stared at the bottle. Dad had drunk the first one so fast. That meant they'd be here for hours, maybe the whole day.

"Want some?" Dad asked, misreading Bobby's stare as interest.

When he didn't answer, Dad slid the bottle over the bar. It left a trail of condensation, like a slug's path, on the table.

"It's all right," Dad said. "Just a sip."

They'd done this before. The taste was always sweeter than he expected, not like cigarettes. The sip tasted bready and cold.

"Hey," Candy said, coming around the corner. "What are you doing?"

"Relax," Dad said.

"He's just a kid," Candy said.

"He's twelve."

Bobby had turned thirteen the month before, but he knew not to correct his father, especially not in public.

"We could lose our license," Candy said. She made a gesture, waving for them to leave.

Dad gulped down the rest of the beer. He left most of the paper, taking the time to tear out a page.

"Hey!" Candy said as he stood. "You haven't paid!"

"Put it on my tab," Dad said, laughing as he led Bobby out of the bar.

"Deadbeat!" Candy called before the door closed behind them.

"Dumb bitch," his father muttered.   *he feels like Adam can feel*

The comment slid something cold and oily into Bobby's guts.

They drove for a while. Dad circled through Guthrie, looking at roads. At one point he got out and used a pay phone, looking at the ad he'd torn from the paper to get the number.

Bobby stared out the open truck window. The day was sunny. He liked getting out of the trailer, away.

Dad was smiling, happy, but Bobby didn't trust it. He knew how fast that wind could shift.

The truck rumbled along through more turns. They left the city and drove some more. Bobby wondered if Dad was trying to buy firecrackers. He had a few years ago, and they'd launched bottle rockets. Dad had stood holding a Roman candle, firing blasts from it like he held a wizard's wand. Mom had watched, wide-eyed, at a distance, biting down a warning about blowing off his hand. *Demarcus Not- Maoz*

Finally, they came to a place not unlike their own, a trailer behind a wire fence. There were fewer fields, more sandy soil and grass than their three acres of red mud and rattlesnakes.

"There it is," Dad said.

He pulled to a stop at a cattle gate. Bobby didn't see any cows.

A man came down the steps from the trailer, waving for them to drive in.

"Get the gate, Son," Dad said.

Bobby jumped out, unwound the wire holding it shut, and followed the truck as Dad drove in.

The property had a gravel driveway, though the rock was fresher, less beaten down into the mud than the Binders'. Bobby caught up to the truck, where his Dad talked to an old man in a droopy, but crisp, wife-beater. The smell of dry clay and sunburned switchgrass was the same as on their property.

Dad extracted Mom's bills from his wallet and traded them for a set of keys.

"She's behind the house," the man said.

"Be right back," Dad told Bobby with a wink. He disappeared behind the trailer.

An engine sounded, too low and loud to be a car, too rumbly for a motorbike. Bobby tensed, uncertain what he'd see until Dad rode up on an ATV. It was muddy, a little rusted out, but it was an ATV—a real four-wheeler.

Dad revved the engine a few times, each putting a warm bubble in Bobby's chest. Dad climbed off.

"Go on," he said, gesturing for Bobby to take the seat.

"Really?" Bobby asked, unable to suppress a grin.

"Yep."

Laughing, he bounced over the ground, bits of grit and insects sticking to his face. Dad waved him back and they loaded it onto the truck, driving it up a makeshift ramp of boards. That feeling of lighter-than-airiness stayed with him as they drove home. It faded like warm sunlight behind a cloud when they parked and Mom came down the steps,

Adam clung to the back of her leg, pale and quiet. Bobby closed the passenger door and leaned against it as Dad opened the tailgate and waved to his purchase like a horse he intended to set free.

Mom said nothing, but her eyes shone.

"Bobby Jack, come help me with the boards," Dad said.

Dad drove the ATV down and watched as Mom squeezed her eyes shut. Opening them again, she scooped Adam into her arms and walked inside.

Bobby knew she'd stare at the cabinet, at the close-to-empty mason jar. She wouldn't say anything, wouldn't risk blowing the wind in the wrong direction. Bobby swayed a little as Dad gestured to the ATV and said, "Go on, take her for a spin."

"Can Adam ride her?" Bobby asked.

He felt the branch creak when Dad narrowed his eyes at the trailer and said, "He's too little. Too weak."

13

ADAM

Adam's eyes cracked open, and he groaned. He felt sunburned, exhausted, and kind of surprised he wasn't handcuffed to the hospital bed.

Whatever he'd done to save Vic had left everything hurting. Vic was short for Vicente, not Victor. He did not like being called Vince.

Wait. Adam blinked. *How did I know that?*

Other thoughts, things he shouldn't know, drifted in.

Vic was named for his great uncle on his father's side, Vicente. Vic had never met him. He'd died in Mexico, in Guadalajara.

Adam forced a stop to the stream of unbidden knowledge and opened his eyes to find Bobby standing over him.

"Goddamn it, Adam," Bobby said, anger thickening his accent.

"I didn't do anything," he said, wincing.

"You stole my badge," Bobby said. "You broke into a private room."

"Yes, I did." Adam lifted his hands in supplication. Everything felt heavy. "But I didn't—"

"Shoot that cop?" Bobby leaned closer. He opened his fists

like he might actually choke Adam. Then he clenched them, sat back into his chair. After a long exhale he said, "They know that. The other one told them what he could, that you didn't do it, that you hate guns. How does he know that?"

"Shit," Adam said, drawing out the curse. The connection went both ways. He was getting things from Vic, and Vic was getting things from him. Not good. Really not good.

"He was the cop who gave me the tour this morning," Adam said. He did not want to explain about the magic, the Reaper, or what he'd done to save Vic.

"Why did the other cop shoot him?" Bobby demanded. "Why did he shoot himself?"

"Do you want the real answer?" Adam asked, facing his brother, eye to eye, though he wanted to sink back into the uncomfortable bed. "Are you ready to believe me?"

Bobby nodded.

"Okay," he said.

"The spirit took control of him," Adam said. "Faster than I've ever seen."

Bobby gripped the arm of his chair, steadying himself. Quietly, he asked, "Can it do that to Annie?"

"I don't know," Adam said, pushing himself back into his pillow. He felt even heavier, telling Bobby this. "I don't know what let it take control of the cop."

"But could it?" Bobby asked. "Make her walk into traffic or hurt herself?"

Adam bit his lip and gave a little nod. Bobby paled, all the fight and disappointment draining away at the same time.

"How is he?" Adam asked. "The cop."

"Dead, Adam," Bobby growled. "He shot himself in the head."

Adam remembered Carl, struggling against the spirit's control, fighting it long enough to put a bullet in himself before he'd let it force him to kill Adam.

"Not him," Adam said. "The other one."

"We don't know. He won't wake up, a lot like you wouldn't wake up. They found him bleeding, babbling about what happened. Then he slipped into a coma. He shouldn't have been conscious. He should be dead." Bobby shook his head. "Why isn't he?"

"I tried to save him," Adam said. "I wasn't sure it would work."

"It must have," Bobby said, shaking his head, shaking all over. "He's stable."

Adam had mixed a strand of his life with Vic's, a stranger's, on a whim. He'd saved the guy's life, and from the sound of it, his own ass, but he didn't know the cost, what would happen.

Vic didn't get a choice

The connection between them hummed like a guitar string. Adam might be able to sever it, but he did not know what that would do to either of them. Their link might be the only thing keeping Vic alive. It was the right thing to do. He still felt that, but it added one more damn item on his to-do list of impossible things.

"If you can—" Bobby started. He leaned close, voice almost pleading to ask, "Can you help Annie? Can you keep her from hurting herself?"

"I'm trying," Adam said. "That's why I needed those records, why I was in there. But I underestimated it. It's not stupid. It's watching me."

"Did you find anything?" Bobby nibbled his lip, likely wanted to chastise Adam but managed to hold back.

"No," Adam said. "I didn't get into the records. So far the only thing I know is that the victims all worked at the hospital. But Annie didn't, right? So why is it attacking her?"

"Adam," Bobby said, his face pinching. "I met Annie here. She was a nurse."

"What?"

"She was a nurse here when I was an intern. She quit when we got married." *She dedicated her life to something she may never have*

Adam put air through gritted teeth. He should have asked earlier. This crap between them was going to get someone killed. Adam sank. It already had.

"So can you help her or not?" Bobby asked.

Adam chewed his lip. No, he could not. He did not know what he was up against. Ignorance had almost cost him his life. The spirit had killed Carl. It had tried to kill Adam and ended up almost killing Vic. He had to stop messing around.

"Yeah," Adam said, throwing himself back against his pillow. The spirit had possessed hospital employees. The hospital had a dead zone. He squirmed. "But I have to talk to somebody."

"You look scared," Bobby said. "And you don't scare easy, *outta character* Adam Lee. Who is this somebody?"   *How TF would he know*

"Do you really want to know?" Adam asked.

His brother sighed and shook his head. "I do not."

Adam smiled, but he had to admit it hurt. He could always count on his family to withdraw when Adam pressed too hard or tried to show too much of his self to them.

"Whatever it is you did," Bobby said, "you've landed in it this time. A man is dead, Adam. A cop. That's serious."

No shit. So is a spirit the size of a house.

"Am I going to be arrested or anything?" Adam asked. He could spirit walk from a jail cell but didn't relish the thought and his body wouldn't be safe there.

"I don't know," Bobby said. "I've called my lawyer, but nobody has said anything to me yet."

"Thanks," Adam said. And he meant it.

He didn't like any of this. It wasn't hard to see that something had put him on this road, drawing a clear path to Denver and his confrontation with the spirit. Adam shook his head, but the sense of something, some things, watching, lingered like the memory of spider legs on bare flesh. He almost called up his Sight, checked the room for spies, but Bobby was right. He was afraid.

14

ROBERT

"Let's get right to it," Ms. Geen said. She leaned back into one of those modern office chairs with chrome arms and mesh instead of cushions. Behind her, the window framed the Denver skyline, mountains and office buildings.

"To say the least," Geen said, "this situation is highly unusual."

"It is," Robert agreed.

He hadn't interacted with HR since Mercy had hired him. This new director was very polished, with light lavender nails and a fitted gray suit. She had a symmetrical haircut. Sitting across from her, Adam beside him, Robert felt pretty certain he wouldn't like what was coming.

After three days in the hospital, Adam had recovered from the complete exhaustion that had knocked him down. Dressed in a blue polo, dark khakis, and a blazer, he looked almost respectable, like he could work at a bank. Robert had sent their mom to buy him clothes. He couldn't risk Adam screwing this up. Robert had worked so hard. Mercy was his dream job.

"We could fire you, Doctor Binder," Geen said. "Your brother used your badge to access the records room."

"He stole it from me," Robert said.

"I did," Adam admitted without any sign of guilt.

"There's no proof you didn't help him," Geen said.

"He didn't get into any records," Bobby said, holding up a finger for emphasis. "No law was broken."

"True," she said.

"And he had nothing to do with it," Adam said, cutting his eyes sideways at his brother. "It was all me. Really."

Geen's head dipped. "I believe you. But there is the matter of the policemen. One dead. One shot."

"I—I didn't kill him." Adam stuttered.

Robert was glad to see Adam's cockiness waver. He'd approached all of this like nothing could touch him. Maybe magic and spirits were real, but that didn't mean Adam could do as he wanted. *why not? What makes Bobby's laws stronger*

"We know, Mr. Binder," Ms. Geen said. "We have the security footage. Did you know that all records access is tracked by federal law?" Pausing, she sighed. "The hospital looks very bad in light of the officer's actions. Legal asked me to speak with you."

"So you need to cover your ass," Adam said.

"Adam." Robert almost kicked his brother.

"Exactly," she said. "So I am going to do you two a favor."

Adam bristled. "What sort of favor?"

"You told the duty station you were looking for HR, for work. It just so happens we're hiring," she said. She slid a clipboard with some papers across the desk toward Adam. A job application lay on top.

"What?" Adam and Robert asked together.

"Come work for us and your brother's job will be safe," she said, clicking a ballpoint pen and rolling it across the desk. "It gives us some deniability as to why you were there."

"That's pretty flimsy," Robert said. He didn't know why he

was protesting. He'd been trying to talk Adam into working at the hospital the day of the shooting, but something about this didn't sit right.

"It's the best we've got," Geen said, her lips pressed tight together. "In addition, you'll agree not to sue the hospital and we'll have you under a nondisclosure agreement."

"What kind of job?" Adam asked, eyes narrow.

But he wasn't arguing.

Robert swallowed his own doubts. He didn't want to lose this job.

"Maintenance," she said.

Adam didn't speak as they left the office. He seethed, quietly until reaching the parking lot. Robert unlocked the Audi with two clicks of the fob. The doors had barely closed when Adam said, "You knew about this, didn't you? It's what you wanted all along."

Robert seethed and started the car. "You seemed okay with it back there."

"It's a way into the hospital," Adam said. "That's all."

Robert couldn't argue with that. It would allow Adam to do whatever kind of investigation he was about, maybe save Annie, but he couldn't help but gently add: "It could be real. You could stay with us for a while, get your own place."

Robert turned them onto Broadway. He tried to decide between the street and the highway, not knowing if he wanted the drive over quickly or not. He'd left Adam behind in Oklahoma. He knew that, but now he had a chance to make it right.

"You could go to college, night classes, online, whatever," Robert suggested, choosing the long way home.

"What college would take me? I'm a dropout, a freak, and a former mental patient. Thanks for that last one by the way." Adam squeezed his fists closed. He looked like he might slam them down on the dashboard but thought better of it. "I don't want to be here, Bobby. I'm not you. I'll take the job to help Annie. That's all we should be focusing on."

"I know," Robert said. "It's just—you need a life, Adam. Not living in squalor with an old woman."

Robert didn't mention the unemployed part. Their father hadn't been able to keep a job either. He'd squander money, leave them without groceries. Mom worked harder and harder, grinding herself down while he pissed her efforts away. More than anything else, Robert suspected that was what had left her so broken down.

"I have a life, Bobby," Adam said, sounding peevish. "People aren't less just because they don't live the way you do."

"I didn't say that," Robert said.

"You think it," Adam said. "You think we're all trash because we don't have nice cars and ugly houses. Life isn't just about money."

His jaw clenched every time Adam said something like that to him. But he had to admit, it wouldn't needle so hard if there wasn't some truth in it. He had hated Oklahoma and everything about their life there. Their mother couldn't leave the land in Guthrie, but Adam could. He could get out.

"But you do need money, don't you?" Bobby countered. "You're barely eating. That car is on its last leg. Anyone can see that."

He didn't mention that he'd snuck a look at Adam's charts and lab results. No STDs or drugs, thank God. He really didn't want to know what Adam had done to survive, especially after he'd run away from Liberty House. Not all gays are prostitutes Bobby

"I'm doing fine on my own, with Sue, whatever," Adam said. "I'm not some kid. I'm sure as hell not *your* kid."

Robert looked his brother over. Adam shook with old rage. They hadn't talked about it, Liberty House. They hadn't talked since then.

But Adam was right. He wasn't a kid, and yet, he wasn't quite

the adult he should be. His time at Liberty House, or the time
after, doing nothing when he should have been in school, had put
him off track. His development had slowed somewhere along the
way. Adam was street smart, and yet, not. *He has no peer access !*

And it was all true. That cop, Martinez, should be dead. *Where's*
Something had caused the other cop to snap for no reason. *the public*
School
Robert had sent Adam to Liberty House because he thought *version*
it was the best thing to do. Hadn't he? Hadn't that been why? *of Hogwarts?*

He remembered the calls from his mother, her frustration
putting teeth into her already sawing voice as every call sounded
the same, Adam missing school. Adam failing classes.

Liberty House had seemed the perfect solution, the best thing
for all of them.

A pressure started behind Robert's eyes. His chest tightened.

"You can quit and go back to the trailer park whenever you
want," Robert said quietly.

"Oh, I will," Adam snapped as they pulled into the driveway.
"When this is over with, I'll never speak to your sorry ass again."

Adam leapt out of the car before Robert had put it in park.
He didn't slam the door, but he closed it with enough force for
Bobby to snap, "Watch it!"

Adam headed for the house. Robert took a seething breath
and followed. The two speed-walking women were passing. As
always, they wore matching sunglasses and track suits. *Glitch in the matrix*

"What?" he demanded. For once he didn't care. For once
he considered flipping them off. That's what Adam would have
done. But Robert was the elder. Mom had told him that his
entire life. He had to be the bigger man, because he was bigger.
He had to be the man.

Inside, Annie faced off with Adam. She stood at the edge of
the tile, just where the carpet started. Her eyes, wary slits, looked
wild and dangerous.

"What are you looking at?" Adam snarled.

"Adam," Robert said, coming in behind him. Robert grabbed his brother's shoulder and jerked him around. "Annie is sick. Don't talk to her like that."

"I wasn't talking to her," Adam whispered.

Tension ran through Adam and into Robert's hand. He looked like he might hit Robert. Part of him would be glad to retaliate, but the sight of Annie standing there, staring like that, bled the heat from his limbs.

Robert squinted, first at Adam, then at his wife. He couldn't see what Adam saw, but he could feel something. The house's oppressive air condensed into Annie. Robert shivered, like the cold ran into him from eye contact with Annie.

Adam jerked free of his brother's grip.

"So what are you going to do about it?" Robert whispered. He watched his wife like he'd watched for snakes in the tall grass around the trailer, listening for danger, listening that Adam was safe when he played.

"That's why I'm staying," Adam said, nodding to Annie. "I might hate your guts, but I'll do what I can for her."

Bobby tensed like he'd been punched as Adam walked away.

15

ADAM

The spirit tendril remained attached to Annie. Its red veins ran through her, pulsing with alien life. They drifted around her in a cloud like exposed nerves. It wasn't at the point the cop had reached, where the spirit was able to control her, but it was close. He'd wasted time, languishing in the hospital, and he could see now that he didn't have long. The spirit's yellow eyes, running up and down the stalk, mocked him with their stare.

Carl hadn't been possessed when he'd opened the records room door. Something was slowing the spirit's possession of Annie, had sped it up with Carl. He needed more information. Adam needed to think, and he couldn't do that here, not with Bobby's disappointment and anger prickling his defenses.

He retreated to the basement. His clothes weren't coming back. They'd been too bloodstained, but he found a plastic bag with his phone, his wallet, and most importantly, his keys. Jingling them, Adam smiled and felt a weight lift.

"Where are you going?" Bobby asked when he headed for the door.

"Research," Adam said.

His days in the hospital had been spent mostly asleep, but waking, he'd missed the Cutlass. She started, and Adam resisted the urge to talk to her.

He hadn't quite gotten to that point with his car, but felt like he could. There were days when Sue and the car, two old ladies, were his only friends. He rubbed a thumb over the stylized rocket logo on the steering wheel.

"Okay, Federal," he said aloud, pulling away from Bobby's house.

He plugged his phone into the car charger. It steered him north.

This part of town was very different than where his family lived. It didn't remind him of Guthrie, being too urban, though it had the familiar shabbiness of home.

All magic had a taste, a scent. Most people were simply incompatible, their power, their life, rubbed at Adam like burlap on bare skin. The warlock, for all his evil, did not. His power and Adam's were of the same flavor. He had no proof the similarity was hereditary, but the only other practitioner he'd felt in tune with was Sue. The idea that he could have blood in common with a torturer made him clench his teeth.

Similar or not, Adam would need to be in close proximity to feel the warlock's power. If the pawn shop was a regular front for such artifacts, he'd find it quickly, though to be honest, Adam needed the drive. He needed to clear his head.

Adam knew what he had to do, but he'd put it off until nightfall, when he could approach the Guardians on Annie's behalf. In the spirit realm, the Watchtower of the North stood straight ahead. He'd turn off Federal before he got too close to it. He did not want to approach by day, without steeling himself.

He stopped at the first pawn shop he found. He didn't have any fond memories of them. His one trip as a kid had been to sell

his PlayStation, one more of Dad's spontaneous gifts that needed
to go away so the family could eat.

You were a real asshole sometimes.

There were plenty of days when Adam didn't want to find his
missing father, when he pushed the mystery of his disappearance
aside. But it always crept back into his thoughts.

Then there was the warlock. Adam didn't even know if he
and Dad were the same person, but finding out would answer his
questions, about his magic, about how he could feel so different
than his mother and brother. He and Bobby could not be related.

Doctor Binder was more concerned with Adam's future than
Annie's. He thought back on all the emails, all the clear signs that
Annie loved Bobby, that she doted on him. If Adam had that, he
wouldn't make the guy his second priority.

He'd—well, he didn't really know what he'd do with a guy in *lol*
the long term. He'd be like the dog who finally caught the car. He *there's*
had no idea what he'd do with a boyfriend beyond the obvious. *no script*
That thought brought an image of black hair and a blue uniform. *for homosexuality*

"Focus, Binder," Adam said, climbing out of the Cutlass. *honey. You*
can do
The shop was open. Used video games and musical instru- *literally*
ments shared space with power tools. A jet ski was mixed in *anything*
with the bicycles. No one stood behind the counter. No one *you both*
greeted Adam, though the door had beeped. His Sight showed *want*
bits of black and blue, a dash of red, lost hopes and betrayals,
clinging to this or that. It reminded him of his mother, of how
she'd faded over the years.

He'd been little when his dad had gone, but Adam remembered his mother, glowing, bright and laughing. That Tilla Mae
and her nicotine-stained smile existed only in fading memories.

The next two shops went the same way. Adam ran a hand over
a rack of beaten hockey sticks and wondered if Tanner's dad had
remembered the wrong street, if the shop had closed. He wanted

to text, get more information, but hesitated. It was best to let Tanner go. Adam didn't want to lead him on. Even if Sue hadn't been right, Tanner wasn't going to do, not for Adam. He was a normal guy. Flesh and spirit. Adam needed both.

Back in the Cutlass, Adam squeezed his eyes shut and tried to shake the little sorrows he'd picked up from the objects.

He hadn't found any answers. His father might be the warlock. His father had vanished. Adam had the terrible, looming impression that it had been his fault. His father had left, and his mother had lost all of her light because of Adam.

Gripping the wheel, he sank into the seat. He felt a warmth, an easing touch, like a hand on his shoulder.

Adam?

That voice again, faint and comforting. He hadn't imagined it.

Adam reached inside himself, felt around, searching for the source. He knew it, knew the oranges and sandalwood scent of that thread as soon as he touched it.

Vic?

No answer.

"Oh, Binder, what have you done?" Adam muttered aloud as he started the Cutlass.

Back at Bobby's, he found his backpack. His mother had washed and hung his clothes. She'd left most of his things intact, but his small stash of weed had vanished. He didn't smoke often, only when he really needed to take the edge off, when the spirit realm pressed too near. *Damn weed can medicate magic*

LoL

With a sigh, he took the small leather sack from the bottom. The tarot cards carried a faint smell of incense and fried chicken, reminding him of Sue and her kitchen. He wished she was there.

Adam waffled on calling her, then finally dialed her number. It went to voicemail. It wasn't unexpected. The trailer didn't get the best reception.

"Aunt Sue? Can you call me? I could . . . well, I could really use your advice."

Other scents rose as he shuffled. He caught a whiff of cigar smoke and jimson weed. A lot of Binders had used this deck. They'd charged it with their magic, left a little of themselves upon it.

Adam didn't expect to have kids, didn't expect he'd have anyone to pass the deck to when he died. He didn't consider himself sentimental, but the thought made his shoulders hunch. *Gifts of blood don't pass on through adoption*

If Annie and Bobby had kids, then maybe one of them would be like him, a nephew or niece Adam could pass Sue's lessons to. The idea was almost pleasant, gauzy but tinged with something gray.

The thought of it ending with him made Adam both happy and sad. Sad, because he loved his family. Happy, because he didn't like them very much. *It happens this way*

Adam wasn't great at tarot, and reading your own cards was often inaccurate. Your own longings and false ideas about yourself got in the way. *Good to know*

He kicked off his shoes and sat on the bed. Careful not to cross any part of his body, he shuffled the cards, hoping some of Aunt Sue's touch lingered in the paper. Adam cut the deck and drew three cards.

The Tower.

The Page of Swords.

The Knight of Swords.

"Bullshit," Adam said.

He glared at the cards like they'd betrayed him. He repeated the shuffle and draw, closing his eyes until he'd laid them out.

The Tower.

The Page of Swords.

The Knight of Swords.

"Shit."

Adam wrapped the cards up and tucked them into his

backpack. He closed his eyes, wondering if Sue had known, how much of all this she'd seen before he'd left Guthrie.

The cards weren't lying. He ran the spread a third time, unsurprised when they came up with the same results.

The Tower. Danger. Sudden change, but in this case literally a tower.

The Page of Swords. Usually his card. Youth, a sign telling him to go forward.

It was the third card, the Knight of Swords, that made him wince. A powerful figure full of life. Of magic.

Adam pressed two fingertips to the card, ran them down the figure's face. The safest road appeared to be the one he knew best but liked the least.

He'd need a gift. He couldn't approach the Guardians without a worthy sacrifice. Adam didn't have anything, but the petition wasn't really for him.

The only thing they don't have is death

He crept upstairs. His mom was smoking out back. Bobby was on the second story, the door to his room closed. Adam watched for Annie as he moved toward the front door. He found what he needed on the coffee table. Heart racing, he moved back to the basement as quietly as he could.

Trying to steady his breathing, Adam laid down atop the coverlet. He stretched out, his arm held to the side with his empty fist clenched as if to hold a blade, invoking the Page of Swords. To petition, he had to come as himself, to invoke the card that best represented him, and Sue hadn't been wrong. It was always swords with Adam.

He sighed and closed his eyes. Man, he hated elves.

16

ADAM

Every city and most remote areas had watchtowers. Monoliths of the spirit realm, the Guardian races shaped them by style or whim, choosing a landmark in the physical world as an anchor. Immortal politics were complicated and possession of a tower changed from time to time.

The tower latched onto a high point, a lonely tree or hill if no building was available. In Guthrie, two were connected to grain elevators, one to the town landfill. The watchtowers were boundary markers and courts, places to petition the Guardians.

The Guardians often changed their appearance to match their anchor. The same spirit might appear as a farmer in Guthrie or a *cute* gangster in Chicago. Adam's best theory was that they worked in aspects, different faces of the same being. A part of them lived in each place while other parts lived elsewhere. *like Skye Bergerson's super power*

He suspected it was the secret to their immortality. If one aspect died, the others would live on. But he wondered if they'd know, if they'd feel the loss of their other selves.

In spirit, Adam strode toward the Watchtower of the North, wondering if that was what had happened to Perak. Maybe he'd died, the aspect of him that had loved Adam had died, and the rest of him didn't know to come looking. It was an easier fantasy than abandonment, the idea that the immortal had simply tired of his plaything.

Adam put the old ache away and spoke the invocation to open the road to the north, "Hail to the Guardians of the Watchtower of the North."

White light, almost blinding, arrived in a blast of freezing wind, forcing Adam to tuck his face to his chest and shield it with his arm.

When things warmed again, he opened his eyes.

Adam gaped at the luminous magic cascading off the tower ahead. He poured all of his will into his defenses, but still they buckled, shining like a nimbus around him.

The elves, Adam's bane and main annoyance, had chosen an amusement park as their Denver anchor. His Sight worked in reverse here, letting him peek across the veil and see the mortal world. The park, while well lit and with running rides, looked full of faded 1920s glory. A roller coaster ran with the creaks and splintery groans of old wood. He frowned at the dilapidation, but the tinge of blue cooled his nerves as he walked on.

The aspect of the looming watchtower became more real than the mortal plane. The tower's old-fashioned light bulbs went from hazy to clear. Everything shone, new and white, like he'd stepped into the past.

Adam entered the park. The magic intensified, crashing around him like a wave. He could no longer see across the boundary.

Stiffening his spine, he fought the urge to run back to his body. He had to do this for Annie.

None of the elves approached him, but Adam could not help but be aware of them moving through the glossy night of the spirit realm. Smooth-skinned, with perfect hair and eyes like

Interesting

jewels, they strolled the park in couples or sets of three. They always seemed to dance, like they heard a music he couldn't, which was entirely possible. All of their senses were greater than his. Perak had loved to tease him about it, distant things Adam couldn't see or hear.

They were so beautiful, so perfect in a way he'd never be. It almost hurt to look at them. And they would last forever, untouchable, except when they weren't. Adam knew with a deep ache that they were never more beautiful than when they lay with you. *Jesus when he fucked you he was sensing your corpse robbing both cradle and grave at the same time*

He'd gotten lost before, entranced by beauty and eyes so pale that they stole the color from flowers or the red from his skin when they tussled. He fought to shake off the memory and the blush it brought. He would never repeat that mistake. He was here on business.

Adam straightened with a jerk when a classic car, a boat of curving metal in black and gray, raced into the parking lot. Adam gaped as it roared to a stop.

"Is that an Auburn Speedster?" he asked, unable to stop himself.

"1935," the driver said. She had a clipped accent Adam associated with old movies.

Come to think of it, the whole place felt like an old movie, classic, cast in black and white, unreal and dangerously fantastic. He had to remember he could die here.

Tall and willowy, the woman towered over him.

"Do you like my dress too?" she asked, twirling. The garment, a slinky number with fins along the skirt, was cut from salmon-colored silk. It floated around her as she spun.

"Yeah," he said. His gaze caught on the wrap of black feathers draped about her shoulders. It quivered in the spirit breeze, more alive than plucked, even when she came to rest, still and elegant as carved marble. "It's, uh, pretty."

In truth Adam never understood why anyone asked him

about women's clothes. He wasn't a drag queen or any kind of fashionable. Just because he was gay?

He caught a sense of the woman's power, the full effect of what stood before him.

All elves possessed more magic than any human, but they weren't all the same. Adam did not know what determined their power, whether it came from age or existed from birth. They were ruled by queens and kings, so it made sense that bloodlines were involved, but he wasn't even sure they had babies.

Some elves wore their magic like fine silks. From others it radiated like a too-strong perfume. Perak had been closer to human, safe to touch.

The wisps of power leaking through this woman's glamour *burned*.

Seeing him realize his mistake, she tilted her head. A cold little smile pursed her lips. Adam took a backward step. Eyes darting side to side, he sought an escape. The elves, all dressed in classic suits and vintage dresses, ceased their strolling. As one, they turned to watch, their jewel-toned eyes focused on the exchange, their heads slightly cocked to the side.

Every nerve in Adam's body thrummed in warning.

"I mean to say, my lady"—Adam made an awkward dip to one knee—"that it is most lovely and reminds me of more elegant times."

That seemed to mollify her.

"You've come to petition the Court?" she asked.

"How did you know?"

She waved a hand, indicating the park.

"You're a mortal practitioner," she said. "The rest are gone."

Only elves walked the dock beside the lake or rode the iron Ferris wheel. No humans strolled with them. No practitioners or supplicants, no refugees from the mortal world.

She put her hands on her hips and said, "Get on with it then. Petition me."

"Oh shit," Adam gasped, looking away from her. "You're the queen."

"You may call me Argent, if you like."

Her smile expanded like an unsheathed blade. Adam averted his eyes as her glamour fell away, but for less than a heartbeat he saw more of her true self, the aspect of her whose full glory could blind or kill him. a God

He glanced away in time, but the image still branded his memory.

She wore a bodysuit of woven steel, unbreakable chain mail. The cut-out shape of a longsword opened at the high collar of the form-fitting dress atop it. It ran down, just past her belly, baring a line of perfect skin. The cross guard exposed a modest amount of cleavage. A great wheel of naked swords fanned out from her back in a terrible halo. A similar band of upraised blades marked her brow in a crown that would make brushing her hair an exercise in horror. The long strands were the color of polished steel. Its sheen reflected her eyes, so pale they could only be the whitest of gold.

She held a massive sword, its blade as wide and long as Adam's body, as if it weighed nothing. To her it likely didn't. He had no doubt she could cleave mountains with it. She laughed, a white sound, like winter, and his defenses, the layer of armor and wards he'd conjured to keep himself sane, cracked. Why doesn't she? what restrains her?

"Hail to the Guardians of the Watchtower of the North," Adam said without hesitation, closing his eyes before he saw more, before he lost his mind or worse. "I seek your wisdom."

"No," she said, interrupting. "You seek my brother. We'll find him in the ballroom."

"You do not want to hear the rest?" Adam asked. Eyes still closed, he rose to his feet. He'd practiced it for hours, alone, with

Perak—learning how to speak to royalty for occasions such as these, occasions he'd hoped would never arise.

"Not really," she confessed. "I know most immortals like titles and ceremony, but all that bores me so."

Adam liked her—or thought he would, if her towering presence didn't make him want to cower in terror.

He heard a click, the close of her little clutch of a purse. Magic rushed around him and subsided, her magic hidden beneath her glamour.

"You can open your eyes now," she said.

He did, and the terrible queen had become the elegant flapper again. She offered Adam her arm.

He took it and found his own clothes transforming as her magic, cold and quick as snow melt, ran over him.

His jeans and tee had changed into a black suit, with a stiff front crease on the pants and a fedora atop his head. Everything fit perfectly.

"Silk underwear too," she said with a wink. "Just in case it comes to that."

Adam swallowed hard. He didn't say anything, but he clenched his fists that she'd toy with him. He clung to his anger, and the memory of Perak's abandonment, determined not to be charmed.

The queen's heels clicked on the cobbles as she led him toward the tower. Square, over a hundred feet tall, it shone, its thousands of white lights incandescent above them. He thought again how much it felt like a black-and-white movie, leeching the colors away, though his hands held their pinkish, human tint when he examined them.

Squinting, Adam forced his Sight to show him the mortal side. He had to fight for it, to press his meager skill past the heavy magic. On the Other Side, the tower remained. It had seen better days. Many of the bulbs were out, and the structures around it

were shuttered or partially collapsed. The ballroom at the base
was boarded up.

"Lovely, isn't it?" the Queen asked, following his gaze into the
mortal world. "It is a shame your people do not restore it to its glory."

"It is," he agreed, a little surprised he meant it.

The elves had their flaws. They had little respect for mortal
property or their brief lives, yet they clutched the past to their
hearts. Die-hard preservationists, they loitered near ruins and
hoarded ancient things. *Interesting. Reminds me of my politics*

Adam could admit he had a streak of their fixation. He loved
the Cutlass, despite the pains it took to keep her running. He
loved the tarot cards Aunt Sue had given him. Even the asylum,
Liberty House, had appealed with its crumbling brickwork when
he'd first arrived, before the days locked in isolation in a room
with torn, padded walls and ungentle orderlies began. Adam had
hit one of them once, and they'd bound his hands, hung him from
a hook, arms stretched above him, balanced on his toe tips, for
hours. He rubbed his wrist now, remembering the soreness and
the chafing of the rope.

The queen released his arm and opened the ballroom doors
with a slight shove. A wooden floor of gleaming planks stretched
beneath a blue-painted ceiling that floated above a colonnade
of alcoves. Dancers spun in waltzes, which Adam felt had to be
inaccurate. The elves loved period cosplay, but they often got *LOL*
the details wrong. He thought they had the clothes right, but he *they wouldn't*
was no expert. Even if they didn't, and even if they looked old- *stoop so*
fashioned, they were beautiful. *low as to google it*

For all their faults, elves weren't small-minded. Men danced
with men. Women danced with women. In one or two cases, three
ooooh hey wow or four waltzed together in a way that made his eyes hurt when
he tried to follow their footwork. Their grace could be painful.
He remembered lying on a bed of flowers, entwined with smooth

skin and contented smiles. Adam shoved the memory away. He had a reason for coming here. He wouldn't let their games, or his past, distract him.

A young man sat playing the piano, a gleaming white beast of a full grand. It stood against the colorful backdrop of the bandstand. Dressed in a suit of cloth the color of platinum and a fedora with a white satin ribbon, he emanated power. He had to be the knight. An aching feeling swirled through the crack the queen had put in Adam's defenses and he forced himself to unclench his jaw. The emotion wasn't his own. He would not let it rule him.

Queens, kings, knights, and pages. They were titles. Sometimes the relationships were unclear. They might not even be family. Argent had called the knight her brother.

Feeling Adam's gaze, or simply bored, the man stopped playing. The dancers stopped in place, as fixed as marble statues, their feet frozen, some lifted in midstep. None of them breathed hard, as though their long turns through the hall were effortless. Perak, too, had rarely shown any sign of physical effort, and Adam had considered it a point of pride when he could bring the elf to it.

Adam mentally pinched himself. He had to stop thinking about Perak. He had to focus on the here and now.

Business. Business. He reminded himself as the queen greeted the man.

"Silver. Brother. I bring you a gift." She unfolded her long arm in Adam's direction. "A mortal practitioner. He carries a petition."

Adam knelt again, keeping his head low as the elven prince rose from the piano bench. Like his sister, he hid his true nature behind illusions. The Knight of Swords pressed a hand to Adam's head. The cool fingers ran through his hair once, twice with a wash of magic. It didn't quite burn, but it flooded him with warmth. That thrumming in Adam's nerves ran ever deeper. He didn't like the presumption, that Silver thought he could just touch him like that. Adam wrapped his defenses tighter, lest Silver sense his anger. He needed their help.

"Rise, Adam Binder, Witch of the Plains, and tell us what you seek."

Adam forced himself to breathe, to not bare his teeth. He'd felt hands like those, slim and graceful, on him before.

"You know my name, lord?" Adam asked, scrambling out from under that touch and finding his feet.

He shook. It had happened. They knew him now. They'd want things, alliances and fealty. They'd want him to fight for them or spy upon their enemies. Scheming things, elves. Pretty, deceitful, and likely to vanish when you needed them most.

"The ether buzzes with whispers of the practitioner who dared challenge a Reaper," Silver said.

Adam could not suppress a flinch. He wanted to avoid any kind of fame, but especially the sort that could get him killed.

Silver looked Adam over, hat to feet, his expression amused and maybe a little concerned. Either way, Adam felt the gaze burrow beneath his skin, into his spirit. Sounding a bit angry, like something he saw there perturbed him, the elven prince asked, "What do you want, Adam Binder?"

"I want to know about the spirit," Adam said. "The thing in the sky over Denver."

"Are you sure?" Argent asked. "It killed the other practitioners."

"It has already tried to kill me," Adam said. "And failed. But it has possessed someone. I need to make it let them go."

Adam kept it vague. They less they knew the better. Knowledge. Power. Asshole elves.

Silver and his sister exchanged a glance. It was only a moment, but in it, Adam felt certain they clashed, two tidal waves contending over a seagull. He'd never know what passed, was said, or who won what—but he felt certain he was the seagull.

Silver gave a tiny nod.

"Walk with me," he said, pulling a straight cane out of the air. He led Adam out of the ballroom and into the night. Silver tapped his cane on the floor and the music resumed, the piano keys moving though his hands no longer touched them.

Cowed by that little flare of magic, Adam walked beside the knight, his head slightly ducked. He appreciated Argent's gift of the hat. It let him hide his face and the crease he knew must mark his brow.

"Where are we going, lord?" Adam asked as the night air, colder than in the mortal realm, struck them. Silver's scent, a faint cologne of fresh-cut grass and lemon, reached him on the breeze. Adam tried to remember what Perak had smelled like, had tasted like. He'd thought he'd been in love.

"I need a drink," Silver said. The cane tip rapped on the wooden steps as they descended to the tower's base.

An elf in a crisp white shirt, bow tie, and black vest manned the bar. A silver-and-marble art deco edifice, Adam did not peek at it in the mortal world, expecting to find it ruined.

Sometimes the overlay could be disturbing, like the time he and Perak had tumbled in a field of teal flowers singing lullabies to the moon. On the mortal side, his Sight had showed a field of long, bleached cow bones. Seeing it killed the mood, especially for Perak. Elves had a complicated relationship with death.

Silver took a stool and watched as the bartender mixed something into a martini glass. It looked clear, with just a bit of lemon in it. Sugar sparkled along the rim.

"Lemon drop?" Silver slid the glass in Adam's direction as he sat.

"No, thank you," Adam said with a bob of his head. It was unwise to eat or drink in the spirit realm.

Silver smiled. "I had to try, beautiful mortal. It is good to see you know the rules."

"I don't appreciate the games, lord. I came in good faith, and I need your help."

"Then you know you have to bring me a gift." Silver toyed with the glass's stem, sliding a fingertip up and down its length. "A sacrifice."

Adam took the car key from his pocket and slid it along the bar. The mirror behind it showed a pretty picture, a lovely young man in platinum sitting beside Adam, who wore all black. They matched in opposite, down to their hats, gray and black with satin and black silk ribbons. Adam wondered if Argent had meant some trick or insult by the way she'd dressed him, having his clothes mirror Silver's in opposite. He shook off the curiosity. Elves were pricks. That's all he needed to remember.

"Oh my," Silver said, spinning the key atop the marble bar. "More my sister's style. But I do like the color."

"Can you, will you, help me?" Adam asked.

Silver waved a hand. A thread appeared in the air. Adam bit down on a gasp. He felt, naked, exposed.

Adam instantly knew that this was the line connecting him to Vic. It ran, straight and taut, through the wall.

Silver trailed a finger along the strand. The sensation thrummed, too intimate, beneath Adam's skin.

"Follow that," Silver said with an angry note. Like a hawk seizing prey, he gripped his drink and downed it in one long swallow. He stood, hefted his cane. Tilting his hat at Adam, he added, "And mind the Reapers."

Adam woke in his bed.

"What the hell was that?" he asked, shaking from the sudden dismissal. Silver had banished Adam without warning. It didn't hurt so much as it'd shocked, like rolling out of bed and hitting the floor. Okay, it had hurt a little, the knight's magic wrenching him from spirit to consciousness.

Adam felt his body, checking that everything was where it was supposed to be. Something wasn't right. Beneath his jeans, the silk underwear remained.

"Elves . . ." Adam muttered, unable to resist a smile at Argent's joke.

The door to his room opened. His mother stepped inside. She stood at the foot of the bed, glaring down at Adam, the faint smell of a cigarette wafting off her.

"Adam, sweetie," she said, putting a little bite on the endearment, telling him she knew before she asked, "Did you do something to your brother's car?"

17

ADAM

"How am I supposed to get to work?" Bobby asked. He kept circling the empty driveway, like he could summon the Audi back.

"You can take the Cutlass," Adam said from the edge of the driveway, trying to keep the guilt out of his voice. "Or I'll drive you."

"I don't want Dad's piece of shit," Bobby snapped. "I want my Audi."

The police had already come and gone. They'd asked their questions, none of which the household could answer.

"You didn't hear them take it? It vanished sometime around three a.m.?"

Bobby had nodded and shook his head. Adam hadn't said anything. He'd stayed in the house, sipping his mom's coffee. No dose of milk would tame its bitterness. He sat on the couch near the door, craning his ear, waiting for the cops to ask him, for Bobby to ask him.

"It's pretty common, sir," the cop had said. Adam had examined him from a distance, comparing him to Vic and finding him lacking. "They likely took it for a joyride. We find them all the time, usually without any real damage."

"How?" Bobby asked. "How does this sort of thing happen here? It's a nice neighborhood."

"We'll do what we can, sir," the cop said. "But honestly, it's not a lot."

Underwear gnomes — Adam wondered how many of these car thefts were the elves' fault, if the Queen of Swords took joyrides before leaving the cars by the side of the road.

"I'll drive Annie's car," Bobby said. He collapsed onto the driveway, falling to his knees where the Audi had been. The concrete, pristine, was unblemished by oil stains. Bobby looked like he might cry.

"Bob—Robert," Adam said, suppressing the need to duck his head. "Come inside. You're making a scene."

And Adam knew too well how much his brother hated making a scene, that his reputation meant everything to him. Adam almost seethed that Annie seemed to just be window dressing in Doctor Binder's perfect life.

Still, Adam's words snapped Bobby out of it.

He marched indoors, his feet heavy on the stairs. Adam's mother remained on the porch, puffing away at a menthol. She had a red plastic cup of something in her other hand—it could have been iced tea or boxed wine. With Tilla either was likely before noon.

She waited until they heard Bobby's bedroom door close before she said, "He's going to kill you when he figures it out."

"How did you know?" Adam asked, leveling his eyes to hers.

"I know when you're skulking, Adam Lee," she said.

"I didn't have any other options," he said.

"Was it worth it?" she asked.

"Not yet," Adam admitted with a shrug. "I got a lead, but I don't know where it goes yet."

His mother shook her head.

Adam took a few steps away, into the perfect grass of Bobby's perfect lawn.

He felt for the thread and whispered, "Vic."

The thread flared to life.

It had shocked Adam for Silver to touch it, but he'd also showed Adam how to sort it from the other feelings running through him.

The thread called to him, like a radar blip echoing through the city or the first note of a long guitar solo.

Heading inside, he washed his face and resisted the urge to change his shirt, but still he wet his hair and ran a squirt of gel through it, giving it what few spikes he could.

"I'm going," he told his mother.

"Will you be back for supper?"

Adam nodded.

"Adam Lee," his mother said. "Will you be back for supper?"

"Yes ma'am," he said. "I should be."

She dismissed him with a wave of her cigarette and muttered something about the Lord giving her strength.

*****

Traffic crowded the highway, but it remained too fast, so Adam took side streets and back roads. He needed time to locate Vic, to follow the thread and try to understand its meaning. It led him far from Bobby's house, north, into a very different part of town. The houses were smaller, but they had real backyards, not a postage stamp of green. Most were clad in brown brick, not heavy siding. Low chain link fences separated them.

Adam reeled in the line. Each tug brought pain, a flare in his chest, and soreness. He'd lain too long in a bed, wanted to move more, but each shift hurt his stitches.

Despite the complaints, a warmth passed to Adam as well, comfort at being in his old room, his old bed. A sense of being loved wrapped him like a thick blanket. More than anything else, that feeling was alien.

The impressions grew stronger until Adam could almost see the other man.

He nibbled his lip, uncertain what Silver was playing at. The elf had pointed out the connection, but the spirit hadn't attacked Vic. He wasn't involved in what was happening to Annie. Something else was in play. Adam looked over his shoulder, extended his senses. He could almost sense eyes watching him, something spying, but saw nothing with his Sight.

Adam turned onto a side street with old trees, weathered wooden trim, and faded paint.

A lot of cars were parked on the street, though only a sleek SUV sat in the narrow driveway of his destination. Adam found a space big enough for the Cutlass, parked, and checked himself in the rearview mirror. Lifting his shirt partly over his head, he used the inside to muss his dried hair, breaking up the spikes, and immediately wished he'd kept them.

Adam checked the house with his Sight and flinched.

Seven Reapers stood on the front lawn. Arranged in a circle, they neither scythed nor bent but stood unmoving, with the cold wind of the otherworld ruffling their inky robes. They didn't seem to present a threat. They didn't seem to notice Adam at all.

"What do you want with him?" he asked the nearest Reaper, but he received no response.

Were they waiting for the line to snap, for Adam to let Vic go so he could die?

With a shudder, Adam shook his head to shut down his Sight and approached the house.

An old storm door, the kind with a scalloped pattern cut into the metal, let light into the house.

A massive pit bull ran for the screen, leaping and barking before Adam could ring the bell.

Adam jumped back with a yelp. He almost shrieked, and clamped his mouth shut when a voice, gruff and male, called out in Spanish. A large man, Mexican and shirtless, came around the corner. Tattoos sleeved his bulging arms, complex floral patterns and words in a font that made it hard to read them. His chest, equally developed, had a trail of black hair Adam tried not to follow to his jeans.

"Chaos!" the man called, switching to English. "Bad girl!"

Heart still in his throat, Adam forced a smile and double-checked the thread. This was the right house.

"Yeah?" the man barked, sounding as ferocious as the dog. "You selling something?"

"Is, uh, Vic here?"

"Who wants to know?" the man asked, eyes narrowing to slits.

"I'm here to see Vic. I'm Adam," he said. "Adam Binder."

The man paused long enough that Adam thought he might need to leave.

"You're the white boy," the man said, brown eyes widening. "The one who saved him."

"Uhhh . . ." Adam stuttered. He didn't know what to say to that. A little curl of excitement tickled his throat but he wondered how much Vic had told his . . . brother. This was Vic's brother, the one he'd mentioned at the hospital.

Jesse.

Jesse unlatched the storm door with one hand. The other gripped the dog's collar.

"Don't be scared. She's a baby," he said, pushing the door open. "Come on. Lock the door behind you."

Adam did as he was told. Jesse, still clutching Chaos's collar, marched her back into the little house. Adam followed past a kitchen painted in greens and yellows. The large dining room table shone with fresh polish, the same lemon oil Aunt Sue used. The familiar smell pulled a little tension from Adam's shoulders.

So many pictures crowded the walls that Adam almost couldn't see the rich purple paint behind them. The tan faces smiled, indicating a familial ease Adam couldn't fathom. There weren't that many Binders in the whole world. His mother had never been big on photographs. After their dad had vanished, she'd put away the few group shots they'd had, erasing him from their lives. Seeing Vic's family, the idea of being part of something like it, put a hitch in Adam's throat.

Then he spotted Vic.

Teenage Vic stunned. He had black hair, always short, so dark and glossy it shone almost blue, the color Aunt Sue called sloe. The Vic in the photos aged until his graduation from the police academy. He remained gorgeous, but he'd added a bit of edge, a toughness that made Adam's heart do a little flip. He realized he didn't know the other man's age. *Twenty-four*, their connection said without prompting.

"Mom was so proud," Jesse said, noting that Adam had paused.

Adam swallowed hard. He flushed to have been caught staring.

He nodded to a picture of Vic flanked by two older people sharing his complexion and features. He wore his uniform and white gloves.

All of them beamed. Adam found himself smiling back at their glossy faces.

"Come on," Jesse said, waving for Adam to follow.

They walked down a little hall.

"Jesse!" a woman called, her Spanish accent heavier than her sons'. "Put a shirt on."

"Mama," he said, becoming bashful. "Vic's friend is here."

"Friend?" the woman from the photo asked, coming around a corner. Her eyes, the same deep brown as Vic's, widened when she saw Adam. "Oh. The white boy who saved him."

Adam blanched. "I just, uh, wanted to see if he was okay."

"He's better than expected," the woman said. "He was in a coma, but he woke up."

Yeah, me too, Adam thought. He suspected Vic's state had been a result of the connection between them, not the gunshot.

"This way," she said. Looking Adam over, she poked his belly. She wore jeans and a teal tee embroidered with a white, scrolling detail. "You're so skinny. Doesn't your mother feed you?"

Adam felt the blush run through him. "Uh—"

"You should stay for dinner," she said. "We're ordering Chinese."

"Uh—"

"What?" Jesse asked. "You think it's all tacos and piñatas around here?"

"Jesse," his mother chided. "He's here to see Vic. Take Chaos outside. And put a shirt on."

She gave Adam a little shove through a bedroom door and closed it behind him.

Vic lay on a narrow bed, his eyes closed, his breathing steady but a little ragged. Bandages covered most of a bare chest, leaner than his older brother's. Adam's shoulders sank to see gray dulling Vic's golden skin.

Uncomfortable, he examined the room. About half the size of where Adam slept in Bobby's basement, it had a worn, well-loved feel. Thick paint slathered the walls, smoothing their texture. The baseboards were probably real wood somewhere under all those coats of white. A framed poster from *Return of the Jedi* hung over the bed. A bookshelf in the corner overflowed. Adam could feel the concern from Jesse, the confident love of Vic's mother. All he'd ever felt from Bobby and his mother were guilt and an aching concern, like Adam may not survive the world.

"Wondered when you'd get here," Vic said, voice creaky, his eyes still closed.

"Came as soon as I could," Adam said.

"I know."

Adam didn't like that their connection went both ways. The line between them, the thread, made him, made both of them, vulnerable.

"I—I came to see if you're okay," he said.

"I think I've been shot," Vic said, opening his eyes.

"Funny."

Vic looked like he wanted to shrug but thought better of it. "Come over here."

The words pulled somewhere beneath Adam's belly. He wanted to narrow the distance, to remove it completely. He resisted and felt a little tickle of pink confusion and gray disappointment from Vic.

"Okay then," Vic said. "I'll come to you."

Adam felt the pain, the pull of stitches as Vic forced himself to sit up.

"Stop," Adam said, moving forward. He didn't want to sit on the edge of the mattress, to intrude or be so near, but there wasn't anywhere else. Adam eased himself down, perching gently, aware of how that barest movement hurt the other man. This was his fault. All of this was his fault.

"It's that bad?" Adam asked. "The pain?"

"Doesn't have to be, but I'm trying to keep off the meds," Vic said. "Don't want to need 'em too much."

"How's that going?" Adam asked.

"Not—well," Vic rasped.

"Can I get you some water or something?" Adam asked.

"Just be here," Vic said, closing his eyes again.

His pain passed to Adam and brought with it the leaden weariness of healing, the blue drowsiness of the medication, and beneath all that, a curiosity, an anticipation trained on Adam.

"I feel stronger with you here," Vic said. "You want to explain that to me?"

Adam contemplated lying. But Vic would know, and everything he'd seen and felt in this house—Vic just might not think him crazy.

"It's magic," he said.

Vic squeezed his eyes shut. He exhaled, then nodded. Adam felt his acceptance, that he believed Adam's simple, ridiculous-sounding explanation.

"It's weird," he said. "Having you in my head."

"Same," Adam admitted.

They sat there, neither speaking, neither needing to, for a good while.

"It's only been a few days," Adam finally said. "Should you be out of the hospital?"

"I'm healing quickly," Vic said. "Just gotta be careful with the stitches. Is that the magic too?"

"Yeah," Adam said. He put a hand to his own chest. He could feel the ache, the bullet wound.

The pull did not subside. Adam could have stretched out beside Vic, gone straight to sleep. He did not know if it was from having pushed the magic into Vic or just the long spirit walk to the North Watchtower, but he felt bone weary. For both of them.

"Sorry I'm not great company," Vic said after a bit, eyes flicking across himself and the room. "Not a lot to work with here."

"It's all right," Adam said. "You've got a good excuse."

Vic turned his hand over, palm up, offering it to Adam.

Adam cocked his head.

"What?" Vic asked. "Too fast? I know you like me."

"What is this, high school?" Adam asked. "I do not *like* you."

"Yeah, you do," Vic said with a hard tug on the line between them. "And I heard you, what you said, there in that room."

Adam flushed.

Maybe it's the uniform. Maybe I think he's hot.

Adam should have known his cockiness would come back to bite him on the ass.

"What else do you remember?"

Vic's eyes flicked to his waiting hand. A smirk played at his lips.

"Fine," Adam said.

Vic's grip felt weak, too weak, his palm too warm. Adam moved a little strength through the thread between them and felt himself sway, like he'd lost a lot of blood.

"Thanks for coming," Vic said with a sigh.

Adam did not know if Vic could feel what Adam was doing or not. Sensitivity to Adam likely didn't bring sensitivity to magic.

"Something cold, but hungry," Vic said quietly. "Worse than ice, worse than winter, like a frozen sea that wanted to swallow me, but you wouldn't let it."

Adam went cold.

"Then I felt you," Vic said. "Between me and it. I felt you save me."

"You told your family that?" Adam asked. "Your mother and brother?"

"Yeah. I tell them everything and they tell everyone else. Jesse's the worst." LOL, Daisy

Adam wasn't sure how to take the idea that Vic's family might know about him, about the magic. Bobby wasn't the only one who might commit him. And yet, Vic didn't seem worried. He seemed to feel they'd believe him.

"You close to your family?" Vic asked, pulling Adam back before his thoughts drifted to Liberty House.

"Not really," Adam said, shrugging, trying to imagine how he'd explain himself, his past, to Vic.

"Are they like you?" Vic asked. "Magic?"

"No," Adam said. "My Aunt Sue is. Kind of. But my mother and brother aren't like me at all."

Vic's brow wrinkled, no doubt he felt the mix of things Adam felt when he thought of Tilla and Bobby.

"My family is complicated," Adam said.

"Why?" Vic asked.

"Because I'm complicated." *Because you complicate them*

"Getting that," Vic said. His eyes closed. They were slow to reopen.

"You need to sleep," Adam said.

"Yeah," Vic agreed. "Meds kicking in."

"I'll go," Adam said.

Vic gave Adam's hand a squeeze. "Thank you. For coming, for what you did."

Adam watched Vic settle into sleep. He waited for the intensity of the conversation to ebb. It didn't.

He'd thought about Vic a lot, especially in the hospital, but this sort of instant connection—what had he done? And why had it pissed Silver off?

Vic let out a little snore. A bit of drool beaded his lip.

Adam stood, careful not to wake Vic.

I'd do it again. Save him again.

Leaning in, he left a quick kiss on Vic's forehead. The contact felt electric.

It lingered as he took quiet steps to the hallway. The feeling was so different than kissing Perak. The elf had felt cool and soothing,

Vic's mother waited in the hall.

"You saved his life," she said, no question.

"I—" Adam stuttered. "How much did he tell you?"

Mrs. Martinez, *Maria*, shook her head, leading him back toward the living room. Adam ignored her silent invitation and kept moving toward the front door.

"He said you saved his life, that you risked your own for his"—she paused, fumbling for words—"I thought it was the drugs at first. Then they let him come home early, days ahead of time."

Adam still did not know how much Vic understood. He had to explain, just as soon as he understood it himself.

"Then there's the roses," she said.

"The roses?" Adam asked.

She gestured for him to follow her outside.

"It started as soon as we brought him home," Maria said.

The backyard held several bushes. They drooped with blooms, flourishing in the Indian summer. The smell was intoxicating, and the late bees seemed to think so too. Some of the trailer lots back home had little gardens, a bush or two. Their colors never failed to make Adam smile. But these, these were black, jet and glossy, sloe, like Vic's hair.

Adam shifted his Sight. Another six Reapers stood on this side of the house, completing the circle. Thirteen total, watching, waiting.

They issued no challenge, didn't draw their scythes or offer a threat.

Still, Adam didn't stay for Chinese food.

[handwritten margin note: To avoid scandel maybe]

18

ADAM

Adam didn't know what to expect from a day at the hospital, so he decided on his black T-shirt with the drawing of a heart dissection that said "Bad Luck" and his best pair of jeans.

He didn't intend to stay long, and certainly didn't intend to perform maintenance, cleaning clogged toilets and mopping up all sorts of fluids. He'd put up with the job only as long as it took to learn what he hadn't been able to before.

He half-expected Bobby to try dressing him. Doctor Binder probably considered it, but was still too pissed about the Audi, even if he hadn't pieced together Adam's involvement in its theft.

Adam emerged from the basement to a silent breakfast table where Bobby sat with a cup of coffee and another newspaper. An actual watch ticked away on his wrist. Adam wanted to ask Bobby when he'd joined the AARP, but knew his mother wouldn't tolerate sniping at her table.

Adam's heart wasn't really in it anyway. That bit of time with Vic's family had given him a taste of what having a mother and brother could be like, and what it was like put a vice around his heart and took the joy out of getting a rise out of Bobby.

The clock read six in the morning as his mother moved pans around the stove, stirring and shifting bacon to a plate with a paper towel to soak up the grease.

She'd made eggs and bacon with a side of fried potatoes. Adam smothered the potatoes in ketchup, the way he had as a kid, but now he found the taste too sweet and wished he'd held back. Meals with Tilla Mae were a special sort of torture. She'd always insisted they eat together when they could, but she didn't let them enjoy it. Adam didn't remember his mom laughing or joking. His dad, though—Adam remembered his dad laughing as he played the airplane game with a spoon full of cereal or did this really dumb magic trick where he pretended to pull a paper napkin through his ears like his head was hollow.

His mother's fork clinked against her plate. She didn't smile. She didn't speak. Dad had been angry a lot, but he laughed too. Their mother was just . . . there. Present but not, unless one of them disturbed the peace.

"Are you ready to go?" Bobby asked, folding the paper and setting it aside. Straightening, he pushed his chair back.

Adam considered the offer as he crunched a piece of bacon between his teeth.

"I'll ride with you," he said.

Their mother sat with her coffee and her own breakfast. She'd given each of them three pieces of bacon, having only taken two for herself. She'd always done that, Adam realized, put her sons first.

Adam knew he couldn't have been easy to live with, especially in high school. He cringed at the memories. His Sight or sensitivity would overwhelm him at the worst of times. The spirit realm would catch him without warning, draw him in and trap him.

Listening to Bobby, she'd taken him to doctors who diagnosed him as narcoleptic and schizophrenic, though in truth Adam had known he was neither. He'd toss the pills they prescribed, but then midterms or upcoming dances would raise the stress level of his fellow students and their feelings and their hormone-fueled anxieties forced their way into him, became his. *Empath*

Adam would have given anything to be like the other boys, whose biggest concerns were girls and sneaking their dad's beer. Even if he'd been straight, Adam's father had vanished, and he couldn't drink without his Sight making him crazy. *Schweibert?*

Eventually he'd lost all ability to function or pay attention in class, and off to Liberty House he'd gone.

His mother hadn't stopped Bobby from locking him up. Hell, she'd signed the papers. And she hadn't listened, hadn't stopped the drugs, the tests, or the endless counseling sessions and group therapy, which had been the worst of it. He'd absorbed the horrors of the others and he'd fled further and further into the spirit world.

Adam swallowed hard, forcing the past back down and stood to take his plate to the dishwasher.

"Thank you, Mom," he said.

She nodded, and Adam followed Bobby to the garage, to Annie's car, a white box geared for child safety. Adam thought it looked like a refrigerator on wheels.

"Where did you go yesterday?" Bobby asked.

"Out," Adam said. "I had a lead to track down."

He didn't have to justify himself to Bobby. He didn't mention his search for their vanished father and his complete lack of leads. And he didn't bring up Vic. He didn't want Bobby to know about his visit to the cop. Whatever was happening with Vic was his. He wanted it to be just his.

Almost idly, Adam wondered what Vic was doing. Sleeping probably. He could press the thread between them, know for certain, but he let it lie.

"Did you hear about the corpse flower?" Bobby asked. "I was just reading about it in the paper."

"What?" Adam asked, some of his scattered attention drifting back to his brother.

"The Botanic Gardens has a corpse flower. It only blooms every ten years. It bloomed yesterday, years earlier than it should have." Uh oh

Adam blinked.

"It smells like rotting meat," Bobby continued. "That's why it's called that."

"Damn."

"What?" Bobby asked.

"Symbols—portents, Aunt Sue called them that. She likes her fancy words."

"What about them?" Bobby asked.

"They're happening. When the normal world starts to get glimpses of the magical one, things are out of balance."

Like black roses, he thought with a cold punch to his gut.

"But what does it *mean*, Adam?" Bobby asked. "How is it connected to Annie?"

Hadn't Adam just explained it? Was Bobby being dense on purpose? He held in a sigh.

"The spirit world is leaking into the physical," Adam stressed. "The thing that has Annie—it's throwing off the natural balance."

Adam twisted to look behind them, to see the tendril marking Bobby's house.

"What do we do?"

We?

Adam cocked his head at Bobby.

"We go to work."

Bobby shot Adam a sideways glance.

"I have to find out what I can about the hospital," Adam said. "The spirit is connected to Mercy, and crawling around its guts is the best idea I've got right now."

He hadn't gotten into the records, but the magical void had to be related to the situation.

He could go back to Silver, try to get more information, since his trip to Vic had only brought more mysteries.

He'd done the thing he didn't want to do and petitioned the elves for help. They hadn't aided him, and he was back to square one.

They parked in Bobby's spot. The place hadn't changed, but Adam regarded it with a wider eye. He wasn't looking forward to whatever "maintenance" was, but he hoped it at least gave him the chance to plumb Mercy's secrets.

They rode the elevator together.

"*Behave*," Bobby mouthed when the door to his floor opened.

"*Fuck off*," Adam mouthed back.

"Ready for your first day?" Ms. Geen greeted as soon as he walked into HR.

"Uh, yes?" Adam said.

"Not too eager, are you?" she asked. She wore the same suit she had the day she'd met him. "This way."

"It's just, I'm not sure what I'll be doing."

She pushed open the door to the stairwell. The gloss vanished, replaced by worn paint and scuffed floors.

"The job description has you making rounds, checking the status of everything from light bulbs to plumbing," Geen explained, leading him downstairs. Her heels clicked on the tiled steps. "We'll provide you with some coveralls and an ID badge."

"How old is this building?" Adam asked. He'd have to find a chance to slip away, to see if he could find an end to the void, a clue to the spirit's origins.

"Mercy's been here since the 1800s," she said. "So you can imagine it needs a lot of upkeep."

They went through a door and down a hall. The drop ceiling

above was dusty, water-stained in places. Water ran through a pipe and dripped somewhere unseen. Adam could smell garbage, acrid and earthy. He cringed. At least they were paying him.

"Who will I work with?" he asked. He remembered the janitor-Reaper.

"While there's a whole maintenance department, you'll mostly work alone." Geen paused at a door. She pushed it open. "In here."

Adam expected a broom closet, or a desk with rows of light bulbs, maybe a wall of tools. Instead he found a teeming forest. The treetops vanished into the clouds. The light of a full moon broke through the leaves. Spirits raced like fireflies among the branches, leaving trails in the twilight.

"What the—" Adam fell back.

"I can't believe you fell for that," Geen said, closing the doors behind them.

He registered the change in her voice. Less reedy, it sounded richer, more steely and familiar.

"Argent," he said, tensing.

She shed Geen's form like mercury, flowing until she resolved into the Queen of Sword's more familiar shape, though she still wore the suit and heels.

"I don't understand," Adam said. "You've been here the whole time?"

"We had to monitor the situation," the queen said. "I came as soon as the spirit appeared."

"Why didn't you tell me?"

"There are rules, Adam Binder. You had to petition us." Argent said. "You certainly took your time. We don't have much of it. The situation is getting worse. You need to be close to the situation, so we'll set you up here, get you whatever access you were so clumsily plodding toward."

"What about Bobby?"

She looked taken aback. "Everything I said is true. Your brother's job is safe. And we are paying you—quite well, might I add."

Adam wondered how much the elves knew. Quite a lot, probably. They were sly, as Argent had proven by insinuating herself into the hospital. He didn't trust her, didn't trust that her presence and his were a coincidence. Elves were experts at binding others to them through favors and gifts.

"What's it going to cost me?" he asked, arms folded over his chest.

Argent tapped her lips with a finger. "Your soul, of course."

19

ADAM

Adam felt the color drain from his face.

"I'm kidding," Argent said. "Of course I'm kidding."

Adam glared at her.

"You're teasing me."

"Yes," she said.

"You're a sword-wielding being of immense power, an immortal. And you're teasing me."

"Yes, I am," she said. "What use would I have for a mortal soul?"

"I don't know," he said.

"I'm not some sort of petty hoarder," she said. "Not like dragons."

Her eyes narrowed with real dislike before she focused on Adam again and said, "We need this thing stopped."

"So stop it," Adam said, waving a hand about them. "You have more magic than anyone."

"We've tried," she said, her voice quiet. "Magic is not what's called for. At or least, not only what is called for. It's not a matter of power. It killed those we sent against it."

"The void," Adam said. He could still feel it, the emptiness centered on the hospital. He realized its source then.

Elves had gone to fight it. The closest thing he'd met to gods, supposed to live forever—for one to die, it felt like he'd learned a species had gone extinct.

"Yes," Argent whispered, all the light draining from her features. Her eyes dipped to the floor. "This spirit is not magic, or at least not magic as we know it. Thus it cannot be fought with magic as we know it."

"Because it's not alive," Adam said, remembering the feel of the thing. "It's a spirit, right? Spirits are ghosts. They were alive."

"They are remnants, bits of living beings that cling to your world. This one is not. It is neither dead nor alive as we define it."

"Is it Death?" Adam asked. The entity who controlled the Reapers was a great mystery, a secretive power serving creation itself.

"No," Argent said, sounding impatient. "And we have checked."

She led Adam to the base of a tree. A table ringed it like a counter. Atop that were scrolls, books, and the occasional tablet computer. He could not read most of the languages laid out before him.

"So what do you want with me?" Adam asked. "I don't have any magic."

"We need you to stop this thing, as we cannot." She waved a hand over the books. "My brother suspects that less magic, not more, is what is needed. Of every practitioner who has faced it, you're the only one to walk away. Coincidentally, you're the weakest being on the spectrum to confront it."

"No offense," Adam said, back stiffening. He forced himself to take a breath. Argent might play games, but she remained the Queen of Swords, whether she needed his help or not. "But by that logic, won't teaching me—giving me more magic—make the problem worse?"

"No," she said. "The idea that knowledge is power is mostly metaphorical. You can get closer to it than someone more powerful. We need you for reconnaissance, to examine it, to learn more. We cannot even determine if it is sentient. Our guess is that it has a primal intelligence, slow and more instinctive."

[handwritten margin note: like the weird flesh network in Stranger Things]

"No," Adam said, veins icing at the memory of it looking at him, looking through him. The elves had underestimated it, but he had too good an instinct for self-preservation to say so. "That's not right. The way it attacked me at the hospital. It tried to kill me. It's smarter than that. It's doing something, watching. It's aware."

He'd felt its magic, the sticky stain of its touch on Annie, and didn't think it was the presence he'd sensed watching on the way to Vic's.

Argent nodded. "Then we must watch it back."

"I have my price," Adam said.

"Name it," she said.

"It has my sister-in-law possessed."

"We shall help her," Argent said. "However we can."

It would be selfish to ask for more, but this might be his one chance to get assistance from the Guardians. He had to step carefully. If he told Argent, an elf, about the bone charms, the immortals might hunt the warlock down before Adam had his chance for a reunion and to ask his many, many questions.

"There is another matter," he said. "A pawn shop on Federal was trading in magical goods a couple of years ago. I need some help tracking it down."

Argent cocked her head to the side, pondering his request.

"This is not related to the spirit?" she asked.

"Not that I'm aware of."

"I will make some inquiries for you, but we can agree that the spirit takes precedence?"

"Yes," he said. "Annie, Bobby's wife, doesn't have much time."

"We've seen some of those it has possessed. We neither know how this thing works nor how it holds them," Argent said. "Some can resist it. Some cannot."

"Then how can you help?"

"If we cannot give her more time." Argent dipped her shoulder in a graceful shrug. "Then we must take her out of it."

"That's not possible," Adam said. "Is it?"

The queen laughed.

"I almost forgot you are mortal," she said. "I must speak with Silver and the Gaoler. We will bring your sister to the watchtower."

"Why don't we go now?" Adam asked.

Argent made a sound like "pft" and waved at the stacks of books.

"Because your shift is starting."

*****

Adam spent the day leafing through texts, most of them bestiaries, but none of the creatures or horrors he found matched what floated over the city. Feeling like he'd emptied his brain, Adam stumbled out of the hospital, uncertain if he should wait for Bobby or try and get a bus.

Outside, he looked for a tree or a bit of grass where he could sit and shake off the day's tedium.

Spying a large park, Adam started that way but turned at the blare of a familiar horn and grinned.

His mother had come to get him. In the Cutlass. Adam had never been so happy to see his car. He climbed into the passenger seat, shutting the door hard and not even caring that he wasn't driving.

They went several blocks before his mother said. "I don't know why your brother hates this car. It's a classic."

"It is," Adam agreed, running a hand over the cracked,

sun-faded dash. He'd restore it if he could. He'd restore all of it.

Sure, it still needed a lot of work, from the crunched front panel to the engine. It could break down any day, and almost did. Adam often pushed his magic into it, willing it to hold together, for his luck to hold until he reached his destination. It was a beater of a car by any measurement, but the Cutlass felt like home, in a way that nothing else did.

"Bobby is too hard on it," he said.

"And you're too hard on him," his mother said.

She braked for a light. The Cutlass wasn't quick to stop, but his mother surprised him. She knew how to handle the car's mass.

He didn't answer her remark. She picked up speed again as the light changed.

The Cutlass was the oldest thing on the road. Adam felt a bit like the elves, a piece of history in motion, an anachronism in a crowd of glossy SUVs and urban assault vehicles. Adam finally felt the tension give. He sat up straight, pressed himself into the bucket seat.

Adam knew her tricks. Like the elves, his mother was sly. She'd circle back to the subject of Bobby soon enough. But he could be sneaky too.

"You know how to handle her," Adam said.

"When he left," she said. "I never wanted to see this car again."

"You asked Sue to take it," he said, wondering how he could get her to circle to the topic of his father and the details he needed.

"Yes," she said. "I couldn't bring myself to sell it, but I didn't want it around either."

"Did you feel the same way about me?" he asked, keeping his tone even. "When Bobby dumped me at Liberty House?"

"Adam Lee," she said, her tone sawing that way it did to warn him he was near a line. As a boy, it would have earned him a spanking or a lengthy time out. "You are my son and I love you."

"You're not answering the question, Mom."

"You're not easy, Adam," she said, her back stiffening. "You're more like your father than you're like me."

"Magical?" he asked. He sincerely wanted, needed, to know. It was hard enough to get his mother to talk about his dad. She'd never given any hint that his father might be a witch.

"Stubborn," she said. "And a smart ass."

"You don't talk about him," Adam said, his voice quieter.

Most of what he could remember was anger, temper tantrums. He remembered a flare of crimson when Bobby called their father "Daddy," not Dad. He'd backhanded his eldest. When Adam had asked Bobby why, all he'd muttered was something about John Wayne and an old movie. *→ not explenative*

Jesus why?

Remembering it now, Adam touched his own cheek and struggled to pull the real memory out from the decade of time that had eroded it and layered on confusing notions. His father was angry. His father loved him, adored him, made him laugh, and called him "tiger." His father hit his sons. His father left.

"There's not a lot to talk about," his mother said, oblivious to the scene Adam had relived. "But Bobby was older. He knew him better. Maybe you should ask him about your father."

Adam sank further into his seat. The cushioning had almost given out. He could feel the metal frame digging into his back. The old cloth was time-stained, with black starburst burns from cigarette ashes. Once, two people, his parents, had ridden in the car and smoked together. Once, they'd been happy. Now, he knew next to nothing about his father. Maybe he was the warlock Adam had chased across southern Oklahoma. Maybe he wasn't. Argent was his only hope on that front. And as he had wondered so many times, Adam wasn't certain their father should be found.

"Maybe I will," he said, knowing he wouldn't.

Their dad was a tough topic between the brothers. Bobby avoided talking about it with Adam, like he was too delicate to handle it. Sometime, long ago, Bobby had decided Adam couldn't handle emotional discussions, like his sensitivity to magic or strong feelings from others meant he was too delicate for anything too heavy. Adam resented the hell out of that.

maybe Mom feels that way

After a while, when they'd turned onto Broadway and neared the suburbs, his mother said, "I know you are still mad at him, over Liberty House, but he only did what he thought was right, what the counselors told him to. That's all he's ever done, what he thought was right."

"I'm not mad, Mom, not like I was. But what he did, locking me up, it broke me." Adam didn't think he'd ever put it all out there before. Liberty House had changed him, not for the better. He'd met Perak. He'd learned magic, to control his powers, but he'd never been able to get over feeling like a freak. He'd never felt at ease in his skin.

"I've always found it strange," his mother said, looking to the back door in a way that told him she longed for a cigarette. "That you weren't as angry at me."

His mom turned to face him. She crossed her arms and met his gaze.

"I was your parent, not Bobby. I signed the papers. Yes, he talked to your counselor for me. I was working. I was always working, but I could have made a different decision."

"Then why didn't you?" Adam asked, thinking that maybe, yeah, he would try being angry at her for a change.

"I didn't know better," she said. "And your brother didn't know better either. I think you need to forgive him. And if you can't, I think you need to be mad at me too." *Smart mom*

Adam had never thought about it before. He'd never doubted that Bobby deserved his anger. He couldn't really say why he didn't the feel the same way about his mom. But it was Bobby who'd held him during Dad's rages, Bobby who'd sworn to keep

Adam safe. Mom had just stood by during the beatings. She'd cowered, and maybe that had been her Liberty House, the time that had broken her, left her incapable of mothering him at all.

"Maybe I should be," he said.

"Bobby thought he was doing the best thing for you when he put you there," she said. "We both did."

"Are you sure it wasn't just the best thing for you two?" he asked.

"I can't say," she said.

It was more than he'd expected from her, but still, it wasn't near enough.

20

ROBERT

Robert collapsed into "the chair" as soon as he got home from work. They'd fought about it, gently, the ridiculous cost of the poufy, floral-patterned thing. Annie had insisted it tied the room together. He'd never seen her sit in it. In fact, he was pretty sure no one had used it until he found his mother reading in it one day. He pressed down into its firm, plush fabric and remembered how much he'd looked forward to their kids vomiting on it. The thought still brought a little smile.

He very badly wanted a drink, but Robert never drank. Too many on-call shifts, too many chances for the memories to catch him if he slipped into that particular fog. *He has the genes*

His mother warded the past off with a box of cheap wine in the kitchen, sipping it through the day as she picked out passages from her bible. Robert pretended not to notice the wine. He didn't approve, but he understood. *Where's that understanding for Adam?*

Adam approached the chair. He came cautiously, like he had as a little boy, like Robert might explode. He nodded, and Adam perched on the edge of the ottoman like a bird. Whispering, so quietly that Robert almost shouted at him to speak up, Adam explained the plan. Robert could not absorb half of it. He wanted that drink. He wanted two.

"When?" Robert asked.

"They'll come for her at midnight," Adam said.

It would be so easy, to just let Annie go with them, to excise the problem and pretend all was well, the way he'd thought all was well with Adam in Liberty House, despite the whispers that said otherwise.

"Us," Robert snapped. "They'll come for *us* at midnight."

Adam opened his mouth to protest but Robert cut him off. "I'm not sending my wife to some magical asylum without checking it out first."

He wouldn't make the same mistake twice.

He heard the anger in his voice. He hated seeing Adam cringe, like he had so often when he hid in their room, under the frame of the plywood bunk bed when he was still small enough to squeeze beneath it. He was cocky, so headstrong as an adult. Robert had thought it then, and perhaps he still thought it. Adam might be too delicate, too breakable for the world.

"I don't know what you'll see," Adam said. "Or how much."

Adam was so eager for Robert to know, and all Robert wanted was to get on with being Robert, to be nothing like his little brother or their father.

He'd tried to forget. He'd tried to move away and leave it behind, but here it was. Here they were—his mother, his brother. The past wouldn't stay buried, would not let him move on.

Robert sort of wanted to explode, like Dad had exploded, with shouts and thrown objects and holes punched into the walls. He forced all that down, swallowed it, though it filled his guts like tar.

He didn't want to see things that weren't there. He didn't want to hear what wasn't said aloud, but maybe it was all real. Maybe he'd been wrong all along, about so many things.

The room felt gloomy, the lamplight heavy and slow as Robert sank.

Adam would show him this hidden world. After all, that was the plan, take Annie to the spirit realm and freeze her in time. If this was real, he was going. If this was some kind of con, the people running it would pay.

Robert unfolded himself from the chair.

"I'll get ready," he said.

He could have dozed off in the ugly floral chair, but he fought the lethargy and stood. Magical beings were about to take his wife to the Other Side, the "spirit realm," as Aunt Sue and Adam called it.

They'd spent a Thanksgiving or two with the woman, at their father's insistence, at their mother's reluctance. She wore floral house dresses and proudly served them TV dinners. She'd always lived in squalor. Robert could scarcely believe the old bat was still alive.

love her

Now he was sounding like her, preparing for some adventure out of make-believe.

All he truly wanted was to sleep through it, but he would not let them take Annie without being there. He needed to see where they'd keep her.

He'd delivered Adam to Liberty House, and he'd seen it for a modern, clean facility. Mostly. When he looked from the corner of his eye, there'd been mold on the walls. More than a few of the fluorescent bulbs buzzed and blinked, but if he stared, if he looked directly at things, they seemed fine. Robert had taken Adam to Liberty House and left him there, looking back once to confirm that his brother would be safe. He'd never been able to bury the doubt he'd felt since.

Heavy limbed, heavy footed, Robert trudged upstairs. He became Bobby again, for all intents and purposes, all control and cultivated order lost. He heard his mother whispering to Annie as she dressed her in the guest room that had become hers.

Robert did not know what to wear. Adam would wear worn jeans and an ironic T-shirt with a flannel over it. Robert cared quite a bit more. He found a pair of jeans with the tags still on them.

They were new, unworn. It made sense. He had two uniforms lately, two looks: what he wore to work, and sweats. Robert pulled on a button-up, white with blue lines in a grid pattern. The night wasn't cool enough for a jacket, but he tugged one on anyway. He'd need the pocket. Robert found the hiking boots he'd purchased when he'd first reached Colorado, intending to go to the mountains every day off and enjoy the outdoors. They were almost new. He pulled them on and laced them up.

Then he loaded the gun. *oh please that won't help*

Adam and his mother thought he'd forgotten all about where they came from, the red dirt and scrub oak of the backwoods, but Robert remembered. He remembered the stories about feral dogs who'd tasted human flesh and escaped convicts hiding in the woods.

The gun, like so many things, had been his dad's. A Ruger .22, so old it couldn't be registered. *Nice*

Robert kept it clean. He promised Annie he'd use a small gun safe and a trigger lock when the baby came, even before the kid could crawl. Still, she hated that he kept it in the house. But Robert remembered—his father, red-faced, screaming. He remembered hiding beneath the bed, first alone, then with Adam clutched, shivering and pink, in his arms.

And he remembered standing in the way as Adam hid, letting their dad explode onto him, battering him with fists and cursing until, rage expended, Dad stomped outside to have yet another beer while Robert nursed his fat lip.

Safety on, the gun went into the jacket pocket.

Dressed, Robert returned to the living room. Adam sat with Annie on the couch. She looked alert, awake, more focused than he'd seen her in a while, just when he would have preferred she didn't know what was happening, what they were doing.

Their mother sat in the den, bible open. She'd left most of the lights off.

The doorbell rang, shattering the quiet she'd drawn over the dark house.

Adam opened the door. A woman strode in. She looked like an old movie star, all curves and beauty drawn in white and silver. There was something familiar about her, and Robert might have sworn he'd seen her once on an old black and white movie, the kind their mom had let run on channel thirty-four while their dad worked on the Cutlass.

The woman ran a hand through her perfect hair. It didn't upset the careful upswept style, but it revealed the dagger point of her long ear. That little touch of inhumanity made Robert freeze. They said spirits didn't like iron. He'd see how they felt about lead. _LOL._

"Lady," Adam said with more deference than Robert had ever heard him show anyone. Adam bowed, actually bowed, to her in a graceful, old-fashioned way that he had to have learned from another old movie.

There were times when he felt his brother wasn't his brother, that they could not have come from the same place.

"How did you get him to do that?" Robert asked. Adam shot him a look of warning, no—fear. What was this woman that she could make surly Adam Lee sit up like a puppy?

"Oh, Adam Binder," she said, swinging her purse off her shoulder. She beamed at Robert's brother like he was some pet who'd performed a trick. Robert tensed. "Aren't you going to introduce us?"

Adam stepped in front of Robert and said, very carefully, "Lady Argent of the Winter, Queen of Swords and Guardian of the Watchtower of the North, I present my brother, Robert Jack Binder, doctor, eldest of my generation. Second of his name."

The way Adam spoke, with such care, gave Robert pause. Kings and queens—he felt like he'd been dropped into Comic-Con. The woman moved with an impossible, avian grace, but she was real. Those pointed ears were not fake. He felt the weight of the gun in the pocket of his jacket.

"There's about five more, but we don't have the time," she said.

"I don't want to not show the proper respect," Adam said.

"You act as though I would eat him," the queen said, her gray eyes sparkling.

"Would you?" Robert asked.

"Robert," Adam hissed in warning.

"Elves are vegans," she said. She glanced at the watch on her wrist. "We should get going. We need to be downtown and traffic is horrible these days."

"We're not going to the watchtower?" Adam asked.

"We are not going to the Watchtower of the North," Argent said. "To save your marriage-sister we must take her out of time, and time is the purview of the East. The Gaoler shall keep her safe."

"Gaoler . . . jailer?" Robert asked. "You're going to lock her up?"

"In a manner of speaking," Lady Argent said. Her neck moved with too much grace, too much flexibility, like an owl or hawk.

"But we don't have all night," she continued with a little tap of her foot. "And you just *had* to live in the suburbs."

Robert shot the elf woman a glare and leaned over Annie.

She sat on the couch, staring blankly into space.

"We're going to go now, okay, Annie?" Robert asked.

Annie lifted her head, cowed and furtive. She nodded, but did not speak. His heart twisted to see his Annie, so proud and capable, reduced.

Argent frowned.

"You were correct," she said. "She doesn't have much time."

She led them outside, to a plain white van parked on the street. It looked like the perfect vehicle for a kidnapping.

Mom closed the door behind them. She did not watch them walk to the curb. She had not said much about any of it, just retreated into her Bible and muttered prayers. Adam frowned, but Robert understood.

He did not know what to say to Annie as he held her hand and guided her along. Soothing noises and soft whispers poured out of him. He realized he'd been saving them up for the baby. With each muttering, each spend from that piled stock, he felt the dream, their perfect life, recede a little farther.

The woman, Argent, took the passenger seat, riding shotgun beside another elf, this one dressed like a chauffeur.

Robert helped Annie into the van. Reaching over, he fastened her seatbelt.

"No," Annie said. "I don't—I don't want that."

Tears brimmed in her eyes.

"You can't make me," she said.

"Shh," Robert said. His heart felt like glass, cracking and breaking into cutting shards. "We're going to make it better."

21

ROBERT

He didn't know if he was lying to her. He held her for most of the drive up the long stretch of Broadway toward the small copse of tall buildings comprising downtown Denver. Adam sat behind them, silent.

Annie pushed Robert away. She stared at him, trying to focus, trying to see him through the haze that had darkened their life. He closed his eyes, hoped she did not see him struggle to swallow it all down and keep it off his face. But his gut had no more room. He choked up, couldn't find air, drowning on dry land.

She did not struggle further, did not strike him or speak. When she relaxed, the pressure in her hands letting up, he opened his eyes. Downtown loomed.

The slight canyons of lights and buildings swallowed them. The driver pulled the van into an alley.

"Stay with the van," Argent told the driver.

The four of them, Annie, Robert, Adam, and Argent, filed out into the bustling night. Denver always seemed busy these days, even this late on a weeknight. People walked in pairs or groups. Most of them were college-age. Some of the young men, skinny, in jeans so tight that Robert could almost tell their religion, might have been gay. They looked happy. Robert shot Adam a look, trying to say *that could be you.* He wanted to see his brother free, not weighed down by the shadows and visions that swirled around him.

There was a nearby campus, shared by three colleges. Adam could go there if he wanted. He could get his GED, go to community college. He could be happy, could leave it behind too. It was all Robert had ever wanted for him, and maybe the past would fade if Adam left it behind.

But Adam didn't seem to notice the sights or even the young men. He kept walking, following the elven woman toward the clock tower.

Robert expected it to be locked, but others were inside, waiting for the elevator. The sound of campy music and laughter rose from the basement.

Argent pushed the up button. Robert wondered that none of the people in the lobby gaped at her, but none seemed to notice her ears.

"Going up," Argent said when the elevator dinged.

The four of them filed in.

When the elevator doors closed, Robert asked, "We're not invisible are we?"

"Us?" Adam asked. "No. Argent is. Sort of."

Robert glared, prompting Adam to explain.

"Magical beings, it's like they're on another television channel. They leak through a bit, but they don't come in clearly. Someone with the Sight can see them, really see them. Sensitives, people with a little magic sometimes can. It depends on how much power they have."

Robert could see Argent as clear as a painting. He blanched, feeling all hope for normalcy evaporate. Argent winked at him.

The elevator dinged and they stepped into a clock. Not the

clock tower observation deck or the mechanical inside of some small space. Robert had expected that. Instead they stood on an actual clock face, a round floor wider than the entire tower. At a distance, gears turned and cogs clicked. The works hung in space, unconnected to anything, floating beyond reach.

They'd gone somewhere *else*, and Robert hadn't even felt it.

Annie hadn't reacted, hadn't changed expressions. It was like she'd shut down, was waiting for something to turn her back on.

Their perch hung from an unseen ceiling by several thick cables, the steel kind used to maintain suspense bridges. Though black and dust-encrusted, they looked steady enough. Robert strained to hear over the grind of gears and faint ticking, but he felt certain water lapped against a rock. Beneath the iron and char of machinery, limestone and brine laced the air.

Adam stretched out a hand, measuring his distance to the clockwork or to ward off something Robert could not see. Argent beamed. At Robert's side, Annie stood fixed in place. He suspected the sights around them were invisible to her. He could not fathom how she even stood here, why she, so much more real than all of this, didn't slip through the floor and drown in the sea hidden below.

A bit of air unfolded, a slice of space blurred, and a trio of creatures stepped onto the clock face. Robert tested his footing in case they had to run. He resisted the urge to check his gun. He didn't want to give the weapon away. He might need the element of surprise.

The surface underfoot felt too slick for speed, like glass or crystal. The massive minute hand shifted slightly in their direction, as if to eventually pinch them between it and the hour hand.

The creatures looked like elderly people, except for their squat height and bulbous noses.

"What are they?" Robert asked Adam in a whisper.

"Gnomes," Adam said. "And they can hear you."

Robert hadn't even noticed their ears. Large, pointed, they resembled outstretched bat wings.

Their anatomy, the broad ears, the small dark eyes, indicated an adaptation to underground living. Biology failed him after that. They did not map to what he knew.

"This is the prisoner?" one of the gnomes asked.

"The patient," Robert snapped.

Argent's humor dimmed. "The Gaoler expects us. It was arranged with him, not you."

"We are his servants," the gnome said, its voice taking on a hiss. "Mind your manners, elf."

Robert looked to Adam.

Adam shrugged and said, "They don't all get along."

"Sometimes we even war," Argent said with an edge that reminded Robert of sharp ice. "Take us to the Gaoler. *Please.*"

Still sneering, the lead gnome nodded. Somewhere, a crank turned. The cables shuddered. The clock face descended. If Robert peered upward, he could see the winches that lowered them into the dark. He kept near Annie, did not move closer to the edge of the clock face and risk falling. Adam looked like he might go see. Robert tensed, ready to throw out an arm if Adam moved in that direction and wondered how his willful brother would respond to a soccer mom block.

Argent perched on the hour hand, treating it like a bench. She affected a bored, distracted air, but Robert could tell she watched Annie from the corner of her eye. Robert inched closer to Annie. He did not trust these people, if they were people.

Maybe I'm the one in Liberty House. And this is all a delusion, a psychotic breakdown.

No. He was here. This was real. The pounding in his ears, the rushing blood, said he was here.

No one teetered off the clock face, though Robert held tight to Annie's arm just in case. It stopped its descent with a bit of rumble. He risked a peek over the edge, made certain Annie took no steps in that direction. They had not reached the bottom. Gloom shrouded whatever lay below. A cable bridge set somewhere near the twelve mark, led on into the dark.

Adam looked nervous, skittish, all his bravado gone, like he'd been as a boy, the little brother under the bed, hiding from the monster.

"Where are we really?" Robert asked, sidling up to his brother.

"Here," Adam said. "In the clock tower, but not in our world."

"You've been here before though."

"Not this exact place," Adam said, shaking his head. "And never physically. I don't have the power, not enough to step between places. This is where I go when I spirit walk, when you think I'm just sleeping."

Robert nodded toward Argent. "But she does? Have enough to bring us here physically?"

"In spades," Adam said with a hint of his earlier fear and what sounded like envy.

So that was it, why Adam didn't apply himself to life. He wanted to be more here, in his other world. *Ding ding ding!*

It was like drug addicts, chasing their high. Lips curling into a frown, Robert took it all in. Whatever it was, you couldn't live here. The carnival had to end sometime. *Says the tourist*

The gnomes stepped aside, letting their visitors first approach the bridge of heavy, rusted pipes and planks of untreated wood. Robert helped Annie onto it, testing it with ginger steps. It swayed slightly in the mist-veiled darkness but held their weight. Clockwork giants, vaguely man-like, moved in the dark beyond them. One wheeled into sight and blinked eyes made of gear wheels and incandescent bulbs down at them.

Argent moved to Robert's side, her steps so light the bridge didn't tremble. Pausing there, arms folded over her chest, she glared up at the thing. It rumbled away and their group walked on.

Robert caught Argent's expression from the corner of his eye. She looked predatory, ready for a fight.

The mist kept parting, teasing what lay beyond, until the bridge connected with a cave, a hole in the side of a granite cliff. The air felt damp on his face. He smelled salt mixed with coal, but he felt no ocean spray, heard neither wave nor wind. The air warmed. Annie grew more animated, more alert. She looked about at the stone walls, their surface lit only by the dim light ahead and behind.

Robert smiled to see her perk up. She hadn't been interested in anything—life, him—in months.

The rock walls glistened with water.

"Do you remember, Annie?" he asked her. "It's like that mine tour we took."

It had been a good day. A hike, pizza in a small mountain town, one of their best dates. It hadn't been anything specific or special. She'd just laughed at some dumb joke he'd made, and he'd known she was the one. He wanted to marry her.

Annie didn't respond, but she flashed a knowing smile. She was still in there, the vibrant girl he'd married. Maybe everything would be all right.

The sound of grinding gears, great and ancient machinery, rumbled around them. Robert felt the tons of rock and earth, incalculable, pressing in, pressing down, upon them. They were not beneath Denver. They were not beneath anywhere. This place was impossible, something he wouldn't have believed before tonight.

The passage ended. The dim lights brightened by a shade or two. The four of them, followed by the gnomes, stepped into a smooth-floored cavern, a domed amphitheater larger than Robert's house. Faceless, skeletal clocks, their gears and hands exposed, hung around them on cables. They curtained the room. Their numbers glowed, making a little more of the light his eyes craved. All were stopped.

Stalagmites lined the back wall, like the uneven teeth of some monster sleeping with its mouth closed. They looked like mud dripped and dried, like the sandcastles Adam used to make on the shore of Lake Liberty. The cave had the same dampness as the hollows along the lake, the same kind of soggy air tinted with rot.

He remembered their dad fishing while their mother laid out a picnic of potato salad and peanut butter sandwiches. No jelly. They couldn't afford it.

Squinting, Robert saw the forms trapped within the stone.

"Gaoler!" Argent called. "We've come to fulfill our agreement."

The distant rumble thrumming through the floor grew louder, closer. Bits of clock assembled into a mix of brass and black iron. Two faces for eyes, a dozen tiny cogs for teeth. It had minute hands for fingers.

Robert took several steps back as it rose. Lumbering, it stood twice his height.

It lifted a hand and pointed to a circle of sand beneath a clock face, a gap in the row of stalagmites.

"Place her there," Argent told Robert, her tone gentle. "The Gaoler will keep her until we have an answer, a way to remove the spirit."

"What will it be like?" Robert asked. "What will she feel?"

"She will sleep, out of time," Argent said. "It will not pass for her." NICE

Robert stared at the plinths. He saw then the faces and fingers, the forms trapped within the stone. The wall behind the Gaoler was a forest of such plinths, some of them as large as a house. He began to shake.

"This place is a prison," he said.

"Yes," Argent said. "The watchtowers guard the boundaries against threats, but we do not destroy when we can preserve."

"Boundaries," Robert said. "Do you keep things in or out?"

Argent said nothing, but the spark in her eyes, the faint star-light twinkle, glinted. He would not get an answer, but he had scored a point.

"This is the only way?" Robert asked Adam.

"I don't have any other ideas," Adam said, looking small and sad.

Robert sighed. "All right."

He turned to his wife, "Come on, Annie. It's time to sleep for a while."

Annie writhed like a child fighting a too-tight jacket, or a patient against restraint. She put her wrists together and shook, struggling against the thing that had her. Then she looked at him with eyes the color of blood. With a laugh, an inhuman choking sound, she drew Robert's gun from her jacket pocket and fired several shots.

oh fuck like the other officer at the hospital

22

ADAM

The gun flashed. Thunder boomed in the cavern. Bullets split the air, then froze.

Adam watched the spirit tendril inside Annie swell. It raged, held in place as the Gaoler held back the flow of time. A crushing amount of force came into play, squeezing the air from Adam's chest. The bullets, paused midair, were aimed for Bobby. Adam moved, glad he still could, and pushed his brother out of the way. He slapped the gun from Annie's hand.

The spirit unleashed a wave of force, breaking the Gaoler's hold. Time snapped back. The bullets sailed on into the darkness. Adam felt a rattling tingle throughout his body as Argent drew her sword.

"Lady, hold!" he shouted. He did not look at her, but held up one hand and wrapped the other over Bobby's eyes.

"Let me go, Adam! Annie!"

"Don't look," Adam said. "It will kill you to see her."

Even with his eyes squeezed shut, white light burned Adam's lids. He turned his head.

"Lady!" Adam shouted. "You said magic could not hurt it. It wants you to strike it."

He risked a peek at Annie. The spirit tendril had frozen. It had heard him.

"You're done playing dumb," he said. "I'm on to you."

Argent paused. The world paled as she sheathed her blade and put aside her terrible aspect.

"Put her in the sand," she said in her normal voice. She still sounded terrible and commanding, the voice of a queen, but the ground no longer shook.

Bobby, trembling as hard as Adam, helped him walk Annie to the circle. While her body had returned to docility, the spirit looked at Adam through her eyes with pure hatred.

It didn't fight them.

The energy around Annie, angry and red, had dimmed.

Adam felt for its power, and it seemed weaker. "You used up your strength against the Gaoler," he told it. He turned, looked to Argent. "That's why you wanted her to attack you, so you could drink her power."

Annie's eyes tightened.

"I'm right, aren't I?" Adam asked.

He flipped it off.

Annie stepped into the circle. The sand came to life. It ran, bubbled, and swirled over her like a tiny storm. It settled into place, hardening into a shell. The tendril remained connected to her, but it had faded. It didn't move.

For all her power, Argent was impetuous, too used to being the biggest threat on the block. The spirit knew it too, and it had laid a trap.

Adam could sense it watching him, a subtle focus a more powerful witch would not have detected. He took a few slow breaths, let them out. His gut churned. He had to end this thing.

Adam looked to Bobby and found him gaping, his eyes shone with tears.

"You can't see it," Adam told his brother. "But she's already better. Its hold on her has weakened."

"But not broken," Argent said. She eyed the tendril like she still considered cutting it. "We must sever its connection and root out the influence inside her."

"How?" Adam asked. "Your blade won't hurt it. What will?"

Argent did not answer him. Instead, she turned to the Gaoler and opened her hands, cupped, a gesture of supplication. She clutched a glass box. Fireflies glowed inside. "The payment for your aid."

The Gaoler lifted its arm, unfolded its minute-hand fingers. Argent opened the little box. The fireflies flew. One perched for a second on Adam's hair before it joined its fellows. They rested on the steel fingers. One by one their lights blinked out as the Gaoler absorbed the magic they carried.

"Wha—" Adam started to ask.

Argent silenced him with a sharp glance.

"Let us go," she said, leading them back through the cavern entrance.

They did not have to take the elevator. A steel door stood where the bridge had been. They stepped through, out into Denver's downtown, but still on the Spirit side.

Downtown, here, teemed with life and spirits. They drifted and danced. A giant couple, dressed like a gunslinger and a Victorian lady, strolled toward the theater district. Smaller things scuttled to avoid the sweep of skirts and falling boots.

If Bobby could see it, it did not wow him. He followed along, shoulders slumped, staring forward as Argent led them back toward the car.

"It's crude to discuss money in public, Adam," Argent said.

"What did you give them?" he asked, looking at the brick-work buildings, the old-fashioned lights, and trolley cars.

"What they most crave," she said. "A few centuries of time. Gnomes aren't like us, immortal, and there is more than a little resentment about it. They build creatures like the Gaoler to outlast them and perpetuate their work." *[handwritten: like people]*

"You can trade time like poker chips?" Bobby asked.

"More or less," she said with a flourish of her hand.

They paused at the crosswalk to let a pumpkin-shaped carriage drawn by giant kittens cross. Adam blinked. He'd never get used to magical beings and their oddities.

Argent continued when the mews and hisses had died down. "The gnomes will live a little longer, and in truth, I don't mind. Life is life. It is to be preserved."

Bobby looked like he doubted her, but he said, "That's why I'm a doctor."

"And yet you brought a gun," she said, her tone sharp.

"You brought your sword, right?" Adam asked.

"I am not a healer," she said. She exhaled, her expression cooling as she did. "But I see your point. We will do whatever we can for your wife, to keep her alive."

"And the thing that did this to her?" Bobby asked.

Adam flinched at Bobby's tone. He never could leave well enough alone. He didn't understand what Argent was, that disrespecting her was dangerous.

That was it. Bobby didn't respect any of this.

He'd gone to the Other Side without finding any of it interesting or awe inspiring. He really was that small, that unconcerned with anything beyond the little kingdom he'd built.

"We shall see," Argent said. *[handwritten: imagine if he did have power like Argent...]*

23

ADAM

Adam drove to work early, more than ready to research the spirit and escape the house. It felt lifeless without Annie. *He'd never even known it with the real Annie there*

He checked in on Vic, reaching for him through their connection and taking some warmth from it.

The English texts Argent had set aside for him were so old that it hurt his head to try to discern their meaning.

The rest were in Elven. Written in spirals, the script wound in and out. He would have strained to read it even if he'd known the alphabet.

He flipped through another book. This one, at least, had illustrations. It reminded him of comic books, with colorful drawings and vibrant figures. He wondered if it was an Elven children's book, then figured it couldn't be when he stumbled across a scene of naked figures entwined in a pile. *LOL*

"Nope," he said. "Not for kids."

Not all the figures were elven. Adam scanned the scenes, *pointy peens?* noting which bits were and were not pointed. After those pages came detailed vivisections of animals and people. Adam closed the book with a grimace.

Turning to one of the tablet computers, he found it was logged into the hospital's record system. Adam blinked. This was more like it.

It took him a while to sort through the interface. It wasn't as easy as a web browser, but he cross-referenced the list of names he'd put on his phone.

It didn't take long to confirm that they'd all worked at the hospital, but he couldn't find another connection. Nothing else linked them—no history of reprimands, nothing fishy to indicate possession. One of the men, an EMT, had a sexual harassment complaint from a few women in his department.

Creep.

Annie was there, under her maiden name, Johnson. She'd been a nurse in the psychiatric unit. Adam checked the other names. Yep, they'd all worked in the psych unit, the center of the void, so far as he'd been able to determine.

He paused, shook his head, and brought up the file for the dead cop. Being contracted through the city, there wasn't as much information, but he'd worked security in the psych ward for years.

Vic was there too. Adam's finger wavered over the open button. He wanted to know, needed to know, but not like this. He wanted Vic to tell him about himself, not read about him on a screen.

Adam had found a pattern. He needed to talk to Argent, but Geen wasn't behind her desk when he reached HR. A pleasant-looking woman popped up from behind a cube wall when he entered.

"Is she coming in today?" Adam asked, jerking a thumb in the direction of the empty office.

"I don't believe so," the woman said. She lifted a hand-painted coffee cup that said "World's Best Grandma" in sloppy ink strokes. "Did you need to see her?"

Adam didn't think she was another elf in disguise, so he said,

[handwritten margin notes: "Explains her very kindemails to Adam, she considers him ill" and "Daniel"]

"Yes, ma'am. If you can please tell her Adam Binder stopped by?"

"Okay, Mr. Binder," she said.

He couldn't sit any longer. He needed action. He checked his phone. He'd taken pictures of the employee records, their names and addresses.

Might as well start with the creep.

*****

William Parker, age forty-two, had just stopped showing up for work. According to his file, he lived in an apartment in a suburb called Littleton. Adam had no trouble discerning if William had changed addresses. A tendril drove through the roof of his three-story building.

Adam parked a block away, approached on foot.

You should have brought backup, a sleepy Vic said in his head. The message came with a purplish, worried feeling.

Adam exhaled. He was getting used to the cop being able to talk to him this way, like a text message with feelings attached instead of pictures.

I'm not going to confront him. I just want to see, Adam thought back.

He walked casually toward the building, doing his best to look like he belonged there. It wasn't like he was trespassing or breaking and entering.

He kept his head down, his Sight off. That meant shutting Vic out too, but he didn't want the spirit sensing him, and he most definitely didn't want it sensing Vic. Adam was going to have to deal with the protectiveness he felt for the cop, the pull between them, but right now he remembered the too recent roar of bullets and shoved it aside.

Adam let the tiniest thread of awareness in and was unsurprised by what he sensed. A void, like at the hospital. This thing was eating magic.

That's why it had tried to lure Argent into attacking it. And he was willing to bet that's why it had killed the Denver practitioners. It was working its way up the food chain. The elves it had killed at Mercy must have been quite a coup. No, not killed. Consumed. A Black hole

Shuddering, Adam eyed the second story, the apartment where William Parker lived.

What do you want all that power for?

As if in answer, the blinds lifted. He recognized Parker from the photo in his file. Heavier than he'd been, wild-haired and obviously filthy, he glared at Adam with bloodshot eyes.

Adam let a little Sight back in. The tendril was there, as it had been with Carl, the cop in the hospital, as it was with Annie. No magic though. Just like Annie, just like Carl—William Parker was not a practitioner, yet the spirit had grabbed hold of him. They faced each other that way for a while. Then Parker, filled with the spirit's influence, grinned.

He didn't move, didn't shift or shudder. Unlike Annie, unlike Carl, William Parker showed no sign of resistance. It had him, through and through, but something was wrong. Adam could See it. Parker was dying, rotting.

The spirit was burning him from the inside out. It was too much for Parker, for a nonmagical being to hold magic, much like what Adam would go through if he saw the elves in their full glory.

Yet it wasn't doing the same to Annie, and Carl had been able to fight it. Parker was completely taken.

Something pricked the edge of Adam's senses, that same sense he'd felt on his way to the pawn shops. Something was watching. Adam spun about, checked with his Sight. Nothing. No one, no strange thing—if you didn't count Parker and the tendril.

Adam backed away quickly, reached the Cutlass, and drove several blocks before he pulled into a parking lot, his senses still shuttered.

He couldn't do this alone. He'd been admitting it slowly, petitioning the elves for help, letting Bobby come to the clock tower, but seeing Parker like that, knowing it had almost happened to Annie—it was time to stop dicking around. He had to stop thinking he was the only one in the fight, and truthfully, he no longer wanted to be.

Feeling lighter, he drove back to Bobby's and found a familiar black SUV waiting on the street.

24

ADAM

"Hey, Wonder Bread!" a voice called from the SUV's open window.

Jesse. Vic's brother.

"What are you doing here?" Adam asked, climbing out of the Cutlass and walking up.

"I came to pick you up," Jesse said. "My brother wants to see you."

"I'm waiting for—Wait, how did you know where to find me?"

"Vic has your address," Jesse said, sounding a little sheepish.

"My brother's address," Adam said, sounding snappier than he'd intended. He nodded at the wedding cake. "It's his house."

"Well, my brother wants to see you. He would've called, but he's shy." Jesse waggled his eyebrows.

Adam had been thinking about Vic, perhaps a bit too much. He wondered if the bandages wrapping his chest had come off, if he had the same dark line of hair as his brother. And hadn't he just admitted he didn't want to do it all alone?

"Uh, I don't know, Jesse," Adam said, eyeing the porch. His mother wasn't there. "I've got stuff to do."

He liked Vic. Vic seemed to like him, but Adam shied away from the connection, from forming some kind of attachment that would break when it did.

"Look, man," Jesse said, shrugging. "You've gotta help me out here. He's getting crazy."

"Crazy how?" Adam asked, thinking of Reapers and black roses. Surely he would have felt it if—

"Stir-crazy," Jesse said. "He's bored out of his mind. Come watch a movie with him or something."

"What movie?" Adam asked. He exhaled, though the thought of Vic missing him made his heart do a little flip. *aw*

"I don't know, Wonder Bread," Jesse said, rolling his eyes. "Star Wars. He likes Star Wars." *♡ God bless men who love Star Wars*

"Fine," Adam said, reaching for the door handle.

Jesse's black SUV was so clean Bobby would have driven it.

"What do you do, Jesse?" Adam asked.

"Auto repair and detailing," he said. "Got a shop off Federal. You need any work done?"

"Tons." Adam nodded to the Cutlass. "But I can't afford it."

"So?" Jesse shrugged. "That's your ride? A '77 coupe?"

Jesse let out a whistle.

"She's starting to fall apart."

"Bring her in sometime. I'll have the guys take a look."

"Like I said, I can't afford it," Adam said.

"I'll pay you for entertaining my brother, so he doesn't drive me to the loony bin."

"They don't call it that," Adam said a little too quickly.

Jesse shrugged and drove. He didn't know about Adam's time in Liberty House. Why would he?

Vic didn't know either, that was what really mattered. Adam hoped he wouldn't care.

*****

Jesse pulled up in front of the house, but didn't kill the engine.

"Go on, it's open," Jesse said.

"You're not coming in?" Adam asked, climbing out of the car.

"Nah, I've got to get back to the shop," Jesse said. "Mom should be home in a few. Don't let Chaos eat you."

Though he hesitated, Adam checked the lawn with his Sight. All thirteen Reapers remained in place. None reacted to his approach. He wondered about their hosts, the bodies they lived in. These appeared unanchored. Maybe they only took possession when there was work to do. Adam knew too little about how Death worked.

He rapped the front door and got no response, not even from Chaos, who had apparently decided that one visit was enough to decide Adam wasn't a threat. Though he grimaced at invading someone's privacy, he stepped inside and followed the slight buzz of a television into the living room. It was painted a rich mustard color that offset the purple dining room. Adam loved the colors. *Me too*

Vic lay on the couch, half-sitting, half-reclining in a nest of blankets. He wore a pair of sweatpants and a flannel shirt buttoned halfway up. Chaos lay beside him, her big head on his thigh.

"Hey," Vic said, lifting the remote to turn off the TV when Adam slipped into the room.

Chaos opened her eyes, started a little growl, but Vic calmed her with a pat.

"You look better," Adam said, meaning it.

Vic had more color in his skin, though Adam felt a twinge of disappointment to see him dressed. *LOL*

"What are you doing here?" Vic asked, his face brightening.

So Vic hadn't felt him coming. Though his voice remained

weak, he seemed more focused, less drugged out. Maybe he only felt their connection when he was in an altered state. He'd sounded sleepy in Adam's head earlier. Maybe it was a bit like spirit walking. Maybe it had weakened with the passing of time. The idea made Adam a little sad.

"Jesse dropped me off. Said to come watch Star Wars with you."

"Yeah?" Vic perked up. He patted the couch next to him. "The DVD is in the player."

Adam took the seat cautiously, remembering how pained Vic had been by movement last time. Though he tried to hide it, Vic winced a bit when Adam sat. Adam felt it, but dimly. He hadn't been wrong. Their connection had dulled. Vic is at risk

"You've already watched it?" Adam asked.

"Yeah," Vic said. "A few times since Mom moved me out here. But I haven't watched it with you."

"Why?" Adam asked as Vic clicked the remote a few times. "Why do you like it?"

"The heroes are heroic. They're good guys," Vic said. "They aren't assholes."

"Han's kind of an asshole."

"Not really," Vic said.

"To Leia."

"Okay, maybe a little," Vic conceded.

He stretched a few times, awkwardly moving his arm but not being able to fully lift it. Giving up, he nodded to his side and said, "Get in here."

Adam shifted himself nearer to Vic, trying to be gentle. Vic smelled clean, like soap and antiseptic, but with something else, something *Vic*, beneath it all.

Vic settled back with a small sigh of relief. Adam felt it too, that things were right when they touched. The connection thrummed. Adam blushed a bit when it ran through him, pooling downward and stirring him a bit. He had to admit that as little as he knew Vic, he'd missed that feeling.

"There you are," Vic said, turning enough to kiss the top of Adam's head. Adam slid a hand over Vic's belly, where he wasn't hurt. He put two fingers between Vic's shirt buttons, just enough to feel Vic's skin with his fingertips. Vic felt hot to the touch, warmer than he should.

Adam wanted to tell Vic everything in that moment, about the Reapers, about himself. He wanted to warn Vic that he'd never done this, just cuddled up with a guy and just watched a movie. It felt way too normal, too distant from his actual life and filled him with a mix of things that made him a little shaky.

Resting as gently as he could against Vic's shoulder, Adam turned his face up to meet Vic's eyes. Adam had forgotten how much taller Vic was.

Adam didn't really know him at all, didn't know if he liked guys, had ever dated a guy.

He opened his mouth to speak, to ask, but the big yellow letters scrolled up the screen. Vic brought a finger up and closed Adam's mouth. He kept pushing, lifting Adam's face until their eyes met. Adam thought Vic was going to kiss him, but drawing back he said, "No talking during Star Wars." OK

Adam nodded off somewhere before the big battle. He woke pressed against Vic's side. He blinked up at Mrs. Martinez, who stood over him, a finger pressed to her lips. The DVD had reset to its menu. The theme music drifted from a loop on the speakers. Next to him, Vic sprawled, looking dead to the world. He had a little drool on his chin.

Mrs. Martinez gestured for Adam to follow her to the front door. She wore a long black dress and a jean jacket. She had a black fedora atop her head and her keys in hand.

"I'll drive you home," she whispered.

"Okay," Adam said, trying to shake off enough sleep to seem human.

He followed her outside to a black Volkswagen Jetta. He could feel the Reapers surrounding the house.

"How is he?" Mrs. Martinez asked Adam as she unlocked the car with two clicks of her fob.

"You know him better than I do," Adam said as he climbed into the passenger seat.

She gave a little laugh. "Hardly. A grown man does not tell his mother everything."

She tensed. She loved her son. She worried for her son. Adam took a small breath and thickened his defenses so she wouldn't affect him so much.

"He saved my life," Adam said. "That bullet he took was meant for me."

"That's his job," she said. "To serve and protect."

"You don't like it."

"It is not easy to be a cop these days. It's dangerous."

Adam nodded. He did not know what to say, so he asked, "What do you do?"

"I teach history at Metro, one of the downtown universities."

"What kind of history?" Adam asked.

"American mostly, and a lot of Western Civilization."

When Adam didn't say anything for a moment, other than giving her some directions toward Bobby's house, she said, "Vicente said you haven't been to school."

"It didn't seem right for me," Adam said. He didn't want to get into it, and started to scowl before he forced himself to remember that Mrs. Martinez wasn't Bobby or his mother. "I didn't do so well in high school."

"College is very different," Mrs. Martinez said. "Though it's not for everyone. It wasn't right for Vicente. He chose the police academy instead."

"And you wish he hadn't," Adam said. It wasn't a question. She didn't seem disappointed, just concerned.

"I wish he had done something safer," she admitted. "When he was shot, it was the worst thing, my worst fear come true."

"I'm sorry," Adam said, meaning it. While the flow of knowledge between them had slowed to a drip, he could remember how much Vic's mother had protested, how much she hated him being a cop—not because she hated cops, but she'd seen far too many news reports of police killed simply for wearing the uniform.

"I'm not sorry he saved you," she said. "Especially since you saved him back."

"There," he said, pointing to Bobby's house.

She pulled to a stop and said, "I am grateful that he's healing, that he's home already, but I don't understand it."

"I don't either," Adam admitted. "But I won't let anything bad happen to him."

It wasn't just him, he knew that much. Vic kept mending, getting better, and Adam didn't feel the pull on his strength the way he had those first days. The Reapers had to be responsible, but he didn't know how or why. They should be trying to take Vic, not watching over him. Oh fuck, Death is scared

"You can talk to me about it, Adam," Mrs. Martinez said. "Whatever all this is, whatever is going on."

"It is all going so fast," Adam whispered. He meant things with the spirit. He was technically working for the elves, not somewhere he wanted to be. But he especially meant about Vic. What he felt, the thing between them. It ran too hot, too quick. He felt certain it would burn him.

"It can be that way," Mrs. Martinez said with a smile. "Vicente's father and I slept together on our second date."

"You, uh. That's not what I—" Adam made a choking sound as he said thank you for the ride and opened the car door.

"At least give me your number," she said. Pulling a pen and a square of sticky notes from her purse, she shoved them into Adam's hands.

He scratched it out quickly, anxious to escape the awkward.

"You know, Vicente has never dated—" Maria paused, took a breath. "I mean there were girls before. No one serious. But he likes you."

"I—" Adam stammered. He didn't know what to say. He couldn't imagine his own mother saying anything like that.

"And, well, I like you too," she said. Her eyes sparked with mischief. "You can run away now."

With a nod, Adam opened the door and scurried out.
She drove off with a little wave. *where did I get mine?*

"At least I know where he gets his directness," Adam muttered.

He found a note from his mother inside the house. It said there was food for him in the fridge. He microwaved it and wondered how it might be to have a family that actually talked about things. He ate, listening for Bobby, who didn't appear.

His phone beeped a while later.

Goodnight, the text read. *But I want a kiss next time.*

Adam's heart skipped a beat and he smiled. He forced that orange, bubbly feeling down.

"It's the magic," Adam said. "Just the magic." *Embrace it honey this world is beautiful too*

He added Vic to his contacts anyway.

25

ADAM

Adam returned to the hospital the next day, to the magic closet of books and research. He rubbed his eyes and tried to stop thinking about Vic.

Argent snapped her fingers in front of Adam's face, pulling him out of his fixation.

"Are you always so distracted?" she asked.

"There's nothing here," Adam said, waving a hand at the texts. "And I can't read most of it."

The queen made a small *tsk* sound. "Agreed. We've had our scribes scouring the texts for a while now."

"Then why make me do it?" he asked, blinking at her. Adam turned his frustration on one of the books, scowling at it, wishing he could make it burst into flames. Sometimes it was a blessing that he didn't have more magic.

"Humans are different. You might see something we cannot. It works both ways, you know. Just as mortals don't see us, we often do not see everything in the mortal world."

"Wait," Adam said, trying to shrug off his weariness and let her words sink in. "Say that again."

Argent began, very slowly, "We've had our scribes—"

"Not that part," Adam said, too preoccupied to mind his tone. "You said that magic works both ways."

"Yes," Argent snapped. She narrowed her eyes in a way that suggested he should not have interrupted her. Adam flinched as Argent continued, "The veil between our worlds separates them. While some of us can cross back and forth, others, like you, can only see across it."

"But this is a spirit attached to mortals, to people in the real world," Adam said.

Argent scoffed at his use of the world "real," but she unfolded her long fingers into a fan, gesturing for Adam to continue.

"It's a spirit, but it's anchored to people like Annie or William Parker," Adam said. "To mortals. That's how it's keeping itself in both places."

"Yes," she said. "We merely need to sever those anchors and that should stop it."

Adam remembered Annie and the weave of bloody veins through her body. Frowning, he met her gaze and said, "Define 'sever.'"

Argent's smile thinned to a line. "That's what we're trying to figure out."

"Will you kill the anchors?" he asked.

"If we have to," Argent said. "Though it goes against everything we believe."

"Everyone it has possessed was connected to the hospital, to the old psych ward."

"They've finished tearing it down," Argent said.

Adam closed his eyes. He let a seething breath out through his teeth.

"I was hoping there would be clues," he said. "We should have another look."

"Agreed," Argent said. "We'll go in spirit."

*****

In his bed, Adam assumed the position of the Chariot, right side up, hand positioned as if to grip a spear. He pulled his armor on, visualizing an invisible shield around him, pouring concentration and willpower into it until he almost slipped into true sleep. Braced for whatever they'd find, he slipped into the spirit realm.

Adam stiffened when he found Silver, not Argent, waiting for him on Bobby's lawn.

The Knight of Swords took in Adam's appearance, his jeans and combat boots, the black tee and the worn-out leather jacket he'd fished out of the Cutlass's trunk.

"You should dress for battle more often, Adam Binder. It suits you."

"My lord," Adam said, eyes tightening. He could not tell if Silver was teasing him. "I expected your sister."

Though he'd kept the gray fedora, the prince wore jeans of a deep blue with faded patches that showed off his dancer's legs. His white shirt, untucked, was unbuttoned a little at both ends, showing a belt buckle like a mirror framed by blades. He wore a buttoned vest over the shirt that accentuated his lean chest and a tie loosely knotted.

"Lady Argent has asked me to escort you this evening. I hope that you do not mind," Silver said, his chin ducking. As if an elf could be bashful.

"No," Adam said. "Not at all."

Adam did not think Silver liked him very much, but he didn't doubt the prince's power. Pale, cold light surrounded him. Adam had no doubt that, like Argent, Silver carried any number of blades, though he wore none openly.

Adam wished he could read the elf. He looked as if he were around Adam's age, but centuries swam in his eyes.

"This way then," Silver said, gesturing to the street. "I believe you invoked the Chariot to make your crossing?"

"I did," Adam said. He'd guessed Argent would bring a car.

He hadn't realized the elves could sense the type of invocation he used to cross over. Usually it was just the Hanged Man, or his own card, the Page of Swords. They were just a means to focus the mind, to shape his intentions when he reached the Other Side. He hadn't meant to announce them.

Silver led Adam to the curb where Bobby's Audi waited. Adam and Silver stood completely on the spirit side, but Adam glanced back to make sure Bobby couldn't see the stolen car. He saw now that he hadn't imagined it. The house looked duller, like Annie's absence had robbed it of light.

"Buckle up," Silver said as Adam closed his door.

Unable to tell if the prince was joking, Adam obeyed. He watched out the window for Bobby to run at them yelling, "Stop, thief!"

"Can you even wreck a car in the spirit realm?" Adam asked as Silver put the Audi into drive and took off so fast that rubber should have squealed. Adam gripped the armrest. He didn't know if the quiet was an effect of the spirit realm, Silver's driving, or the quality of the car.

"Argent has had several collisions," Silver said. "There is a dragon that lives on Lookout Mountain. It carried off her favorite roadster once."

"Seriously?" Adam asked.

"Yes. A Triumph Spitfire, 1974. She never did get it back."

A dragon versus the Queen of Swords would have been a magical tussle Adam would have liked to have witnessed from a serious distance. Through a telescope. Or on video. Through a telescope on video—somewhere far removed from the blinding damage it would have done him to be anywhere near that much raw magic.

Silver flicked on the stereo. Adam settled down into his seat until the Brit-pop with a dance beat made him perk up.

"I know this band," Adam said. "Years and Years."

"They're quite good," Silver said, smiling.

"I thought you'd only listen to classical music," Adam said.

♡ "Some things are instant classics," Silver said, his gray eyes focused on the road ahead. He tapped the steering wheel as the boy on the stereo sang about being a king under another's control.

Adam reached for the volume, let his hand linger to ask permission. Silver nodded with the smallest curve of his mouth.

The cheery music lifted Adam's mood even if the company did not. They drove, listening in silence, sliding over dark streets lit only by the large spirit moon. Mercy appeared, limestone and glossy windows. The past shone through in the spirit realm, so much more than in the mortal world. Buildings tended to reflect the intent and spirit their creators and inhabitants imbued them with. Sad institutions twisted and crunched together, imploding from weight. Other structures glowed. Some broke apart, but did their best, their pieces orbiting one another in a slow death dance.

The spirit floated over Mercy, closer, bigger, like a gory second moon. Adam shuddered and pulled his defenses tight, making sure the thing couldn't spot him. Silver had done the same, though it was hard to conceal so much power. A little leaked through, like a sliver of moon behind the clouds.

The physical anchors for the watchtowers did not correspond to their distance in the spirit realm. In the mortal world, they were a ways west, toward the mountains. Here, the towers were equal distances from Mercy, equidistant from the menace and where Adam needed to go.

"It's at the middle," Adam said.

"Dead center," Silver confirmed.

Adam had wondered why they'd driven. "You wanted me to see this."

"No," Silver said, shaking his head. "But I needed you to."

"What's the difference?" Adam asked.

"One is required if we're going to stop it. The other means deepening your involvement, something I would not have done had I other options."

"You don't think I can handle myself," Adam said, straightening. His back pressed into the leather.

"The spirit bested you before," Silver said, his tone even.

Adam couldn't really argue. From the beginning, he'd underestimated the thing. He'd known he didn't have the magic to face anything so powerful, but he'd let Argent convince him that his lack of power was an asset. Still, he snapped, "I didn't know you cared."

"No," Silver said. "No, you didn't."

Adam looked sideways at Silver, trying to process the exchange. That led him to recounting all of his conversations with the elves since he'd gotten to Denver. Remembering Bobby's question, asking if the towers kept something in or something out, Adam reversed what he thought he knew about the Guardians and whispered, "In. You're keeping it in."

"We have been, I think," Silver said.

"You don't know?" Adam asked, turning to face the prince.

"Not for certain," Silver said. "There have been a lot of Guardians, many changes as the Towers shift ownership. We don't always know which things are locked in the basements, so to speak. My father may know, but he will not answer me on this matter. I may never know, not even when I assume my full mantle."

"Huh," Adam said. "What does that mean?"

"I am a prince," Silver said, the light around him growing colder. "Someday I will be king."

"You don't sound too happy about it," Adam said.

Silver's grip on the steering wheel loosened. "When I wear the crown of the King of Swords, I will change. I will be something, someone, else."

"What are you saying?" Adam asked. "That your aspect, this you, will go away?" Identity must be important if you don't age

"You are perceptive, Adam Binder," Silver said. "We have many selves. I happen to like this one."

"If it helps, your highness," Adam said. "Your father is immortal. I doubt you have to worry about it happening anytime soon."

"Let us hope not," Silver said.

They drove the rest of the way in silence. Adam watched the twisting, fun house mirror versions of the trees and buildings go by. Little was static. Only the streets seemed normal, though occasionally their white lines grew centipede legs and scurried out of the Audi's way with a hiss and show of fangs, like possums would.

Adam pondered what Silver had confirmed, that the immortals worked in aspects. He liked being right. The feeling was rare enough in his life.

And yet, there was something sad about the way Silver discussed his father. It mirrored something in Adam's own feelings. His father had been missing for so long. He had no way of knowing if they were different or similar. He hoped not, at least when it came to magic. To twist life and bend it into bone charms. But if Adam could find him, perhaps he'd come to understand him, bridge the gap between the laughter and rage.

Silver pulled to a stop outside the hospital. Looking to Adam, he raised an eyebrow. "You are silent, Adam Binder. That is uncharacteristic."

Adam was thinking, trying to remember if Perak had ever mentioned any kind of conflict with his family. Adam ducked his head. He'd never asked about the elf's relations, what struggles he faced with them. Adam had been selfish, thinking such conflicts unique to his life.

"I just thought family squabbles were a mortal thing," Adam said.

"And I suspect you learned to argue from us," Silver said. The elf paused, his mouth open a little, like he had something else to say. Then he closed it again. Instead he nodded and said, "Happy hunting. Be most careful."

Adam didn't know how to read Silver's odd body language, but his step lightened to know he wasn't joining him. Elf or not, prick of a prince or not, Adam would not see him destroyed. The spirit could do that, and he suspected it wanted to. Adam set off toward the hospital.

26

ADAM

The streetlamps bent and twisted. The hospital did not look like a single building but rather several floors, each floating but connected by stretched electrical cables and copper plumbing. Some of the walls remained, but others opened into space, like the back of a dollhouse. They had yet to clear all of the construction debris. Chunks of it orbited the site, floating and slowly spinning in the breeze.

Adam walked around the outside of the hospital's property, hoping the fences would be less of an impediment on this side of the veil. His suspicion proved right. The posts were bent and twisted like the streetlamps. Adam squeezed between two, a feat he wouldn't have managed on the mortal side if he kept eating like he had. Still, it was nice, not going to bed hungry. He had to give Bobby that, being a doctor paid for food atop the dickish cars and ugly houses.

The hole gaped like an open wound in the earth. The construction equipment stood nearby. In this place their teeth seemed longer, their yellow paint rustier, but they did not writhe with life. Things of metal, iron especially, usually didn't.

Adam knelt to better examine the ground. He'd always suspected the earth of sentience, of at least plant-level intelligence, if not something greater. He imagined it watching him, much like the spirit had. If the earth felt pain at the construction, then he didn't want to know how much man's other activities, like strip mining and deforestation, upset her. With a shudder, Adam shut down that line of thinking.

Spirit walking never felt like a dream. This body felt real. It could be hurt, it could feel pain or pleasure. It could bleed. It could come. And if he died in the spirit realm, his body would die too. These were the things Perak had taught him. That too, the old ache, was something he didn't have time for as he approached the site. They'd dug into the earth, taken out the old foundation, and exposed a basement.

He risked an upward glance. The spirit hadn't focused on him. It floated, untethered to the hospital. It seemed as uninterested as a sleeping cow ripe for the tipping. Adam didn't buy it. The thing had some sort of consciousness, more than plant. Animal at least. Cunning.

Still, he had come to see the site from the spirit realm. Adam climbed down and immediately froze.

What is that?

A disk of glassy stone, about the width of the Cutlass, was set in the ground. Adam blinked, made certain his Sight wasn't wrong.

He could not read the symbols carved into the obsidian, but they spiraled over the large disk, unreadable to his eyes.

And they were broken. Someone had taken a hammer to the disk, cleaving off shards. The discarded tool lay nearby, glowing with familiar enchantment. The magic imbuing it was sick, familiar. The taste of battery acid and rotten blackberries wafted from it.

Adam lifted a long piece of the stone, ran a finger over the elven writing. This was their script, a form of it, he was certain.

He had to get this to Silver, to Argent. Maybe there was

something in those texts about the disk that could tell him what
it was for.

A flash of yellow warned Adam. A tendril fell from the sky.
He managed to dodge as it drove into the earth. Eyes opened
along its length. They blinked and focused, at first without any
unity, then turned on Adam like he'd shouted. The obsidian shard
had gotten its attention and it looked mad.

Another tendril dove, a third.

"Oh shit."

Adam looked for the edge of the pit, intending to run, but
a tendril lashed around his waist, tripping him. He dropped the
shard. Threads of the tendril, slimy and muscled like earthworms,
wound about his hands and legs.

He didn't have time to curse again as it bound him. The
tip wriggled free and darted for his nostril. Wet and pulsing, it
reached inside, burrowing, burning as it pushed toward his brain.

Everything went red as the spirit wired itself to him. With it
came memories, images of its ancient past, and Adam glimpsed
what it had been. A giant beyond giants, towering higher than
the redwoods. It wasn't a god. It came before the gods. Moving
through the world, it stomped out villages, kicking over hills and
sacred groves.

Adam recognized the elves, though they were clad more in
leaves and mud than anything like cloth. They approached the
humans, whose own state was even poorer. The spirit felt nothing
for them, thought nothing of them. Alien

Their alliance, the first peace between spirit and flesh, was
formed to end that common threat.

The giant, the titan, could not imagine them a threat, that
the tiny things it had swatted were capable of massing an army.
It took them all, elves and humans. It killed so many, but on
they came. They *swarmed*, and so many more of them died

when it fell, collapsing atop them with force enough to shake mountains.

Yet they had brought it down. Then Adam felt its rage and secret terror through the red haze of its assault on his mind. The spirit pushed into him, trying to wrest control of him. Adam pushed back with all his willpower and spite.

They screamed together. In the spirit's memories, the army of immortals and mortals tied it down with ropes and vines. Adam felt every knife, every nick and slice, as they carved it up and burned its pieces. Its memory of the moment weakened it and gave Adam strength. He pushed it back, willed himself to remain who he was. It would not have him. *This thing is trying to feed him hopelessness*

In the past, in the memory, the battle raged. Reduced, it became a horned skeleton whose tail could sweep villages from the map. Still the powers, the mortals and immortals, cut it from both sides of the veil. They whittled it to parts, flesh and spirit, until only the last part, its massive heart, remained.

The thing had tried to kill Adam. It had possessed Annie, shot Vic, and killed Carl—yet what Adam felt through their forced connection was too familiar. Tears welled in his eyes at the aching loneliness, at being the only of its kind, opened inside him.

The elves must have seen it too. ~~When the time came for the final blow, they hesitated. Ever the preservationists, they could not let it fully die.~~ *maybe Adam's strong enough to kill it maybe Bobby is*
They buried its heart, bound it in obsidian, deep in the earth. Sleep crept in, and the memories, its awareness of the outer world, faded.

Adam watched the elves withdraw to their side of the veil, ceding the world of flesh to humans and other races, other things. It was not a simple departure. Bonds had been formed, children of mingled mortal and immortal blood birthed. The elves decided that any children would stay with their human parents.

A blood vessel burst in Adam's eye, ripping him back to himself, back to the present. He screamed. The spirit hadn't possessed him. He'd staved that off, but the tendril had him. It wormed into him. Everything burned, like his blood was lit afire.

And yet he didn't burn. He was stronger than he'd thought, than he'd realized. Adam pushed the spirit back, though he did not know how long he could keep it out of his mind. His strength wouldn't last much longer.

Heat filled him. Then the tendril binding Adam splintered. He felt the spirit recoil as their connection broke. With his hands free, Adam ripped the vein from his nose. It came free in a bloom of blood and agony.

Silver landed on the ground beside Adam, the shard of obsidian in his hand. The prince crouched, a hand pressed to the ground, a reedy jay ready to take flight.

"Run!" Adam shouted.

Another tendril dove toward the prince. Adam had none of the elf's avian grace, but leaping, he pushed Silver aside. They went down in a tumble of limbs as the tendril hit the ground. Others came as Silver grabbed Adam around the waist and ran with supernatural strength and speed.

They'd never reach the car.

"We can't outrun it," Adam gasped, the breath short in his chest.

"My thoughts exactly," Silver said. "Close your eyes."

"What?" Adam asked.

"Now is the time to trust me," Silver said. "I must reveal myself to save us."

Adam obeyed, but the light still burned through his closed lids.

The next thing Adam knew, he was underwater.

> like beholding the Ark

27

ADAM

Adam's spirit flattened and stretched. All the air was knocked out of him. He'd felt it before. The memory rose from somewhere dark, newly clear, swarming with feeling, as if fresh.

They'd gone down to the lake, to the little homemade dock they'd fish from. Adam had been too little really, so he'd watch the dragonflies, blue and shining, dart over the water. He'd eaten an orange, left the peel in pieces in the brown mud by the water. The zest of the first bite lingered on his tongue.

Dad had made a similar pile of beer cans. Such piles littered the lake's edge.

"Adam," Dad said. "Do you want to learn how to swim?"

He'd nodded. He did, and he'd asked before, but Bobby had always warned of snakes, said they weren't supposed to. Adam's eyes darted to the end of the dock, scanning for beady eyes.

"It's okay, no water moccasins today," Dad had said. "Come here." tick repellent

Adam had obeyed. He wasn't wearing shorts, just jeans and long sleeves. Dad, too, was fully dressed. He scooped Adam up, like he often did when he was playful, but this time he waded into the lake.

"Hold my arm."

No other warning. No other instruction. Dad pushed Adam down into the lake, to the bottom. Adam tasted foul water and mud. He saw bubbles, colors, and sparks.

He remembered lying on the little dock, coughing. He heard his parents arguing, feeling his mother's concern more than understanding her words as the water ran out of his lungs.

"He wanted to learn," his dad said. "He said so."

The memory faded, and Adam was drowning again.

There were planes beyond the Spirit and the mortal. Elves could move between them, but Adam hadn't known they could do it at will. Maybe it was a royal ability, unique to the most powerful. Maybe it was unique to Silver and Argent. Maybe they all could do it.

He imagined the planes like a sandwich. If the mortal was the meat, lying thick above the lower crust of the hell dimensions, the spirit was the condiment, the glue holding them together. Elves hailed from somewhere higher, the lettuce. Yeah, that made sense. They were hippies, all green and vegan. This is so good

Adam and Silver hadn't dropped into the water. They'd appeared in it, soaked and floating. Silver's arm gripped Adam's middle like an iron band as he began to shake. Mortals weren't meant to transcend. It felt like what he imagined divers who rose too fast went through. He wondered how much of it came from the stretching of the distance between his consciousness and his body. He couldn't feel it, his flesh. And he couldn't feel Vic at all. If the connection between them snapped, then Vic might die. He might not yet be healed enough to live on his own. His heart knocked in his chest at that. He cast about, eyes seeking light but finding none.

Be okay. Please be okay.

Distant music called him, faint and slightly metallic, like a symphony of flutes and harps. Adam couldn't name the song.

The warm water ran up the channel burrowed through his nose by the spirit. Pain seared through his skull.

On some planes everything broke apart into fire, or so the colorful drawings in Argent's texts implied. In the other direction lay ice. He hoped Silver hadn't just placed them in endless water.

No, there was light above them, but he could not tell how much ocean filtered it. Taking some comfort in Silver's grip, that he wasn't alone, Adam kicked toward the surface. His lungs burned. His sight flushed red and black, his throat about to burst.

Adam broke into the light, gulped air, in and out.

The air tasted clean, salted, but so clean. Silver breathed hard, his chest rising and falling against Adam's back. He focused on the sun, warm, but not burning. It did not hurt his eyes to stare at it. The light had a liquid quality, like the spring days he'd walk with Bobby down to Lake Liberty, the leaves bright green on the scrub oak.

"Light doesn't have flavor," Adam muttered.

"You are in shock," Silver whispered in his ear.

"Probably."

"You will be all right, Adam," Silver said, his lips brushing Adam's ear. He dragged Adam toward the beach, one arm around him, the other clutching the obsidian shard.

They collapsed onto a ribbon of perfect white sand. Silver rolled to a crouch. His open vest showed a soaked, transparent shirt that left nothing to Adam's imagination. He had the body of a track star. He'd lost his hat, revealing a haircut with short sides but longer on top and in the bangs. His chest, pale, only finely haired, rose and fell. Adam shook himself to focus. The pounding in his heart eased.

"Where?" he sputtered, looking away from Silver and up the beach at a pristine forest of pearl-barked trees with leaves too green for even the word emerald to do them justice.

"Specifically? In English, this place is Starlight's End," Silver said. "In general? This is Alfheimr. Elf home."

"It's beautiful," Adam said, meaning it.

"We come to the sea for retreats," Silver said. "Holiday and contemplation."

Adam nodded. He tried to imagine the elves on a beach vacation and could not. He'd never seen the ocean—movies had not prepared him for the brightness, the liquid sapphire of the ever-shifting water.

Adam tried to dismiss the image of Silver in swim trunks.

"Did I get it all out?" Adam asked, lifting a bloody nostril for the elf's inspection.

Silver chuckled. "Yes. It dissolved soon after I cut it."

"How did you do that?" Adam asked. "It killed the other elves."

"Concerned for me?" the prince asked, his tone mocking.

"Yes," Adam admitted, surprised to find it true. He had a lot of questions. The elves were beings of immense power, and yet they'd risked themselves for Adam. Silver had risked himself for Adam.

what will he ask for in return?

"I used this," Silver said, holding up the shard. The broken end had a fine edge.

"What is it?" Adam asked.

"I don't entirely know," Silver said. "But I guessed from its reaction that the spirit would not enjoy being cut with it."

"It's Elven," Adam said. "Isn't it?"

"The script is old," Silver said. His head whipped around. "Oh. Adam—I'm not supposed to be here, especially not with you."

"What do you mean?" Adam asked.

"Keep this safe," Silver said, putting the shard into the inner pocket of Adam's jacket, his eyes never leaving the cliffs. They rose high above the glittering sand, green with growth, where marble towers spiraled into the sky. Stairs, with nothing to moor them but magic, drifted in the air. Adam tried to see whatever approached from that direction. Though he found nothing but the slowly orbiting towers, a deep shudder began somewhere in his spine.

Silver cocked his head to the side, listening to something Adam could not hear. He gave a little nod and said, "Come here, quickly."

Silver pulled the silk tie from around his neck. "You must not see what is to come."

"What is it?" Adam asked. The shudder had reached every part of him. He felt it in the tips of his hair, a faint vibration that moved downward until the tiny hairs across his body were standing on end. It felt like the moment he'd seen in videos back home, the guys in mullets taking funny pictures right before the lightning struck them dead.

"I will do my best to shield you, but—" the prince trailed off.

Adam saw doubt behind Silver's eyes, but he nodded and obeyed. If another of Silver's people came upon them unveiled, the magic would burn Adam to ash. Silver bound the tie around Adam's eyes. There was no way to know if the other elves would think to raise a glamour for Adam's protection.

He felt something else, liminal, soft—Silver's light, his power, weaving a bubble around his spirit. The feeling wasn't uncomfortable, just dimming, like ear plugs at a loud concert.

"Why?" Adam asked. "Why are you protecting me? And why are you hiding the shard?"

"I would not see you harmed," Silver said gently. "And I am not yet certain what the shard means."

Though soaked in seawater, the tie smelled of lavender and rosemary. Blind, Adam reached out a hand, felt it land on Silver's heart, his wet shirt a thin barrier between them. Awkward, he shifted it to the elf's shoulder.

Then magic cascaded over him. Adam was certain that if he

could see, he'd find every hair on his arms raised. He'd never felt anything like it, never been near to a source so vast.

"What is that?" he asked, the question almost a gasp.

"My father is nearly here."

"Your father?" Adam asked. "The King of Swords?"

"Yes," Silver said as he finished weaving his ward.

The bubble fell into place with a subtle chime. It was a graceful magic, slightly cold and so very elven. So very Silver.

Tensing, the prince stepped away, just when Adam could have used him most. Adam drew up his armor, all of it, just in case, and felt his defenses sync with Silver's, chain mail and plate layered together.

The force of the King's arrival slammed against Silver's wards. Enough leaked through to buffet Adam's defenses, a tornado wind diverted by a wall of trees. Adam shook against the strength of it, but he kept to his feet. The feeling leeching through was white-hot rage, anger worthy of a tidal storm, worthy of an elven king.

Silver and Argent were one thing. They were used to shielding mortals from their nature, but the King of Swords was unused to curbing his power for humans. More of that anger broke through and Adam fell to his knees. Any more and he would start to burn.

Several clomping sounds, hoofbeats Adam guessed, announced the arrival of riders. He desperately wanted to see if they looked like something out of Tolkien. Maybe the elves rode unicorns. Maybe they were centaurs in their natural state. That led to a perverted thought and a mad laugh almost escaped him.

Still in shock then.

A voice boomed in a language Adam didn't know.

He wished Silver had blocked his ears as well as his eyes. Silver answered in kind, his voice like reedy music in his native tongue.

Though Adam could not understand their words, the King barked at his son, his sentences short and jabbing. Adam squeezed his eyes shut to hear Silver's contrite responses. The anger did not abate, and Adam felt it was meant for him especially.

The king said something, short and decisive.

Silver protested, loud enough that Adam cringed.

A viselike hand seized his shoulder. He hadn't heard the elves approach.

"Hey!" he shouted.

"Do not fight them," Silver said in English. "Let them take you and do not look at them!"

"Where?" Adam asked.

"To a dungeon," Silver said over the shuffle of bodies as they gripped him.

*****

Adam stumbled once, twice—then one of the elves simply lifted him and threw him over a muscled shoulder. He didn't fight, and worried that the shard would slip free as they jarred up and over what had to be hundreds of stairs, probably the ones leading up the cliffs. He could feel the spray on his bare skin. His damp clothes cooled around him. Everything smelled of salt.

They set him down with more gentleness than he'd expected. The shard's weight still rested in his pocket.

A door closed. A bolt clicked.

The cell didn't feel dark or dank, none of the things he'd have expected from a dungeon. It smelled like lilies. He couldn't sense another presence. The temptation to peek nearly overwhelmed Adam but he waited.

He didn't need to pee. He didn't feel hungry or thirsty. That would come though, and with it, he'd be tempted. There were many old stories about eating food from other planes. Everyone, starting with Sue and Perak, had warned him to never eat or drink anything

Does semen count a food in this conte

offered to him in spirit. To consume a bit of that other world would make him part of it, bind him to it, and trap him there.

And he had to get home. If the king ordered him imprisoned forever, if Silver could not take him back—Adam fought a fit of breathlessness.

"Screw this," he said, reaching for the necktie.

Thin, firm hands seized his. Adam yelped. He'd thought himself alone. He hadn't heard anyone else in the cell.

"Let me," a voice, familiar and almost forgotten, said. Adam hadn't heard it in so long.

His heart dropped and soared at the same. It couldn't be. How could it be?

"Perak?" he whispered.

"I'm so sorry," the elf said. "I didn't want you to find out like this."

Hands pulled the tie away.

Adam blinked as much from the light as to focus on the face of his first love, the elf boy who'd left a lonely teenager alone with nowhere to turn. Slimmer than Adam was now, with hair in shades of purple and blue that shifted even when he wasn't moving, Perak was a like a dream. His skin was pale, but spotless, almost unreal. He hadn't changed by even a day. His eyes were exactly the same—pale, almost colorless, they were like water with just a drop of gray in them. They picked up the shades of his hair, so at the moment they were almost lavender.

Adam had found the burned-out church, their usual meeting place, empty. He'd run through the spirit realm, searching. He'd even asked the trees, and they hadn't answered. Adam balled up his fist and punched Perak in the gut.

The elf folded with an *oof.* He threw up his hands in surrender.

"It wasn't my choice," he said. "My father found out. He was furious. He forbade me from seeing you, kept me away."

"Your father?" Adam asked.

"He would not have his son consorting with a mortal. He sent me to teach you, and I did—but I tarried too long, gave myself, us, away." Perak ducked his head, giving Adam a better look at the purple-blue hair that had captivated him. It shifted colors like a thing alive. "Then he knew how I felt about you."

Adam wanted to punch Perak again, and kiss him, and punch him again. It flipped back and forth in his chest until he took a deep breath and forced himself to stop spinning, to remember Vic, to remember the contact between them.

He seized on which of Perak's words hurt the least and asked, "Why did he want you to teach me?"

"We had been looking for mortal practitioners for a while. The thing out there, the spirit—we knew we could not combat it. We knew it would take witches to fight it."

"The Denver practitioners," Adam said. "You sent them against it."

"We did," Perak confessed. He bowed his head. "It killed them."

Adam forced himself to focus on the topic, to keep his brain working on what it could handle, not on seeing Perak again. "It's been free for a while then. For years."

"Yes."

"I saw some of its history when it attacked me," Adam said. "Mortals and immortals, that's how you beat it before."

"We are not what we were then. Neither are humans. The Denver practitioners agreed to help us, and we led them to their deaths." Perak trembled as he spoke. "It killed them all, Adam, elves and humans."

With a hard swallow, Adam took Perak's hand and traced a finger over the smooth skin of his palm. The flesh pinked and faded back to pale beneath the pressure. The flesh felt clammy.

"You're afraid of it," Adam said. "The spirit."

"I'm terrified."

"Yet you fought it," Adam said. "At the hospital. You risked your life . . ."

"For you, Adam," Perak said. "I did it to save you."

His eyes, so pale, stole the color from Adam's and turned a little blue. An illusion, a mask.

"You can stop now," Adam said. "You can show me. Be yourself."

Another nod, a shift in features, almost liquid. Perak faded. Silver emerged. Not his true form, but probably, possibly, the one he wore most, and as he'd said, his favorite.

Adam let out the breath he'd been holding. Silver gave a sad little smile, his lips bent to a thin line. He looked relieved, like he'd put down a heavy weight.

"What's going to happen to us?" Adam asked.

"Father has yet to decide," Silver said, his voice his own, though a trace of Perak's lilting tones remained. Perhaps they'd always been there, hoping for Adam to hear them. "He is very angry. That must cool before he'll speak to me again, before I can plead for our release."

Silver was the Knight of Swords, and his father was angry enough to imprison him. It was that bad, and Silver had cared that much, risked that much. For Adam.

It was almost too much for Adam to bear. Something inside him cracked and most of his anger drained away, fading from red to purpled blue.

"How long will that take?" Adam asked. Squinting, he looked for traces of Perak in Silver's features. They were there, subtle but present. Adam suppressed a sigh, but could not stop shuddering. Perak had not abandoned him, not willingly, and Adam really didn't know what to do with that.

"The last time he was this enraged, with Argent, it took eighty years for him to calm."

"I don't have that kind of time," Adam said. "They'll put me in a hospital. I'll be dead, or at least really old, when I get back."

"I'm glad to see your priorities are in order," Silver said.

"Shut up," Adam snapped softly. "I'm still pissed at you."

"Noted."

A witchlight lantern floated by the window like a bloated firefly.

"Wait," Adam said, wondering what would happen to Vic while he was trapped. "How much time has passed? I know the stories. Time moves differently here."

"We're in the Shallows, not too far from the mortal realm, but if we went deeper into Alfheimr, time would pass on Earth very quickly. Your body would age."

"Is that going to happen?" Adam asked. "Taking me further?"

"I do not know. My father may order it."

"I don't want to die here," Adam said. Out the window, the waves brushed the beach. The salt air, cleaner than any he'd tasted, scrubbed away some of the anxiety.

Adam examined the room. A bed, low to the ground like a futon, with comfortable blankets, took up most of it. There was a basin, and even a pot that he expected would serve grosser needs, but he could not eat here. He could not drink here. The little table where they were supposed to dine held a few implements of silver. Two pairs of utensils. Two chairs. One bed.

"This is pretty comfortable for a dungeon," Adam said. He wasn't going to mention the room's arithmetic.

"These towers are what you'd call 'roughing it,' but we aren't savages to treat our prisoners poorly."

"And you are a prince," Adam said.

"And I am a prince," Silver agreed.   Nice

"Your father left us only one bed." Adam mentioned it. The blanket looked like velvet, glossy and thick, but it flickered with the light. Adam wondered how they wove it, if the plants they used were unique to Alfheimr. He resisted the urge to reach out and touch it, afraid that the rich texture would tempt him to ponder things, the memory of things, other than sleeping.

Silver sighed. Currents of darker metal swam in Silver's pale eyes. "He assumes that since we are here together, that we are *together.*"

Adam exhaled and felt a little churn in his gut.

"I will sleep on the floor," Silver said. "Prince or no."

Adam paused. It was right of Silver to respect him, to keep his distance, but a little tug on his heart reminded him of sleeping beside Perak in fields of flowers. But that was then. This was Silver. There was Vic. Adam could not feel him, not over this distance.

He gave a little nod and pulled off his boots and socks. One touch of the fabric confirmed that he wanted to undress completely and feel the cloth all over, but he stopped with his jacket and shirt.

Silver settled onto the floor without a blanket or pillow. He curled into a long C, like a cat.

Adam sniffed.

"Adam?" Silver asked.

"Yes?"

"Do not strike me again."

"Okay," Adam said, blushing that he'd had the balls to do it in the first place. Although he still kind of wanted to.

28

ROBERT

Robert had the day off, but he couldn't do anything. He needed to shop for a new car. He could rake the backyard or go for a hike. None of those would distract from Annie's absence, from the dread he felt at having trusted her to Adam's world.

"Adam Lee!" their mother called from kitchen. The sound was so familiar he almost smiled.

Robert found her at the dining room table, sipping her coffee, her bible open to some verses inked in red. The worn book was her constant companion lately.

"Go check on him for me," she said, her voice taking on the impatient edge he'd heard too often in the trailer, when he'd come home from school for the weekend and found her angry with Adam.

It had been almost too easy, filing the paperwork, letting Mrs. Pearce, the guidance counselor at school talk him through the options. Adam had been more an inconvenience than a risk, but at the time it had felt like the perfect solution, the best way for Bobby to move on, to escape.

His teenage brother had been sullen and spacey. It had driven both of them nuts. He'd leave the water running, threatening to break the well pump. Or he'd open the refrigerator and just stare into its light, running up an electric bill that their mother could barely pay.

"You know, I never thought about what it must be like for you," he said. "Being stuck in a metal box with the two of us."

She grunted. "It was better after your father left. But you two were never quiet. And when you started fighting, you'd shake the whole damn house. More than the wind."

Despite her mention of their dad, Robert smiled as he marched down the stairs. He and Annie had joked about the basement, that it would be the perfect place to banish a brooding teenager to when the time came. He'd never thought that his adult brother would be the occupant.

Already the place felt more Adam's than Robert's. It had always smelled new, fresh paint and unused space. Now it carried the odor of another man, a combination of body spray and sweat that should not have been able to saturate the air in so little time.

Adam lay atop the narrow guest bed. He didn't move when Robert turned on the light. He didn't stir when Robert moved nearer, and something cold and prickly walked up the back of Robert's neck.

"Adam?" he asked.

He slept, fully dressed, even in his shoes, atop the blankets, arms straight, fists closed, like he gripped an invisible bar. Robert shook his brother. He didn't stir. An old, rising ache moved up Robert's spine.

"Adam," Robert repeated, shaking his brother with more force. It had no effect.

Adam had to be spirit walking, Robert felt certain of that. He was alive, but his breath was a whisper. Robert took Adam's pulse, found it steady if weak.

He peeled back Adam's eyelid, checking for activity and found his eye shot with red.

"Shit," he said, leaning in closer. "Mom!" he called over his shoulder. Adam did not stir at his shout.

Tilla shuffled down the stairs.

"What's wrong?" she asked, concern putting an extra buzz into her table saw of a voice.

"I can't wake him," Robert said.

"Your dad talked about it, how Sue would get like that," she said. "Spirit walking, she called it."

"Yeah, but did she ever—" He waved for her to see Adam's eye.

"Jesus," his mother said. She clamped her hands over her mouth and shook her head.

"It's a subconjunctival hemorrhage," Robert said. "Not as bad as it looks. They usually clear up in a few weeks. You can even get them sneezing."

"You think he's sneezing on the Other Side?" she asked.

"No, no. I just wanted to know if you'd seen it before. If it was normal."

She barked out a bitter laugh and said, "My daughter-in-law is possessed and locked in a clock tower. My youngest is sleeping in his shoes and bleeding out his eyes. None of this is normal, Bobby Jack, not even for our family."

"I can call an ambulance," he said. "Put him back in the hospital. It might be safer if he's monitored."

"No," she said, calming after her moment of panic. "Don't move him. Sue told your father it could be hard to find her way back if they moved her."

It had been the same way when Adam had collapsed at the hospital. He'd lay in a coma-like state, unresponsive, but alive. There would come a point, Robert figured, when they'd have to tube feed him, but that time hadn't come yet.

First Annie, now this. The spirit, the thing, seemed determined to take them all. He stared at Adam's pale face. He remained too thin, almost sickly.

"Do you think Sue was right? That we shouldn't move him?" he asked when the silence went on too long, when his imagination had colored the situation with a greater darkness.

"How do I know?" his mother snapped. More quietly she added, "She's nuts."

"What if he wets the bed?" Robert asked.

"Wouldn't be the first time," she said. "Not for either of you."

"Mom . . ." he said. Then, after another long silence, he suggested, "We could call her . . . Sue."

"I don't think she could help us," his mother said, her tone ratcheting toward the bitter.

As far back as Robert could remember, his mom had hated her husband's aunt. Tilla had tried to keep Sue away from them, afraid perhaps that her backwoods hedge-witchery and oddness would infect them.

Robert felt much the same, though he stopped to consider his feelings. He'd taken what he felt about Sue from his mother, but that didn't mean Tilla was wrong.

"She'd probably just suggest drugs. I don't think she's been sober for years." Tilla reached down, ran a hand over Adam's scalp. "I found some in his things you know."

"He's not on anything," Robert said.

They exchanged glances, a guilty look over their prying and snooping. The silence stretched out again, too loud and long for comfort, like it often did when Adam was the topic.

Robert cleared his throat and said, "It's just . . . I brought him here. If he dies—"

"You don't talk like that," she snapped, calm again. The strong one, the one who always knew what to do. "About him or Annie. Where there is life, there is hope."

Robert nodded, but still, to see Adam lying there, unmoving. After all he'd done, everything he'd put them through.

"I'm sorry," Robert whispered. He'd been wrong to send Adam to Liberty House. He knew that. He remembered Mrs. Pearce, the kind smile as she pushed the papers across her desk. "I need to tell you that, somehow."

He'd been wrong to send Adam away to where he couldn't protect himself, where Bobby couldn't protect him. He could have, should have, found a better way.

He wanted Annie back, to be herself. He wanted Adam to wake up. It—all of it—had gone so damn wrong.

"You can go," his mother said. "I'll sit with him, though I don't know if it will help."

"No," Robert said. "I'll stay."

"There's that at least," she said, turning. "You two talking again. I'll make some more coffee."

29

ADAM

Adam drifted awake to find Silver's arms wrapped around him, his bare chest pressed to Adam's back. He felt like moonlight, cool to the touch. Adam scowled at his body's reaction to the contact. Damn elves.

Though he hadn't swallowed the whole of it yet, he had to admit his anger had been misplaced, partly at least. Perak— Silver—had not abandoned him. Or at least, he hadn't abandoned him without a reason. Adam's breath hitched in his throat.

And what about Vic? Adam felt inside himself for the thread connecting them. It had grown so faint, so pale, like a tiny root pulled into the light. At least he could feel it again.

There was connection, interest. Vic had made his clear, but it had to be the magic, giving them a window into each other. Did that make the feelings any less real?

The press of Silver against him, steely, smooth, felt so different than Vic's warmth. Silver smelled of flowers, not the bit of sweat and sickness Vic's shirt had carried. Still, it had been nice, lying on Vic's couch like that, not worried if his mother or brother saw them, not stressing about acceptance or the many differences between them.

The door to the cell opened. Argent stepped into the dark, the moon's glow clinging to her, even more brightly than it did to Silver.

"There you are," she said to Adam.

Silver sprang to his feet. He looked sheepish, embarrassed even. Adam withered at the sight.

Argent didn't seem to notice.

"Let's go," she said.

"But Father—" Silver said.

"Will brood for a decade or two," Argent said, peeling Silver's still-damp shirt off the back of a chair and tossing it at him. "We'll have you back long before he's over it."

"I cannot go back to the watchtower," Silver said. "I must remain here."

"Poppycock," she said, looking at her watch. "Adam has reading to do."

Silver remained to the side, his eyes elsewhere, but not on Adam. Maybe the king had forbidden the prince from seeing Adam, but he'd gone along with it. It wasn't the same, Adam knew that, but if Bobby had told Adam he couldn't see Perak, well he would have flipped him off and walked away.

Holding in a scoff, Adam dressed. "What do we need to do?"

"Follow me," Argent said. She took a fob from her pocket and clicked it as she strode out the door.

Adam heard a beep outside.

A car waited, parked in the air like it belonged there. Adam was pretty certain it was a Ford, but he didn't feel like asking her about the make or model as they climbed in. He took the back seat.

"Sister . . ." Trailing off, Silver looked to the horizon.

"I will handle Father," she said. "He cannot imprison you, either of you, not while that thing is free."

Argent put the car into gear and light flooded Adam's vision. He could feel Silver's ward hold back the force of the shift, and this time, with his eyes closed, the air wasn't knocked from him, though his ears popped.

Adam fell back into his body. Finding himself in Bobby's basement, he gulped air.

He wasn't alone. Argent and Silver stood nearby. The car was missing. It was probably still at the hospital on the Other Side.

Sitting up, Adam felt along his limbs, making sure he could move everything.

"It's all there," Argent said. "At least it should be. Silver, go check."

The elven prince did not seem to share his sister's amusement.

"Father will be furious," he said.

"Yes, he will," Argent agreed. "But he's right about one thing. It's time you assumed your role of Guardian. You can't do that, cowering in a cell every time he has a tantrum. You have to stand up to him. He won't respect you until you do."

"Like you did?" Silver asked.

Argent's eyes narrowed and the siblings exchanged another warring glance. Waves of force slid between them. Adam felt Silver yield, just a little, to his sister. Maybe, he thought, he was starting to understand them.

They didn't seem so foreign anymore, though they still felt dangerous. He wondered what it would be like, to have a sibling you could disagree with, even war with, but still care for. Because he had no doubt Argent cared for Silver. If she disapproved of him, of what Adam was quickly coming to see as his cowardice, it didn't run the depth of Bobby's.

"You could do it," the prince whispered to Argent. "You could inherit."

Adam wondered what he had to give up to take up his mantle. Being Perak? His feelings for Adam? Something gray and crawling, like a moth, fluttered over Adam's heart.

"No," Argent said. "I cannot."

Though her words were firm, she looked sad as she said it.

"Father has chosen you as his heir," she added. "Only he can change that, and he will not."

Silver's chin dropped to his chest.

"Besides," Argent said. "I have a day job. You should get ready, Adam. We don't have all day."

He nodded. He needed to tell her about the shard, but a voice called from atop the stairs.

"Adam?"

Adam looked to the elves, but they'd vanished. Bobby came down the stairs, footfalls knocking.

"What?" Adam called. He shifted so his legs dangled off the bed.

"What happened to you?" Bobby asked, a note of what sounded like real worry in his voice. "You've been out for almost twenty-four hours."

Adam shook his head. "I tried to find out more about the spirit, about where it came from. It didn't go well."

"But did you?" Bobby asked. "Find out about it?"

"Yeah," Adam said. "Quite a bit."

For the first time, he felt hopeful. They knew a little more. They maybe had a weapon.

Adam groaned as he tried to stand.

"You don't have to go," Bobby said, holding up a hand.

"I need to talk to Argent," Adam said, lurching his sleepy limbs toward the bathroom. "But first, I need to piss."

"There's also the matter of your eye," Bobby said. "We should have it checked, just to be certain it's not permanent."

"What?" Adam called before turning on the light and checking the mirror. "Oh, gross!"

30

ADAM

"So?" Argent asked. "What did you learn?"

"Silver and Perak are the same elf. You knew that and didn't tell me." Adam threw up his hands. "Oh, and your father is forcing Silver to be his heir, which he does not want. Now we're both escaped convicts from the universe's nicest beachside prison resort."

Argent tilted her head at him. "You forget yourself, Adam Binder."

Just a few days ago he would have flinched, realized he'd been flippant with the Queen of Swords. Now it felt normal to tell her how he really felt. They were almost something like friends.

"Sorry," he said. "Silver said your father sent him to teach me, to give you another mortal practitioner to throw at it, because all the others died."

"He did," she said. "They did. What else?"

"It's using magic to rebuild itself. That's why it wanted you to attack it."

Argent waved for him to continue.

"Then there's this," Adam said. He laid the shard on the table. It gleamed, black and green.

Argent leaned toward it.

"This was at the site?"

"And apparently it can sever the tendrils. What is it?"

"This is old, older than me, perhaps older than father," she said running a finger over the writing. She sounded reverent when she said, "This magic is lost to us. But I think it was a seal."

Adam nodded. The images he'd gotten from the spirit when it attacked him meshed with that.

"It was broken," Adam said. "Intentionally. Why would someone set this thing free?"

Turning from him, Argent opened a large three-ring binder and began flipping through pages of clipped newspaper articles.

"Sometimes our fixation on the past has its uses," she said. She read and flipped too quickly for Adam to follow. Finally, she landed on an article from five years prior and tapped for Adam to read.

Someone had broken into Mercy. They hadn't taken anything, but when a guard had caught them, they'd killed him and left the scene.

The article included a grainy image from the old security cameras. Adam leaned forward.

It could be him. It could be Adam's dad. The height and shape were right.

"We won't be able to go back," Argent said. "Not with the spirit watching for you. My brother will not forgive me if I risk you again."

Adam nodded to the shard. "Silver used this to sever the tendril connecting the spirit to me. Could it save Annie?"

"Perhaps," Argent said. "It is worth trying."

"When?" Adam asked. "Can we go now?"

Anxious as he was, the idea worried him. He could feel his magic—thin, weak. Another journey wasn't wise, not until he had time to recover from his trip to Alfheimr. He felt it like a bone weariness, shaky and empty of blood, like he was too tired and had drunk too much coffee.

"It will have to be tonight. Our accord with the gnomes requires me to send warning. I will go with you."

Adam looked at her.

"I will come, not Silver," she said.

"Why did you send him last night?" Adam asked, blurting out the question.

"He needed to tell you, and you needed to be told. You weren't taking my hints, and I couldn't stand his moping any longer. He's been morose since Father forbade him to see you. Even the patience of immortals has limits, Adam."

"He could have sent a message," Adam said. "Said something."

"Silver is . . . traditional. He did not mean to hurt you, but he has duties. He must fulfill them. That is part of who he is."

"He saved me," Adam said. "From the spirit. It could have killed him, and he saved me."

Argent closed her eyes, let her head bob.

"He loves you very much. He always has."

Adam exhaled. "I don't know what to do about that, my lady."

"I know," she said. "Neither does he. He won't let it compromise his duty, and he cannot set it aside."

"Tonight then," Adam said.

"Pick me up here," Argent said.

*****

There are no accidents

Adam drove back to Bobby's. The hospital was positioned weirdly, just off the grid where the highway made the most sense, so he took side streets and found them crowded. The heat didn't help his mood. It should have been fall. Where was all the snow to cover the dead, skittering leaves piling along the sidewalks?

Halloween, Vic's voice whispered, quieter than it had been before Adam's jaunt to elf land. *It usually snows by Halloween.*

He smiled to feel Vic there, in his head. It was a warm relief that grayed when he thought of Silver, of waking with the elf beside him. They hadn't done anything, but Adam remembered before.

He wanted a cold shower, for a few reasons, and almost pulled over to take off his shirt, but he didn't want to stop, so he cranked the AC. The Cutlass blew out some dust, a bit of plastic and burnt rubber smell that always accumulated when he didn't run it for a while.

He passed a large park, the green full of joggers and cyclists. Everybody here seemed to do something outdoorsy. Everybody here, Vic included, seemed to be in better shape than Adam.

He stopped at a light, and the Cutlass stalled. He got her going long enough to turn onto a side street and pull over. Adam looked around. These were nice houses, not as new as Bobby's, but they spoke of money. They were old, like the Martinez's, but much bigger.

Adam got out, lifted the hood, and peered inside.

"Vapor lock," he muttered.

Adam examined the engine. He kept it clean, but no one could miss the wear and patchwork repairs. There was as much magic in there as bailing wire. He kept her going through sheer force of will, most days. Right now, he didn't have the strength. She'd just have to cool off before she'd start again.

The Cutlass, usually a comfort, felt beaten up and broken down. She'd be beautiful, if he had the money to sink into her.

Or he could sell her, probably get a few thousand for her. Adam crushed that idea. That was how Bobby thought.

"Besides, then what?" he asked. He'd be out a car and the only concrete connection he still had to his father. He could remember the angry parts, the fits and throwing things. But the softer moments, like the action figures his dad would pinch from Walmart, or walking to the lake to fish, were getting fuzzier.

Then he remembered nearly drowning. His father had tried to kill him. Adam wanted to deny it, but he couldn't. He'd laid a trap for a five-year-old and almost succeeded.

And he killed the guard at the hospital, set the spirit under Mercy free.

As with all things Dad, Adam needed to know why.

And he needed to tell Argent that the warlock and the seal breaker were the same.

The Cutlass started up. Adam made a mental list of parts she needed as he turned onto Bobby's street, a shower and a nap his only plans before he met Argent. The loneliness of the house, what he'd felt from it in Annie's absence, deepened. He thought that maybe places missed people, like cats missed their owners, though people thought they didn't. Maybe this wedding cake of a house missed Annie.

Adam pondered inviting Bobby to come with them. If the shard worked, he'd have Annie back. But if it didn't, he'd have given Bobby false hope.

Then again, Adam wasn't so certain Bobby cared about Annie. The way he went to work, lived his life, Adam was starting to suspect Bobby saw Annie as one more symbol of his success, not a partner.

Adam didn't have much experience with relationships, but he was certain he wouldn't do that to anyone, and he wouldn't be that for anyone.

"Mom?" Adam asked, coming through the front door. He expected to find her in the kitchen, but she wasn't there. He heard her laugh, an alien sound, and took the few steps into the unused den, ears and eyes cocked for trouble.

His mother sat on the love seat, across from Vic, who sat on the couch.

"Oh, honey," she said, looking up and smiling at him. "You're home. Vincent has come for dinner."

31

ADAM

Adam's heart did a little flip as he stepped into the den. His mother and Vic sat across from each other, looking perfectly at ease and normal.

"What are you doing here?" Adam asked. It came out sounding more demanding than he meant. He smiled, afraid Vic would think Adam didn't want to see him. He did, but the visit to the clock tower loomed.

"I thought I'd come check on you," Vic said, squinting with mock suspicion. "You've been too quiet."

Adam's heart dropped a little. He had no idea how to explain about where he'd been or what he'd learned.

"I'm going to get dinner ready," Adam's mother said. Standing, she looked from one to the other. "You are staying, Vincent?"

"Vincent?" Adam muttered, lifting an eyebrow.

"If it's not any trouble," he said. "I can have my brother come get me after."

"Adam or Bobby can drive you home," she said, sweeping toward the kitchen, a faint miasma of cigarette trailing behind her.

"That would be nice of you," Vic said. He leveled brown eyes on Adam and smiled wolfishly. Adam swallowed.

"Vincent?" Adam repeated.

"Your mom can call me Vincent," Vic said. Eyes narrowing, he leaned forward. "Her accent is terrible."

"Yeah," Adam drawled. "We're pretty white."

He flushed with a warmth that started at his center and radiated downward as he took the seat his mother had vacated. He and Vic watched each other for a moment, waiting until Adam's mom started rattling around the kitchen before they spoke again.

"What's up?" Vic asked.

"You seem better," Adam said.

"I'm healing, faster than I should. A lot faster," Vic said. "The docs say I'm young and strong, but that's not all of it, is it?"

Piercing. Searching. Those weren't words Adam had thought he could associate with brown eyes but there it was, Vic's stare, focused and hard. It reminded Adam of Vic's cop face, the one he'd wore when he'd found Adam in the records room. Adam didn't hate it, but he squirmed a little under the weight.

"No," he said.

"What did you do, when you saved me?" Vic asked.

Adam ran a hand through his hair. He didn't know what to say, how to say it, so he let it spill out. "I tied us together."

"How?" Vic asked, eyes narrowing.

"Magic," Adam said with a grimace and a shrug. "I took a strand, a bit of my life, and wove it to yours."

"You can do that?" Vic asked.

"I guess so," Adam said with a shrug.

"Why?" Vic asked. "Why did you do it?"

He seemed almost offended. Adam could feel Vic's curiosity, but not his interest. That had waned. Adam's heart fell. He'd been right. The fading connection had Vic doubting his attraction to Adam. He was resetting to who he should be.

Adam made some awkward combination of a shrug and a cringe. "Because I could."

"Are you sorry you did?" Vic asked.

"Why would you ask that?" Adam said, sinking back into the cushions. "Of course not."

"Then why haven't I seen you?" Vic asked.

It had to be the magic. It couldn't be real between them. Vic would forget about him. Adam would go home to Guthrie, back to the trailer park.

"I went somewhere," Adam said. "It's hard to explain."

Vic's brow furrowed. "Try."

"There's somebody I used to know," Adam said.

"More than know," Vic said. He jerked a thumb toward his heart. "I can feel you, remember?"

Adam nodded with a gulp. "There's a lot to it."

In the kitchen. The sound of sizzling oil flashed. Adam's mom was humming, actually humming.

Vic said, "Start talking, Binder."

Adam explained what he could about the spirit, the way it had possessed Annie, and the cop who'd shot Vic. He tensed during that point, and Adam felt the blue-black pulse of sorrow and grief through their connection. It got harder when Adam explained about Perak, about Silver. He didn't, couldn't, use many words, but when he glanced up to meet Vic's gaze, he didn't think he needed to.

He hadn't known what he'd feel when he started explaining. The longer it went, the more he thought about the way Silver had been forced to abandon him. It mixed up everything, especially Adam's feelings for Vic. Now Vic didn't want him anymore. It churned in his gut. Adam felt tears start to gather.

"Come here," Vic said, opening his arms.

Adam didn't want to. He didn't want to break, or cry, or to need to do either, but that unfaltering gaze reeled him in.

He paused, hesitant, not sure how strong Vic was yet.

"It's all right," Vic said. "Just be gentle."

Adam moved into Vic's embrace, stayed there while the cracks, pops, and meaty smoke of his mother's cooking flavored the air.

"It's going to be all right," Vic said.

"How do you know?" Adam asked.

"Trust me," Vic said. "I'm a cop."

Adam met his eyes, expecting to melt in them, but what he found were skulls, small and white, floating in Vic's gaze. Adam flinched.

"What?" Vic asked, blinking.

The skulls had vanished.

Adam couldn't answer. He could use his Sight, try to see if they'd been his imagination or not. He knew they weren't. He didn't check.

"Nothing," Adam said.

"Why you'd freak out?" Vic asked. "You're the one with the gross eye."

"Is it that bad?" Adam asked, reaching to cover it.

"It's pretty bad," Vic said. "Be glad your mom warned me."

"Bobby says it will go away in about two weeks."

"In the meantime, could you wear an eye patch?" Vic asked. "It's going to be hard to eat with that next to me."

Adam cocked his head at Vic and used his fingers to pull his eyelid open further.

"Okay, okay, parlay," Vic said, waving him off. "I can see why Jesse likes you."

"Jesse doesn't know me," Adam said.

"Sure he does, I mean, a little," Vic said. He nudged Adam.

"By the way, he's not going to shut up until you take your car to his shop."

"I don't have the money for that."

"He doesn't care about the money. He just wants to get under the hood." Vic's voice dropped lower when he asked, "Do it for me?"

"All right," Adam said, yielding under that brown, skull-free gaze. Still, he stared, trying to find signs of the Reapers' touch in Vic's eyes.

Vic caught Adam focusing on him. Or he felt the concern. He leaned back, his sharp-featured, handsome face bending with a frown, and asked, "What's happening to me?"

"I don't know," Adam said, taking Vic's hands in his. Vic gripped him back. He felt so much stronger than he had been the last time Adam had seen him.

"It's part of what you did to me, isn't it?" Vic was starting to understand, starting to realize the implications. Adam didn't jerk away, though he didn't see this going anywhere good in the long-term. The magic would fade, and Vic would walk away, if Adam didn't go home first.

"Yeah," Adam said.

"You risked your life for me," Vic said. He seemed bewildered.

"It wasn't you," Adam said. "I mean, I did it, but it wasn't just you. I—"

"Would have done it for anyone?" Vic asked, pulling Adam closer.

God, he smelled good . . . solid, human. Adam inhaled, his nose pressed to the cloth of Vic's shirt. Adam took a few breaths, thinking. He hadn't known Vic, not really. It had been a cocky move, arrogant even. But he'd meant it. He couldn't let a man die for what he'd done.

"Yeah," Adam whispered into Vic's shoulder.

Vic kissed the top of his head. "Good. You did good, the right thing, without any reason to. That makes you a hero."

"I didn't save Carl," Adam said. Just saying his name aloud felt wrong. "I couldn't—"

Vic added his other arm to his grip on Adam.

"We can't always save everyone," Vic murmured into Adam's hair. "You have to remember that or it will eat you alive."

"Boys," Adam's mother called from a safe distance. Adam wondered if she'd seen them embrace as they scrambled apart. Vic looked confused, but he seemed to pick up on Adam's discomfort and straightened his shirt.

"Dinner," his mother called.

Adam wished very much at that moment to have his own place, to be alone with Vic, that there could be less space, and clothing, between them.

"What are you thinking?" Vic asked, smile bending into a smirk.

"Nothing."

"Right," Vic said. Standing, he gestured toward the kitchen. "Lead on."

"Would you care to say grace, Vincent?" Adam's mom asked when they'd taken their seats at the small table in the dining room.

It wasn't where they usually ate—at the little table in the kitchen. Adam's mother had decided to use the actual dining room. Adam figured Annie had chosen the long table of beautiful hardwood. It looked just right for entertaining a doctor's guests.

Annie had quit working at the hospital after she married Bobby. Adam reached back, but couldn't remember a time when Tilla Mae had only kept house. Dad had been the one to stay at home, and he didn't cook or clean. After he left, their mother only worked harder.

There were weeks when the only times Adam saw her was when Bobby took him to town, to the corner store where she worked. They'd look through the comic books, careful not to fold the corners, and never buy them. Bobby would buy Adam a pack of gum, or a little candy, sometimes. The cash register dinged when Mom rang it up. It spit change into a little cup if you paid with the rare bill Bobby could scrounge up. Adam loved the little slide, the shine of the rolling coins.

Adam wondered if that was when she'd taken up her twin addictions, smoking and bitter coffee. All of his memories from back then were tied to her dark-ringed eyes. Her hair had been a sandy blond, like his, though a bit more straw and less mud. His mother didn't smile often. Dad had smiled a lot, but she didn't yell or threaten or spank him either.

Vic prayed aloud, his accent a little stronger as he spoke with confidence and easy familiarity.

Religion and Adam's mother went hand in hand. It was a background thing, her faith. She didn't make it to church often, not with her work schedule, but they read the bit about the wise men on Christmas Eve, and every Easter she forced the two boys to scrub and shine before she dragged them to an annual sermon, the contents of which he tuned out.

Adam peeked at Vic as he prayed. Catholic, which was really foreign to Adam, but how much of it did Vic believe? Adam was used to being called a sinner, an abomination. Backwoods magic and condemnation went hand in hand. Plenty of the practitioners he'd met had blended the two. Some kept bibles on their little altars. cute

Aunt Sue hung a cross in the kitchen where she read tarot. She told Adam it let people feel better about visiting her if they saw that Sue didn't hate their faith.

He wondered how Vic would feel if things between them went somewhere real. Adam realized that what he'd done, binding them as he had, had deeper implications. He'd saved Vic's life, but Adam hoped he had not broken him somehow, that the magic hadn't made him think he was someone he wasn't.

Sensing Adam's turmoil, Vic said Amen and looked at Adam with a knowing, worried face. Vic shook his head.

You worry too much.

The thought passed between them.

"What are we eating?" Vic asked Tilla. "It smells amazing."

Adam's mother actually blushed a little.

"Macaroni," she said.

Adam cringed. He hated macaroni and cheese, had since his mother had fed it to them for months straight. Bobby had learned to cook it, tried to make it palatable for Adam by adding pepper and basil, leftover hot sauce from the fast food tacos Bobby bought them when he started working at the corner store. In the end it had seared his taste buds. Even now he used a lot of Tabasco sauce.

Vic, sensing that, too, looked at Adam. He leaned forward, opened his mouth as if to ask Adam what he was feeling, and why.

Adam forced a smile and reached for the bowl of canary-colored elbows.

"It looks great, Mom," Adam said. He didn't want his mother to know how much he hated it, even though she'd fancied it up with bacon and spinach. It wasn't her fault that she couldn't afford to feed them anything else back then, though he wished she'd been able to default to something else now that Doctor Binder was footing the bill.

Vic exhaled. Adam saw him shake off his curiosity. He nodded for Adam to pass him the bowl. Adam did not doubt that they'd talk about it later.

Adam couldn't shake the strangeness of it. If anyone had asked him if his mother would be all right with a guy dropping by for dinner, he'd have said no. Adam watched her out of the corner of his eye like she might be the possessed one. She'd surprised him, and he didn't think she had anything up her sleeve but interest in Adam's well-being. She'd changed, he realized, or she'd never been who he had thought she was.

She smiled at him, as if she could read him the way Vic could. It felt normal being with them like this, and Adam found himself smiling back.

32

ADAM

"Is this thing safe?" Vic asked as Adam drove. He took the long way. "It doesn't feel safe."

"It's fine," Adam said. He felt what little was left to the padding beneath his ass and did not sigh. It wasn't nice like Bobby's Audi or even Jesse's SUV.

"Still, you need to let Jesse look at it."

"I don't want charity, Vic."

He meant it. It was bad enough that he had to shop for shirts at thrift stores, that he was used to hunger. Pity, especially from a guy he liked, would be too much.

"He wants to help you. It's okay to ask for things, Adam. It's okay to need or want things for yourself."

"I just—I don't want to be the white trash guy you feel sorry for."

"White trash?" Vic asked. "You're not white trash."

"I grew up in the woods, Vic. I live in a trailer park. I've never had a new pair of shoes, you know that?"

"That's poor, not white trash. Your mom worked hard. Your brother works hard. You're only white trash if you're lazy. And I know that's not you."

It made him bristle that Vic was right. Everyone in their family hustled. Everyone always had, except for Dad. He couldn't be bothered to do the simplest things, not even put garbage where he was supposed to. Long after he'd gone, Bobby ran over a discarded spray paint can with the lawn mower. It exploded and destroyed the mower. They'd been lucky Bobby hadn't been hurt, or even killed, by the shrapnel.

Shaking his head, Adam pulled to a stop in front of Vic's house.

"You don't know me that well," Adam said.

"I know you're a good person." Vic reached over to put his hand to the back of Adam's head. He made a little motion with his fingers. Adam pressed into the touch. Vic raised an eyebrow. "Or do you have a Confederate flag tattoo somewhere I haven't seen?"

"No," Adam said. "Just a monster truck. Oh, and a cow munching grass on my ass cheek."

"Left or right?" Vic asked.

Adam paused, breath held, palms itching.

Vic leaned across the bucket seats. So close, his face inches from Adam's, he paused. Vic kept up that slight pressure, that little movement of his fingers on the back of Adam's head.

Adam wondered if this was how Vic had been with the girls he'd dated. He shut that down, let the sensation carry him until, unable to wait any longer, he closed the gap between them and pressed his lips to Vic's.

The thread, the connection between them, sizzled. It hummed as if to say *Yes. Finally.*

Adam paused to gasp and Vic let him take a long breath before he pressed them together again. Vic parted Adam's lips with his tongue. Their hands moved over each other, down arms, inside Vic's denim jacket. Vic skimmed his fingers under the hem of Adam's T-shirt, brushing skin.

Their eyes stayed locked the whole time.

The blood rushing in Adam's ears and downward cut off all thought. Pausing, he asked, "Am I hurting you?"

"No," Vic said, leaning in again.

Adam believed him. He did not think either of them could lie in that moment, in that strange pretzel twist of bodies, lips, and life threads.

Adam risked a glance out the window as Vic kissed his neck, the tip of his tongue darting against soft flesh. The Reapers were gone. Adam wanted to know more, but he was a bit distracted by the tightness everywhere. He kissed Vic, over and over, their eyes open and seeking. Adam found it then, the bit of doubt layered under all that confidence. He tried to wipe it away with a kiss so long he thought he might pass out. Vic broke first. He ran a fingertip over Adam's lips.

"I'd better go," Vic said. "Before we get too . . ."

"Sweaty?" Adam asked with a laugh. He felt like everything between them was balanced on a knife edge, like he and Vic could drop at any moment into bed or back into their separate lives. He forced himself to exhale and redirect his blood back into the rest of his body.

"Sweaty," Vic agreed.

"Are you sure?" Adam asked, leaning away until his back touched the door.

"Yeah. Don't want to bust a stitch." Vic smiled and ran his eyes down Adam's belly to his jeans. "Either of us."

"Okay," Adam said with another laugh.

"Walk me to the door?" Vic asked.

Adam nodded with a long inhale and moved back to the driver's seat. He climbed out, felt the night breeze cool his hot skin. He stiffened when Vic took his hand. The street was as busy as ever.

"What?" Vic said.

"What if your neighbors see?"

"We just made out in front of my mother's house," Vic said. "You didn't care if they saw that."

Adam blushed so hard he felt it burn his ears.

"Look," Vic said, pausing halfway up the narrow concrete walk. "I don't know where this, us, is going. But I want to go there. With you, okay?"

"You're not worried what people might think?" Adam asked.

Vic shrugged. "Small neighborhood. Jesse has a big mouth. People are going to find out, if they just didn't."

"You're not scared?"

"I'm a cop. This is my neighborhood. I know everyone on this street, and they know me."

Adam shook his head. "It's not like that where I come from. Holding hands with a guy, shit, just anyone even knowing I'm gay. Let's just say it wouldn't go over so well in the trailer park."

Vic wrapped his fingers into Adam's.

"It's not like that everywhere."

"And—what if it's not real?" Adam asked, his voice quiet. There. He'd asked it. "What if it's just the magic?"

What, he thought, *if you don't really like me?* It felt too pathetic to say it aloud.

"Liking you is magic," Vic said, smiling. "What's more magical than a first kiss? Everything doesn't have to hurt all the time, Adam. There is good. There are good guys. Like you."

What about Silver? A little voice asked. Adam crushed it. Silver wouldn't stand up to his own father. Vic was willing to walk down the street with him. Vic was willing to walk with him, holding hands, to his front door. There wasn't a comparison.

"You're thinking again," Vic said, dragging Adam onto the porch. He leaned in to give Adam a quick peck on the lips. "Go home. Think there. You're making my bullet-hole hurt."

Vic sauntered inside. Adam waited a moment before heading back to the Cutlass. He'd driven about two blocks when a voice in the back seat asked, "Do you love him?"

After a yelp higher in pitch than Adam would have preferred, he looked in the rearview mirror to see Argent in the back seat.

"How long have you been back there?" he asked.

"Long enough," she said, climbing over the seats in a lithe, but still awkward way to drop into the passenger seat.

"I was on my way to pick you up," Adam said.

"I got bored. Hospitals are quite dull. Your television shows make it seem like it's all explosions and illicit sex in closets."

"You could have waited."   *LOL*

"Answer the question," Argent said.

"I don't know," Adam said. "I just met the guy."

"Yet you wove a strand of your life force to his?" she asked.

"I didn't want him to die," Adam said. He remained adamant in the decision, and yet it had felt like peeling off a piece of his heart. Remembering it now, he realized that was what he had done. "He didn't deserve that."

"Still." Argent sighed. "It remains a most impulsive way to marry someone."

"Marry?" Adam asked. "I didn't marry him. That's not what I was doing."

"Adam Lee Binder," Argent said, drawing out his full name. "You might possibly be the most ignorant, most arrogant mortal practitioner I have encountered in twenty centuries."

"Is that how old you are?" he asked.

"It's impolite to ask," she snapped, eyes closing to slits. "But yes, Adam, when a boy likes another boy very much, you tie a strand of your life to theirs. You share their pains, their gains, their rise and fall. In sickness and in health, all that."

Argent grew quieter, looked around as if to make sure no one could overhear, and said, "Which is why we do it when we take a mortal mate. It extends their life, lets them stay with us longer, though not forever."

"Does that happen?" Adam asked, trying to sound neutral, wanting to ask if it had happened to her. He remembered what Silver had alluded to, that she'd defied their father, stood up to him once, and been imprisoned for it.

"Rarely," she said. She looked so sad that she answered his unasked question. He wondered who in those long centuries she'd loved and lost. "And not for a long while. We are traditionalists, preservationists. And we are so long-lived. It is painful to see our mortal lovers or children die."

Adam shrunk into his seat. Hands gripped to the steering wheel, he asked, "Is that—Silver. Is that why it hurt him when I saved Vic?"

Argent raised an eyebrow at Adam.

"Quite," she said, examining herself in a small compact. "Silver is more *traditional*. He fit well in your Victorian era. He knew he'd lost you, that father would never allow him to keep you, but that does not mean that he wanted to see you bound to another."

Adam groaned. "I don't know what to do about anything, not Vic, not Silver. I don't know what to do about the damned spirit."

"For now," Argent said. "Drive to the Clock Tower. We have an appointment with the Gaoler, and a chance to free your marriage sister."

"Then what?" he asked.

"When this is done you must decide whether or not you love him."

Adam nodded. He wanted to, but did not ask Argent which *him* she meant.

*****

Adam could not find an open parking space large enough for the Cutlass.

"Stupid SUVs," he groaned.

"There," Argent said with a wave, shifting them and the car, to the Spirit world.

"Thanks." Adam smiled as he pulled into an empty spot. The parking meters had mouths where their coin slots should be. They undulated like hungry snakes, begging for coins.

"How many of you can do that?" he asked. He fed the meter a few quarters. Contented, it tried to lick his face before closing its eyes and drifting to sleep like a cat in the sun. "Move a whole car over?"

Argent arched a plucked eyebrow at him. "Adam Binder, are you trying to be clever with me?"

"No, I'm just trying to learn."

"Asking questions is a start," she said. "But do better."

"How?"

"Ask better questions."

Adam could not think of a follow-up as they kept walking. It seemed the elves would teach him, if he could prove his worth through asking the right questions. It was like taking a test to prove you could take tests.

No wonder I never made it to college.

They'd parked in the theater district. A trolley car snarled past. Curtis Street sported ancient theaters, their signs comprised of light bulbs set to make the letters, shone through the bit of haze that had settled over downtown. They had names like Chop Suey and the Isis.

Tonight the atmosphere felt like a carnival. The spirits walked on stilts or bicycled through the air, suspended by balloons. Dressed in pinstripe suits and evening gowns, everyone seemed headed for the shows. Adam wondered what he'd find within, especially as a pair of well-dressed octopuses tapped their way by, each sporting eight walking sticks.

Adam made a note to come back and look at them more closely. Maybe he could bring Vic somehow. Like a real date.

"What are you grinning about?" Argent asked him.

"This," Adam said, waving a hand as a bear in a fez danced along the street. Argent didn't ask him to expound, and he was glad. He wasn't sure he had the words for what welled up in his heart. She returned his smile.

They neared the clock tower. It stood just north of them, its face glowing like the moon.

A wave of force broke from the building, a cloud of dust and debris. It knocked Adam to the ground.

"Da fuck?" he asked, looking up.

"Language," Argent said before turning to see what he had.

The cloud froze. It hung, unmoving over several blocks. Even the fire, the smoke and flames, stood fixed in place. Then it reversed, compacting before it expanded again.

"Da fuck?" Argent echoed him.

The explosion's pause didn't stop the spirits around them from panicking. They screamed. Adam heard a roar, some beast large enough that its call echoed off the bricks.

"What is that?" Adam asked.

"Manticore," Argent said. She didn't change, didn't unveil her true aspect, but she drew a very long sword out of her purse like a magician might draw a rabbit from a top hat. She wore a hungry expression. For a being that respected all life, she looked quite the hunter—dangerous and ready to draw blood.

The manticore roared again, the sound more distant. She nodded to the tableau of destruction set on pause.

"What's happening?" Adam asked, clearing his vision and focusing on the cloud.

"The Gaoler has contained the explosion," she said, standing tall, all her casual demeanor cast aside. "Likely at the cost of his life."

"What about Annie?" Adam asked.

The Queen of Swords shook her head. "I don't know."

A wave of cold washed over Adam's senses. The spirit tendril pulsed through the sky. It thickened and swelled, a bloody root drinking deep. No, Adam realized, not drinking, feeding itself, pumping its essence, into something, someone. The spirit vanished from the sky.

"Where has it gone?" Adam asked. "What's it doing?"

"Nothing good," Argent said.

She tensed like she might leap.

"You can't," he said. "It will kill you."

Argent seethed. He felt her start to turn her rage on him for his impertinence, but she held back as a shape walked out of the debris cloud, her slim hands pushing aside floating chunks of wall or broken pipes.

Annie. Her eyes were wholly yellow. Focusing on Adam, her face split into a rictus grin. Adam checked the sky. The spirit had gone. It had filled Annie, taken her completely.

He'd lost her. Adam had lost her. What was he going to tell Bobby?

A wave of force broke as the explosion spread.

Argent grabbed him by the collar.

"We have to go," she said.

She pulled Adam back onto the mortal plane without pause. It took him a moment to recover, but it was no trip from Alfheimr, that or being in his body made it easier.

The dark grounds of the closed amusement park shifted into focus around them.

"My car!" Adam said.

Argent frowned. "Oops."

She snapped her fingers and the car landed nearby, burning and crushed, its windows shattered. A large chunk of debris had folded the hood almost in two.

Argent whistled.

Adam gaped. She was wrecked, maybe not completely, but he'd never find the parts. He'd never be able to afford it.

His car.

He paused. There were bigger concerns. Annie. All those people—

"What about downtown?" He craned his ear to listen for sirens.

"They likely felt nothing," Argent said, staring into the distance. "The mortal tower remains."

"And the immortal?"

"Gone. Broken. The spirit is well and truly free, as are the other prisoners the Gaoler had contained."

Argent dimmed. She shook her head.

"It's possessed Annie," Adam said. "It's corporeal now."

"Then we truly are out of time," Argent said.

33

ADAM

Adam could not stop shaking. Staggered, he circled the Cutlass. The front tires had popped when the debris hit. Even if he could just take off the hood, he had no way of driving her home. Totaled. His car was totaled.

Silver ran toward them, guards flanking him like a wing of birds.

"Did you see?" Argent asked her brother.

"Everyone saw," he said. "A watchtower has not fallen in centuries."

Adam tried to breathe. He tried to focus. Okay, his car was wrecked. He'd deal with that later. And Annie—Annie was possessed. Adam had to figure out what do about it, what to tell Bobby.

"The gnomes' prisoners are free," Argent said.

"Envoys have already been sent," Silver said. "Though the gnomes do not answer."

"They're likely dead," Argent said. "The spirit has taken Adam's marriage sister. It has left the sky."

"We have to find her," Adam said. He looked toward downtown. On this side, the mortal side, it seemed calm, quiet and distant. "We have to go back."

"We can't," Argent said.

"Why not?" The shard was cold in his jacket pocket. They hadn't even had the chance to try it.

"The explosion is still happening, still expanding," Silver said. "It's too dangerous."

"And there are things loose that even I would hesitate to fight," Argent admitted.

Adam hugged himself at her admission and the deepening weight of the knowledge that they'd done this. They'd brought Annie to the clock tower, let the spirit in, given it the chance to—All those gnomes, just gone. Adam thought he might be sick.

"You are not to go there," Silver said, his voice firm.

"I am not one of your vassals, your highness," Adam said. "I don't work for you."

"Adam," Argent said, stepping between the two of them. "There is no way for you to shift back to the mortal side. If something caught you there, you'd be killed."

"Or worse," Silver said quietly.

"What about Annie?" Adam asked. "We can't leave her there. She could be hurt."

"The spirit absorbed the watchtower's magic," Argent said. "It gained enough power to become corporeal again."

"And it has enough power to heal her," Silver said. "It needs her alive."

"But not unhurt," Adam said, hearing his voice break. "What's it doing to her?"

He'd felt it inside him, burning him. Fully possessed, Annie must be in agony.

"If it can bring down watchtowers and Guardians," Argent said. "Then there is only one solution."

"We have to kill her," Silver said. His eyes dropped to the ground. "I'm sorry, Adam. I cannot see another course of action."

"No," Adam said. He refused to accept it, even though he'd already come to the same conclusion. "Maybe we can drain its power, make it incorporeal and lock it away again."

"It's too big of a threat now," Silver said. "We must involve Father."

"I will tell him," Argent said. "I am not yet out of his graces."

Adam watched her walk away and turned back to the Cutlass. He wanted to ignore Silver, but couldn't.

"What happens now?" Adam asked. He'd failed. The spirit had possessed Annie, brought down a watchtower. Boy troubles should be the least of Adam's priorities, but the prince remained.

"The other Guardians are gathering to attack it," Silver said. "They will expect us to show no quarter this time. They already blame us for its survival."

"And if you say no?" Adam asked.

"There will be war among the immortals."

Adam kicked the Cutlass's flattened tire. He spat.

"We have to find her before they do," he said.

"And what do we do with her, Adam?" Silver asked. "We cannot contain the spirit. It has a body now. It can die."

"So Annie's just a casualty?" Adam asked.

He expected Silver to say something like, "You forget yourself, mortal," but the prince only bowed his head and whispered, "Yes. I wish it, and so many other things, were different, but yes."

"You talk so much about the sanctity of life, how important it is, but when it comes down to it, you're cowards."

Silver lifted a hand, spread his fingers. Adam expected to die, for lightning to strike him dead after daring to speak so, but the guards vanished. The Cutlass vanished. Silver sent everything but the two of them back to the spirit realm.

They stood alone in the shadow of a sleeping roller coaster.

"That wasn't fair," Silver said. He looked hurt. Anger Adam could have dealt with.

He plunked down onto the concrete. Around them, the night had chilled. The highway north of the amusement park had quieted.

"No," Adam admitted. "It wasn't. And I'm sorry. I don't want to fight."

But they were in one. Every nerve still thrummed from the explosion's aftermath. That grin. Her possessed eyes—the spirit would come for them. Annie would come for them. He felt it in his bones.

"You assume I do?" Silver asked.

He'd returned to his 1920s gangster look. The gray suit, fedora, and cane would have added years to anyone older-looking. On Silver it enhanced his perfect skin and color-sipping eyes.

Adam closed his eyes for a moment. He did not think he would ever not feel grimy and dingy next to the prince. At least he felt real, himself, not some elven illusion or too-beautiful sculpture.

Like Kaiyang [handwritten margin note]

"Are you all right?" Silver asked.

Adam expected Silver to offer a hand, to lead Adam somewhere finer, but the prince took a seat on the ground, in the dust, beside him.

"I'm not hurt. Argent got me out in time."

"Though I am glad to know it, I didn't mean physically."

"I know," Adam said. "What am I going to tell my brother? I came here to save Annie, not get her killed."

"I don't know," Silver said. "I want another way out of this. For her. For you."

"Me too," Adam said. He tried, and failed, to hide his bitterness.

"Of all of this," Silver said, "I find your brother the most confusing."

"Huh?" Adam asked. Silver's proximity didn't excite him so

much as it made him overly aware, like his skin was a little too tight. The sensation bordered on the uncomfortable.

"From what I recall, what you told me before, you did not think he cared about you," Silver continued. "He locked you away."

"He did," Adam said.

"Then why call you here?" Silver asked.

"He didn't have anyone else," Adam shrugged.

"Are you certain?" Silver asked.

"Where are you going with this?"

"Someone set all this in motion," Silver said. "The practitioner who broke the seal knew exactly what to do, where to strike. That is no coincidence."

"You're right," Adam said. He took a long breath and came clean, about the warlock, about the charms, about his father.

Silver did not seem shocked.

"Regardless of his identity, he did it at someone's behest," Silver said.

"Someone is pulling the spirit's strings," Adam said. He felt certain of it now. He'd felt watched since this business started. He still did, even though the spirit was corporeal. He could rule it and Silver out.

The presence was subtle, but it was there. A few weeks ago, he wouldn't have been able to detect it, but Adam had tuned his senses since coming to Denver.

"I think so," Silver said. "And finding whoever freed the spirit is your best approach."

"I don't have a lead," Adam said. "I didn't find anything on Federal."

"Nor has Argent been able to find anything," Silver said. "Without the Gaoler, we cannot look back through time."

"Great," Adam said. All the avenues to victory were closing. They'd reached a dead end. They'd lost.

They sat there for a long time, saying nothing, watching the sun rise. Adam felt he should be doing something, making some move to stop the spirit, to save Annie, but he felt wrung out, bloodless. The days had taken their toll, but at least he knew his next move.

Silver sat next to Adam, staring into the horizon.

"What do you see?" Adam asked.

"The dragon from Lookout Mountain," Silver said, pointing west. The explosion has stirred it.

Squinting Adam could see a gliding shape. It ducked in and out of the silvered clouds.

"What's it doing?" Adam asked.

"Warning thieves off its hoard," Silver said.

They watched it for a while, watched the sun rise a little higher.

"I should go home," Adam said.

"All right."

"Thank you, Silver," Adam said.

The elf ducked his head so the fedora hid his face.

"Close your eyes," he said.

Adam did, and felt the rush of air, a change in temperature as he left the tree shade of the closed amusement park.

He opened his eyes to brightness, to find himself sitting on the curb across from Bobby's house. He looked around, hoping the neighbors hadn't spotted his sudden appearance, but the street was peaceful, suburban, a typical weekday quiet.

The Cutlass sat, wrecked, battered, and leaking all its fluids, in the driveway. Adam's mother stood nearby, nodding to Jesse as he muttered a comment and forced open the folded hood. He whistled when he saw Adam approach.

"Damn, Wonder Bread. What did you do to her?"

Adam smiled despite himself. He wondered briefly, what it would be like to have an older brother like Jesse, someone he actually liked, one who liked him back. Uncomplicated would be nice.

"It's a long story and I don't think you'd believe me," Adam said.

Frowning, Adam's mother asked, "Something downtown?"

Adam blinked, gave a slow nod.

He'd always assumed that he'd gotten his magic from his father's side, but he'd always suspected his mother might be sensitive. From time to time she'd known things she shouldn't. Maybe that was the secret to his uniqueness, the weird blend of bloodlines.

That's cuz she's your mom [handwritten annotation]

Maybe they were about to have a moment of understanding.

"You're lucky your brother went to work early," his mother said, tone chiding, the moment squashed. "He'd have had a heart attack over this mess, Adam Lee."

Like it was Adam's fault. Like he wanted his car wrecked or Silver to put it where it could offend Bobby's delicate sensibilities. But he didn't get into it with his mom, especially with Vic's brother there. Jesse wore one of those long thermals with a button at the collar straining over his broad chest and a Broncos baseball cap.

"She's a real beauty," Jesse said. "Or she was. Will be again."

"I couldn't afford it before." Adam waved a hand at the wrecked car. "And I really can't afford it now."

"You did this?" Jesse asked, pointing to the engine.

"Did what?" Adam asked, coming to look at whatever Jesse indicated.

"The carburetor's been rebuilt."

"Yeah," Adam said with a shrug. "It wasn't hard. Just took it all apart, cleaned it, and switched out what was broken."

"Huh," Jesse said. "What else have you fixed?"

"This or that," Adam said with a shrug. "Whatever I could."

"Where'd you learn to do it?" Jesse asked.

"Internet videos, asked around if I got stuck."

Jesse nodded, musing for a while.

"You're hired," he said.

"What?"

"We'll fix your car, Wonder Bread. Well, you'll fix it. You'll work in my shop. You can pay for the parts that way."

"You don't have to do that, Jesse."

"I know that," Jesse said, straightening. "I don't have to do anything unless my mom tells me to do it. But you keep saying you need money, and I need a part-timer. You can sweep up and man the desk until we've made a good mechanic out of you and you get your car running. I'll have it towed over."

Without further argument, he took out his phone and walked toward the curb.

But Adam wasn't staying. Denver wasn't home. Yet Vic was here.

Adam wondered if Aunt Sue had known. She'd sent him with the tarot cards. It stung to think she hadn't said more of a good-bye, but it wasn't that far, not if he had a working vehicle.

"Think about it, Adam," his mother said.

Maybe he could stay a while, and when he went back he could bring some skills, maybe send Sue a little money in the meantime.

But none of that mattered right now. They had to save Annie.

"When will Bobby be home?" he asked.

His mother squinted. "Why?"

"I just—I need to talk to him," Adam said.

"He'll be at the hospital all day," Adam's mother said.

"Tow truck's coming," Jesse said, looking up from his phone.

"No offense, but why are you here?" Adam asked.

"Vic wanted to check on you," Jesse said, answering his phone with a "yeah?" before letting out a quick a stream of Spanish punctuated by a glance at the house numbers and Bobby's address.

"He's inside," his mother said.

34

ADAM

Adam hadn't sensed Vic's presence. The line between them, the connection, had faded again. That kiss had been electric, burning, but Adam's gut twisted at the new distance between them.

"Hey," Vic said from where he sat in Annie's overstuffed, oversize chair.

"What are you doing in here?" Adam asked, smiling as the screen door closed behind him.

"Still can't stand too long," Vic said.

"Do you need anything? Water?" Adam asked.

Vic waved away Adam's concern. "Nah. Tell me what's up."

"Jesse offered me a job," Adam said, coming close enough to sit on the ottoman, within reach.

"That's great," Vic said. He leaned closer. That scent, his body wash, Adam suspected, citrus and sandalwood, pressed near.

"But that's not why you're here, is it?" Adam asked.

"I'm going a little crazy," Vic said. He scratched the back of his head, made a sheepish expression. "I love my mom, but she can get a little smothery."

"I get that," Adam said. Sue was kind, but there weren't many secrets or much privacy in a single wide trailer.

He was happy to see Vic, but Annie—he had to tell Bobby. He had to do something.

"What's wrong?" Vic asked.

"Let's go downstairs," Adam said. Standing, he nodded for Vic to follow him into the basement.

Adam reached the bottom first and looked back. Vic took the steps slowly, his hand gripping the rail. Framed in the light from the door, Vic looked weak. Adam wondered if their weakened bond had slowed Vic's healing.

"Are you okay?" Adam asked, stepping back up in case Vic needed help. He felt bad for making Vic climb down to him.

"I'm fine," Vic said. "Just not a hundred percent, and really not ready to go back to work."

Adam kept his eyes on Vic in case he fell and asked, "Have they asked you to?"

"No," Vic said, his face stiffening. "They're still not sure what happened. All they saw was the shooting. Carl, he—well, he wasn't the most stable guy, but no one saw that coming."

"Least of all Carl," Adam said, eyes dropping to his feet. "It wasn't his fault. The spirit used him."

"I didn't go to the funeral," Vic said. "I don't know how it would have gone, if I would have been welcome. I didn't want his wife or kids thinking about me, you know?"

"I'm sorry," Adam said, ready to catch Vic when he reached the bottom of the stairs.

"It's all right, but I'm going kind of stir-crazy. I can't wait to go home."

"To your apartment?" Adam asked, feeling a little flush at the idea of access to a space that was only Vic's, without either of their families around.

"Yeah," Vic said, a little smile telling Adam he was having similar thoughts. He stepped close enough that their noses almost touched.

Adam reached out an arm, brushed past Vic to turn on the light.

"Now tell me what's up," Vic said.

"Cold move, Martinez," Adam said.

The weight of it all pressed in.

Vic slid passed him, sat on the bed, and patted it, telling Adam to join him.

Adam sat.

"Explain," Vic said.

He really was intense when he went all stoic cop face.

So Adam caught Vic up. He spilled it all, his father, tracking the warlock, the clock tower, Annie's possession.

"You were right," Vic said.

"About what?"

"You are complicated," Vic said, knocking their shoulders together. "Feel better?"

"I do," Adam said. He shook a little, like emptying it all out had weakened him, like he'd been running for so long and had finally stopped to catch his breath.

"Thank you," he said quietly, meaning it down to his toes.

He wasn't used to that either, being able to just talk to someone, openly. Even Sue, though she loved him, had strong opinions. And he realized he'd been hiding some things from her, protecting her from the warlock's depravity. That wasn't fair of him. She was old, not weak or stupid.

"You know, you smell awful," Vic said.

"Thanks," Adam said. Adam couldn't argue. He was coated in smoke and dust.

Vic laughed.

"Go shower. I'll make sure Jesse doesn't talk your mom's ear off."

Adam was almost out of clean clothes again, but having

washed, dressed, and unburdened himself, he felt better, ready to figure out their next move. And it was theirs. He wasn't alone in this.

Heading upstairs, he found Jesse gone, the Cutlass gone, and a Dodge Challenger black, glossy, and utterly new, in the driveway.

Argent leaned against it, talking to Vic. Hands in her pockets, she wore a stylish gray pantsuit and sunglasses that would have paid Sue's lot rent for a year.

"We have a lunch invitation," she said.

"From who?" Adam asked.

"I think it's whom," Vic said.

Argent looked between them and said, "The Guardians of the West. They say they have a package for you."

"That's suspicious timing," Adam said.

"Agreed, but I think we should take the meeting," Argent said.

"We?" Adam asked.

"I'm not letting you go alone. I don't want you walking into a trap." Argent nodded to Vic. "And I think he should come too."

"Can I drive?" Vic asked.

"No."

"Shotgun," Adam said, before Vic could react.

Vic folded into the back seat with a frown.

"The West," Adam said as she backed out of the driveway. "Who holds the tower?"

"They're not my favorite," the queen admitted, taking off far too quickly for a residential speed limit.

"But who are they?" Vic asked.

"Each watchtower is controlled by a powerful race," Adam said. "They're usually immortal, but not always. Long-lived, surely."

"We prefer to work with other immortals," Argent said. "Those who take their duties as seriously as we do."

"And these guys don't?" Vic asked.

NICE

"The Guardians of the West are leprechauns," Argent said.

"Like, St. Patrick's Day, sports team mascot leprechauns?" Vic asked.

"They would prefer you avoid the stereotypes," Argent said. "But essentially, yes. They are tricksters. They like to make deals, and they aren't above making bargains with unsavory elements."

"A magical black market?" Vic asked. "Cool."

"Really?" Adam asked.

Vic leaned back into his seat. "Maybe it's the pain medication but at this point nothing surprises me."

Adam watched him shrug in the mirror and a warm feeling tickled his belly. It ran downward. Vic caught Adam watching, or maybe he felt it, too, and smiled.

"Where is their tower anchor?" Adam asked, trying to push down his blush, which made it worse.

Argent didn't seem to notice. She drove way too fast. She zipped between cars, shifted them from mortal to spirit and back again, crossing the city at an impossible speed. The day was slightly hazy on the mortal side. The mountains looked unreal, silver and pink. In the spirit, he could see the explosion downtown, still expanding, an obscuring cloud covering the city.

Argent sniffed and slid the car into a parking spot. She nodded to a church-like structure. It was pink with a big fountain out front.

"It's a theme restaurant," she said, her mouth bending into something like a frown.

"Oh no," Vic said. "This place?"

"Security is tight, especially after what happened with the East," Argent said. "We have to enter through the mortal side."

They entered and joined a long line, passing through a stucco hallway with booths high above them.

Adam blinked and checked that they hadn't crossed over. The

place could have used some fresh paint. It was obviously old, but the people waiting seemed happy and the line moved briskly.

The menu wasn't complicated.

"Please don't tell my mother I ate here," Vic said.

"Are we eating here?" Adam asked. He could eat. He could almost always eat, but he hadn't gotten paid yet and cash remained short.

"It's the only way in the door," Argent said. "You can eat. They don't have anything vegan."

"Elves are vegan," Adam told Vic before he could ask.

"Why?" Vic asked.

Argent sighed and said, "They say the average toddler asks three to four hundred questions a day. I see it is the same with your sort."

"His sort?" Adam asked.

"Those new to magic," she said. "Babies."

Argent was hedging. She knew something. Adam wondered what price he had to pay to get her to tell.

"I prefer the term rookie," Vic said, giving Adam a questioning look. "How else am I going to learn?"

"He's got a point," Adam said as the menu, lit screens over the cashiers came into sight. The colors were supposed to be festive, but they lacked the cheery brightness of the Martinez house. They were more like someone's *idea* of Mexico. The crowd seemed to like it, but Adam bristled at their numbers, the press of their feelings. The children were especially hard. They had no control, no reservations, and their emotions broke over him like too many colors, flashing all at once.

"White people," Vic said, nudging Adam, and just that contact settled him into his skin. Vic nodded to the menu. "Get the cheese enchiladas. Trust me."

The line dragged on until they collected their trays from beneath a heat lamp and shuffled forward. Argent carried a single glass of iced tea and wore an expression that challenged anyone to comment.

The host led them to a seat near a waterfall. An actual indoor waterfall that dropped into an actual pool, deep enough to swim in.

"This is really—" Adam started, glancing around, his stomach a ball of nerves about what Vic must be thinking.

"It's fun," Vic said. "Like a carnival in a cafeteria."

Adam took in the decor. It was like a little town. They sat in a booth fashioned to look like a balcony beneath a drop ceiling painted black.

"I will go seek the entrance," Argent said with a disgusted look.

When she'd gone, Adam looked to Vic. "Be very careful with her. She's powerful."

"She likes you," Vic said, using his fork to slice a piece off his enchilada with a mischievous grin. "Everybody likes you."

Adam shook his head and looked around. He didn't see anyone browner than himself. "Doesn't this place offend you or something?"

Vic laughed. "'Cause it's my culture or something?"

"Yeah."

"It's a restaurant. The food's bad, but it's fun. And a family can feed and entertain their kids without spending a lot of money."

As Vic spoke, a diver took to the top of the waterfall. He wore a speedo and with an almost unintelligible song and dance about the height from an MC holding a microphone too close to her mouth, he dove into the pool.

"What is this place?" Adam asked. He checked it with his Sight, made certain Argent hadn't crossed them over, but no, there was a waterfall and a human diver. In a restaurant. The smell of bleach wafted through the air.

The diver climbed out of the pool and up the fake grotto, using the rocks to dive again, this time with a flip. Adam gaped.

"He's hot, don't you think? Vic asked.

"I—I don't know." Adam felt the blush travel up his face.

"What's wrong?" Vic said.

"I just—I don't look like that, you know?"

"So?"

"So what if you decide you *are* gay and—"

"I think I'm bi," Vic said.

"Okay," Adam said.

"I mean, I hadn't really put a label on it, but I guess I've always been equal opportunity, more about the person than the gender, you know?"

"Okay," Adam repeated.

"Say something," Vic said. "This is my big coming out speech. I thought you'd take it better than my mother."

"You told your mother," Adam said, remembering their conversation in her car.

"She's always shopping for Pride flags." Vic said with a shrug.

"I—I don't know," Adam said. "What if it's just the magic?"

"It's not," Vic said, shrugging through another bite. He kept his eyes on Adam "I mean, I've never gone there, but to be honest you're the first guy I've wanted to take the trip with."

"Okay," Adam said a third time. The tea was too old. Aunt Sue would have thrown it out.

"You could say something else," Vic said. "How about you?"

"I've only ever been with guys," Adam said. He watched the diver, wet and scowling with concentration, juggle lit torches. "I've only ever wanted to be with guys."

"Are you worried I'll change my mind?" Vic asked.

"Sometimes," Adam said, nodding to the diver. He would have scowled too if his nipples were fire-adjacent. "Or that you'll want someone like that? A jock."

"You think I'm that shallow?" Vic asked. He looked hurt. "You think I don't see you."

"It's just—I'm not used to this," Adam said. He waved his fork to indicate the connection between them. "Having someone in my head, or talking about it, you know?"

And my heart. Because as little as they'd done, he liked Vic. Adam could sense the fall, the crevasse beneath him. Given time, he could love Vic, and he barely knew him.

Adam took a bite of the enchilada at last. It wasn't as bad as he'd expected, but the cheese had a plastic taste. He dumped the salsa from the chips atop it.

"You think *I'm* used to it?" Vic asked.

"I know," Adam said. He cringed. He had no right to whine. All of this was even newer ground for Vic. "But I mean, to being wanted."

"You didn't date in high school?"

Adam snorted. "No one really wanted to kiss the guy who heard voices."

Vic gave a confused shake of his head.

"It was the magic. I couldn't control it or tune it out until Pe—Silver taught me."

"What about after?"

"There've been a few guys," Adam said, blushing. He remembered kissing Tanner, and some of the others he'd met in Oklahoma. They weren't like Vic. Kissing them was nothing like kissing Vic.

He almost asked if Vic had many girlfriends, but decided he didn't want to know.

"I don't care if you're a jock," Vic said. "I think you're beautiful. Handsome. Whatever."

"Pft," Adam scoffed.

"Shut up and take a compliment," Vic said, a smile playing at the corner of his mouth.

"You're too nice," Adam said. And he was. Vic was handsome,

good. It made no sense that someone like that would be able to see Adam's past, where he came from, and just not care.

"Not according to Jesse. Trust me, he'll give you a long list of my flaws. And Mom, she's got a lot to say since I've been staying with her."

"You can't really want me," Adam asked. "Can you?"

Vic leaned over and kissed him. Adam started to pull away, nervous about the people around them, but no bruise-colored shame or crimson hatred leaked in, not from the diners, the waiters, and especially not from Vic. This was real. *They* were real.

Vic broke the kiss, and settled back into his seat, though he kept his eyes on Adam's.

"I want you," Vic said. "Yeah, maybe I nearly died and would never have thought about it if you hadn't saved me. But who cares?"

They really were from completely different worlds. Vic might as well have been as alien as an elf. He'd realized something about himself, thought about it, and accepted it without the self-torture or endless stress Adam would have gone through. And that, the fact Vic was like that, different, made Adam smile, even if a bit of something like jealousy tinged it.

"I see you," Vic continued. "And I want you. It's that simple."

When Adam chewed his lip, Vic demanded, almost angrily, "Okay?"

"Okay." Adam looked around them, double checking the room.

"Fuck 'em," Vic whispered.

"You know, you're taking all of this really well. Not just the guy-on-guy thing, the magic, the elves . . . all of it."

"Think about it," Vic said. "There's a whole world out there."

"Worlds," Adam interjected.

"That we don't know about."

"It doesn't freak you out?" Adam asked.

"I'm Catholic," Vic said. "When you think about it, it's kind of confirmation."

"That we're going to hell?" Adam asked. He wiggled his fingers. "I'm gay. And I do witchcraft."

"Well, have you talked to God about it?" Vic asked. "You know, taken it up with management?"

"I've never seen proof of God. Gods, yes, but not the capital-G Judeo-Christian one."

Vic looked a little disappointed. "We should ask around. See if anybody's met Him."

"You're really not struggling with all of this?" Adam asked.

"Not yet," Vic said. "But like I said, I'm still on painkillers. I'm kind of waiting for the shoe to drop, you know? Like it's all real, and this unseen world affects me in ways I can't see."

Adam stiffened a little. He wondered if that's how Bobby and his mother felt. Adam could understand. His Sight was weak, but they were mostly blind, so far as he could tell, so far as they'd admitted. He'd been too hard on them perhaps.

"You're going to help me understand," Vic said. And there it was. Vic could ask where Bobby could not. They were nothing alike.

"I can do that," Adam said, smiling.

"What's that grin for?"

"I've never met anyone like you, Vicente Martinez."

Vic made a pained expression. "We're going to have to work on your Spanish."

"They're ready for us," Argent said, appearing with her usual grace beside the table. "Let's go."

"Too bad," Vic complained. "The sopaipillas aren't bad. And I think they're vegan."

Argent arched an eyebrow at Adam and asked, "He's just trying to piss me off, isn't he?"

"I don't know," Adam said. "I can't always tell."

Smirking, Vic said, "You'll get used to me."

"Come," Argent said. "Before I stab one of you out of annoyance."

They followed her down through the restaurant. The place went on forever, and they hadn't even crossed from the mortal side. Adam gaped at the underground, the dining rooms themed like a mine shaft, then a cave. His nose wrinkled as the bleach from the pool followed them. It masked the food or any other odor.

"This place is too much," Adam said.

"It has a little charm," Argent admitted. "But be cautious. Leprechauns like their games."

She pushed open a door to a gilded ballroom.

Golden mermaids held up a mirrored ceiling. A stage curtained in red took up one long wall. The floor shone, freshly waxed. It reminded Adam of the elven court. He wondered if the leprechauns meant it as an insult, that the place was a gaudy reflection of Silver's vintage ballroom. He checked again, but no, they still hadn't crossed over.

"And sidhe are snobs," said a voice with an Irish accent.

Argent lifted her hand with a sigh. The door behind them closed and clicked. They did not shift to spirit, but a short man appeared.

Dressed in a red suit, he sat alone at the center table. A matching red baseball cap rested on the table.

"Hail, Guardian," he said to Argent.

"Hail," she replied coolly.

"Our choice of anchor is not to your liking?" he asked. "I thought you appreciated history."

"We appreciate preservation," she said.

"This place has been here for half a century," the leprechaun said, waving a hand to the gaudy ballroom. "Is that not long enough to be worthy of preservation in your eyes?"

Argent sighed and took the offered seat. "Shall we get down to business?"

"If we must," he said. "These are your mortals?"

Vic opened his mouth to say something but Adam held up an arm barring it across Vic's chest. Vic looked at him, but Adam shook his head and said, "We are not her vassals."

"They are," Argent said, not commenting on their exchange.

"Argent said you have a package for me," Adam said.

The man extended a hand toward Adam. "Seamus."

"Adam Binder." He took the offered hand. Usually immortals went in for titles and lengthy pleas. He liked that the leprechaun didn't, even as he distrusted it, remembering Argent's warning about unsavory elements.

"Let's get to it then," Seamus said. "I have a package. It's been waiting for you."

"What's your price?" Adam asked.

It wouldn't be good. It might even be deadly, but he'd come this far. He'd pay it, he realized, refusing to glance at Vic, though he had so much more to lose now.

35

ADAM

"I appreciate your directness," Seamus said. "But this delivery was paid for in advance."

"I don't understand."

"You did someone a favor, a kindness," Seamus said. "And they paid the price for you."

Adam blinked.

"He said his name was Bill."

"The Saurians?" Adam asked.

Seamus nodded.

"I was hoping to steer you into a bargain," Seamus said.

"Why?" Vic asked.

He'd tensed, going into what Adam thought of as his cop mode.

"Adam is stirring up a lot of mischief," Seamus said. He grinned. His teeth were thick and yellow, like a horse who'd chain-smoked his entire life. "I could use somebody like that." Adam counted to three.

I might have a new contender for which immortals are the biggest pricks, he thought.

Whatever Seamus would ask for, it would be too much.

Adam shook his head.

Seamus snapped his fingers and the curtains on the little stage parted. "But that's all that was paid for."

A long box stood on the stage.

Biting down on a seething breath, Adam climbed onto the stage and stared down at it. A note, addressed in plain letter to Adam Lee Binder, was taped to the top.

"Go on," Seamus said. "It won't explode."

Adam kicked the box so it slid to the edge of the stage. He knelt over it as Vic joined him.

He read aloud.

Dear Adam:

If you've followed the trail I've left, and the trees speak true, then you've found this in time.

There is still time to save her.

You will know what to do.

Adam read it a second time, trying to absorb the words. He didn't recognize the handwriting, couldn't remember his father's scrawl. It wasn't signed.

Adam took a long breath, let it out. Something he'd held onto for years went with it. The warlock was his father. The proof lay in the yellowed pages attached to the letter. They weren't magic themselves, but he recognized their contents right away.

A recipe for bone, glass, and bog iron.

It was the binding charm, hand-written in a rushed, shaky script. Adam read the note again, read the recipe again. On the page it seemed almost innocuous, but it was black. This magic would taint his, rot it. He would never use it, so why would the warlock insist he have the recipe?

"What's in the box?" Vic asked, stirring him from a stupor.

Adam parted the cardboard flaps, expecting to find more horrors, bones or something foul, but the package contained a compound bow, slightly used by the look of it, and several arrows. Adam lifted one into the light.

"No heads," he said, running a finger over the open slot in the arrow's shaft.

"Can you even use that thing?" Vic asked.

"Yeah. We grew up with them," Adam said.

It wasn't like guns. The memories were pleasant. Bobby had taught him to shoot a bow, and they'd shot arrow after arrow into a stack of old hay bales or, when he got better, at the slender scrub oaks. Adam had enjoyed it, and Bobby never made him shoot at anything alive. He wished his feelings for his brother weren't so complicated, so mixed up. Because there was good in there, along with all the anger and hurt. If it swung strongly enough either way, he could walk away or be at peace with having Bobby in his life.

But neither the bow nor the note answered all of his questions. Annie was still possessed.

They were still missing something. Someone had bound Mercy, the spirit. Someone had broken the seal. Adam looked at the box's flaps. No return address, not that he'd expected one.

"I know who sent it, and I know who paid for it," Adam asked, eyes flicking to Seamus. "How long have you had it?"

"Wrong question," Seamus said, eyes gleeful.

"Okay. *Where* did this package come from?"

Seamus smiled, and Adam knew he'd asked the right question.

"That's a bit of information," Seamus said. "I'm not the sort to deal and tell."

"What do you want for it?" Adam asked.

Vic and Argent exchanged a glance.

"Adam . . ." Argent cautioned.

"We've come this far," he said, and he was getting tired of

playing nice. "Seamus has his reasons, don't you? You wouldn't tease it out if you didn't want something. So what is it? What is it you want from me?"

"A bounty," Seamus said. "A head."

"The warlock," Adam guessed, spine straightening.

"He can't be allowed to continue," Seamus said, the lilt in his voice clipped.

"Never piss off your dealer," Vic muttered.

Adam's father, missing all these years, responsible for so much pain. He remembered the pool cue, the Saurians, the other charms he'd hunted down. Each had held a bit of pain, a bit of ache inflicted on a magical being.

"Deal," he said.

He felt the bargain seal, the magic locking in place. If he failed to deliver, there would be consequences.

Argent looked away, her expression sad or angry, maybe both.

"Payment came through the Hanged Tree," Seamus said. "It smelled like sunflowers and sweet tea."

Ice crept into Adam's veins, but he felt for the thread of the watching power, the presence he'd felt from time to time. And there it was. Now that he knew what to look for, the flavor of the magic, it was familiar, so damn familiar. Adam had known it since Sue had introduced them all those years ago.

"Sara."

"Who's Sara?" Vic asked.

"Not who I thought she was," Adam said.

He remembered that first visit with Sue. She'd traded a peach cobbler recipe for the secret to Sara's pie crust. Looking back now, Adam thought maybe he had detected a bit of wariness in his aunt, a bit of fear that he'd mistaken for caution or shyness at the time. Adam wondered how much his great aunt knew, if that was why she hadn't called him back.

"Or what," Argent added.

"We need to go," Adam said, lifting the box. Though long, it weighed very little. "Now."

Argent nodded to Seamus and said, "Guardian."

"Guardian," he answered, somehow making it sound sarcastic.

Adam almost flipped the leprechaun off as they left the ballroom. He ignored the restaurant's carnival atmosphere, the games and face-painting booth, and followed Argent to the exit.

"Someone please tell me what's going on," Vic said.

"We've been played," Adam said. "By someone I thought I knew."

They piled into the car. Adam put the box in the back seat with Vic.

Argent gripped the steering wheel so hard Adam thought she might crush it.

"I cannot go with you," she said.

"Why not?" Adam asked.

"There are accords between us, more rules," Argent said, her sharp features bent with anger—no, concern, or even worry.

Force poured off of her.

Adam had never seen her upset. He risked laying a hand to her shoulder. It was that or have her go full-on queen and kill him and Vic.

"It's okay," Adam said. "I don't think she'll hurt us. She needs us. She wants us there."

"So I'm coming?" Vic asked. From his expression in the rearview mirror, Adam didn't think it was really a question.

"I think you have to," Adam said.

*****

Argent dropped them a short walk from the Hanging Tree. Vic gaped at the scene around them, the ever-present emerald moon, the twilight sky, and the unreachable hills on the horizon.

"You can see it?" Adam asked.

"Yeah, it's wild," Vic said, reaching for Adam's hand.

But still Adam had no sense of magic around Vic. He shouldn't have Sight. Unless the power was so subtle that even Adam couldn't detect it. Another kind of void.

Adam's heart, despite all the weights on it, leapt to see Vic here.

The slow light played over his skin, deepening its golden color. He glowed, just a bit more beautiful than in the mortal world.

"How do you feel?" Adam asked.

"My chest doesn't hurt," Vic said.

Adam wished he had time to show it all to Vic. Maybe he could, when it was done.

"Just remember it's real," Adam said. "We can die here."

"Is it dangerous?" Vic asked, eyeing the landscape with narrowed eyes. The grass here was red, like fresh brush strokes on canvas. Adam felt no breeze, but the stalks waved, alive and possibly listening.

"A little," Adam said, shrugging. "It depends on where we go. There's a lot to explain."

It occurred to Adam that he could teach Vic, explain the spirit realm like Silver had explained it to him. It could even be fun. If they got the time.

They reached the tree with its grim nooses and bark blackened from evil acts. The Reapers, working their field of bright sunflowers, came into view. They paused, ceased their work and straightened. As one, their skull masks turned to stare.

"What are they?" Vic asked. "And what are they looking at?"

"Reapers," Adam said. "And I think they're looking at you."

Knowing it, admitting it, filled Adam with cold. He squeezed Vic's hand, more for his own sake than Vic's.

Vic took in the hooded shapes. Adam felt him tense. His palm sweated a little against Adam's.

"They're familiar," he whispered.

"One came for you, that day in the hospital," Adam said. "They've been watching you, waiting outside your house."

Vic took a step forward, like he might let Adam go. Adam pulled him back with a gentle jerk of his arm and asked, "What is it?"

"I don't know," Vic said. He looked lost. "I feel like I should help them. They need help. *My help.*"

"You mean, like they're in trouble?" Adam asked. He scanned the horizon for danger.

"No," Vic said, meeting Adam's gaze. He looked afraid. "Like there's work to do."

Cold pressed itself into the center of Adam's back. He'd saved Vic, hadn't he?

What had he really done?

"Come with me," Adam said. "Stay close."

They moved along the path to Sara's trailer. The Reapers kept their eyes fixed on Vic as he and Adam passed.

You can't have him, Adam thought. *I fought one of you before. I'll fight all of you now if I have to. You. Can't. Have. Him.*

Adam thought it over and over, as if the thought alone could make it true. He pulled Vic past the fields of scythe-wielding spirits.

This time, Adam didn't hesitate to move past the split rail fence and approach the trailer. Sara watched them. She sat back in her chair, rocked a little, and smiled.

"What have you brought me, Adam Binder?" she asked. "One of mine?"

"Yours?" Adam asked.

She smiled, stood, and never seemed to stop standing. Sara

stretched. Blackness unfurled around her, cloaking her, cloaking everything. The light, always so liquid in the spirit realm, fled from her.

Adam staggered back, tugging Vic with him, but the Reapers had drifted closer. They formed a wall of black robes and bone masks. He whirled from side to side, but came back to Sara as a long robe of shadows coalesced around her.

The door to the trailer opened. The blackness beyond was deeper, more perfect, than anything Adam had ever seen.

"Won't you come in?" Death asked, her voice unchanged, still pleasant, still laced with southern kindness. Sara's spectacles still perched on her face, though no nose held them up.

Vic gripped Adam's hand. He looked like he might bolt. Behind them, the Reapers had not moved, but Adam did not doubt they could. Sara hadn't been keeping them back with wards or spells. She was Death. She commanded them.

Forward, through the darkness, was the only path, regardless of who had led them to it. Adam held tight to Vic. Whatever lay beyond, he wouldn't go alone. Wouldn't send Vic alone.

"It's going to be all right," he whispered. *I think.*

Hands held tight, they stepped through the door.

36

ADAM

Adam had thought Sara's trailer would contain the goddesses he'd always sensed around her. But he knew now that was camouflage, a way to disguise her true nature.

So he wasn't surprised when they stepped out of a crypt and into a cemetery. It looked old. The trees, crooked, were nearly dead. A grove of Egyptian-style obelisks overlooked grave markers carved to look like tree trunks. There was even a log cabin. It smelled terrible. A power plant rose in the distance and an auto salvage yard across the street.

"Is that an oil refinery?" he muttered.

They weren't in the mortal world, and they weren't in spirit. This was somewhere between, another layer in the sandwich, but just beneath the mortal plane. Sights, sounds, and smells, especially smells, leaked through. Adam suspected this was where Death did her work, where she'd been watching him from. No wonder her magic, her real magic, was so hard to spot.

"What is that?" Adam asked, gagging. "It smells like sewage and dog food."

"It is actually," Sara said. "The sewage treatment plant and the pet food factory are both nearby. Not having a nose, I tend to forget."

"Where are we?" Vic asked.

"Riverside Cemetery. Fascinating history," Sara said. "We should go for burritos when our business is concluded. There's a great place a little upwind. Your mother would approve, Vicente."

"You know my mother?" he asked.

"I know everyone," she said, her voice still sunny and southern. "And everyone's mother."

Adam had known Sara for years. And yet, he'd never bought anything from her. The price was too high. Had Aunt Sue? Had anyone? Or was it all just a ruse?

Sara resumed her human form, though she still wore the black robe and her steps left no press in the short, dead grass beneath their feet. She exuded no power at all, appearing even more normal than Adam. In some ways, she felt like power's opposite. A black hole. Like the spirit, but not starved or mad, just naturally consuming, the terminus. The end.

Adam inched closer to Vic.

"You're Death," Vic said.

Sara shrugged. "Yes."

"And all of this is your doing," Adam said. "The spirit, the broken seal?"

"Yes," she said. "I paid the warlock to break the seal."

She'd known him. She knew who he was. He wanted to ask so many questions, but what came out was, "What does Vic have to do with any of it?"

"Oh, he's just a bonus," Sara said. She produced a glass of iced tea from the air. That little fold in space didn't cause as much as a ripple to Adam's perceptions.

She looked at Vic. "You're a Reaper, Vicente. You work for me now."

"That's not—" Adam said. "No."

Sara narrowed her gaze on him. "It's your own doing. When you interfered and saved him, he joined my team. That's how it works. You broke a rule and there are consequences for that. Consequences for both of you."

Adam had known of course. Even with their connection, the days in the hospital, he'd known the price had to be higher. Adam put his hand behind him, tried not to exhale or show his relief when Vic tightened his hold on Adam's hand, but Adam felt him tremble.

"What does this mean, exactly?" Vic asked.

"It means you get to go back to work," Sara said, her smile pleasant. "It means you get to live, be a police officer. And from time to time, when the death is extraordinary, you'll claim a life for me."

Vic looked from her to Adam.

"That's it?" Vic asked. Adam squeezed his hand to send a warning.

"What else would there be?" she asked, dipping a shoulder in a graceful shrug.

"You don't want his soul or something?" Adam asked.

Sara's nose wrinkled, like she'd scented something unpleasant.

"I have no need for souls," she said, sounding offended. "They aren't trading cards."

"Huh," Adam said. That was twice he'd asked about souls and gotten a weird reaction from an immortal. He filed that mystery away for another day.

"So Vic's not a part of it."

"He is now," she said. Her smile was sharp this time. "I wasn't expecting you to do what you did, but I can't complain. You'll need backup for what's ahead and a shoulder for the fallout, I suspect."

"Why did you free the spirit?" Adam asked. "It's killed a lot of people."

Sara's eyes narrowed.

"It was outside the rules," she said. "It had to be corporeal again, alive again, for me to claim it."

"Why Annie?" Adam asked. 'What did she do to deserve this?"

"Nothing, honey," Sara said. "Nothing at all. It wasn't supposed to be her. I thought the spirit would possess your brother. Or you."

"Bobby? Why?"

"It takes just the right mix, you see," Sara said. "Just a drop of elf, diluted over eons. Genetic markers, your brother would call them. Too little and the body can't contain the spirit. It burns out too fast. Too much and the possession isn't complete, the possessed can fight it off. It needed to be complete, alive."

Elf blood. Him? It sort of made sense, that practitioners would have a little immortal in them, but if that was the case why wasn't Bobby like him?

Adam set it aside. Now wasn't the time to obsess about the old questions.

"So you can kill it," he said. "That's what you want to do right?"

"No, Adam, honey, so I can *claim* it. Killing it is your job."

"Why?" he spat. "Why me?"

Surely this fell to the Guardians. They were equipped to fight it.

"The markers. Pay attention. The spirit was supposed to possess your brother. Then you'd kill him. That's why I talked him into committing you all those years ago, so you'd hate him and have no trouble pulling the trigger."

Adam clenched his fist as she continued.

"Magic can't stop it. Mortals can't stop it. It takes just the right mix, the right breeding. I've spent centuries crafting your bloodline, then the damn thing seizes your sister-in-law."

"But why Adam?" Vic asked.

"So he can bind it. You must seal the spirit in the flesh before you kill it. That is the only way to ensure it doesn't escape me again."

The recipe. The arrows. Bog iron, bone or glass. The cost to his soul.

"I won't do it," he said.

"Suit yourself," she said, her smile flattening to a line. "It's already destroyed one watchtower. Give it the chance and it will bring them all down. It will tear down all life. It doesn't matter much to me. In the end, you're all mine. But if you delay, well it'll be a bumper crop this year."

"Why did you set it free?" Adam asked. "It was safe in the ground, where the elves put it. You could have left it there."

He saw real anger in her brown eyes. Her round features, always so pleasant pinched. Adam felt no power, no sign of force, but at her expression, he didn't doubt there was cold steel in her, a core of something hard and unforgiving.

"It broke the rules," she said coldly. "Evaded me, and I can't stand for that."

There was more to it, Adam felt certain, but he didn't press. She wouldn't tell him for free, and he was already shaking from what she wanted of him.

"You have everything you need," she said, her tone sharpening. The light around them dimmed, the graveyard going dark. "Make it quick. Make it painless. But however it happens, it dies. We'll skip the burritos this time."

Then they were elsewhere. No doors, no rush of power or change in the air. They stood in Bobby's basement.

Adam wanted to weep. He wanted to throw himself into Vic's arms or face down on the floor, but they had no time. If Annie was an imperfect host, the spirit would hunt for a better fit.

"We have to get to Bobby," he said.

37

ADAM

It *was* like driving a refrigerator. Adam put the pedal of Annie's white box to the ground.

"He's still not picking up," Vic said from the passenger seat, where he had Adam's phone pressed to his ear.

Adam hadn't asked if Officer Martinez would be able to get them out of a speeding ticket. At least red lights in Denver seemed to mean two or three cars went after they'd changed from yellow.

They had to get to Bobby, to the hospital. In that moment, Adam would have made any bargain to have Argent's power, anything to reach Mercy faster, to save Bobby and Annie.

"Almost there," Adam spat through gritted teeth. The Spanish-style building loomed ahead. "Almost—"

A boom cut him off. The car squealed to a stop, the windows shaking. Screams, car alarms, and a wave of magical force followed the blast.

Vic was making another call, using his cop voice, but Adam was out the door, on the street. He left the bow behind. What point did it have without arrowheads? Annie was here.

Across the street, the pavilion in front of the hospital, where patients were picked up and dropped off, was on fire.

Adam ran for the doors as another wave broke. The hospital windows buckled, rippled, and shattered.

Glass rained down, tinkling like ice, and in the aftermath, a voice sang, "Come out. Come out."

Annie.

Adam started forward, but lurched to a halt when Vic grabbed his arm.

"What are you going to do?" Vic demanded.

Adam pulled the seal shard from his pocket.

"What I have to."

A gunshot sounded. Another. Security had rallied. Sirens sang in the distance.

It couldn't be that easy, could it?

A guard flew. He landed with a wet crunch atop a parked car.

Vic rushed to check on the man, getting his phone from his pocket to call for help.

Adam watched him as if time had frozen. Commanding, concerned, and in charge.

Yeah, Adam could love him, if they lived through this.

He ran for Mercy and found her by the nimbus of magic, the sallow heat haze, pouring off her. She stood between the wrecked pavilion and the hospital's entrance, singing her song.

Annie did not have much time. Adam's Sight showed the spirit overlaying her body, barely contained by her too-weak flesh. It tore, then healed, then tore again. The bullet holes closed. If there were any true mercy, she wasn't conscious. It had to be agony. Adam's heart broke for her, this cheery woman whose only mistake had been to marry his brother and want a family. This woman he had to kill.

He ran at her. A great crack appeared in Annie's cheek. Blood flowed. Then it closed.

Maybe he was the mercy.

Adam drew the shard from his pocket as he ran, intending to drive it into her back, as quick as he could.

Of course Bobby chose that moment to come outside. He walked out of the hospital's main doors, his lab coat bright white.

Annie fixed on Bobby. Bloody, filthy, her mouth opened to a nasty grin. Her jaw slid open, wrong, like Mercy wasn't used to human teeth.

Bobby gaped, eyes wide as the whole truth of the scene settled upon him.

It was now or never.

The car closest to Adam exploded. His ears rang, like a gun had gone off nearby. Smoke and dust filled the air. He could taste burning plastic, burning gasoline.

The force had knocked him to the ground. He thought maybe a few of his bones had cracked, but worse, he'd dropped the shard.

Adam! Vic screamed silently, his worry and panic like a knife in Adam's heart.

I'm fine, he called through their connection. *Stay back, please.*

If she hurt Vic—he couldn't take that, not atop what he had to do.

Annie—the spirit—laughed. She turned, took a step toward him, the spirit tendrils erupting from her like the tentacles of an octopus.

"Adam!" Bobby called.

"Run," Adam spat through gritted teeth.

Annie strode toward him, her face split and closed. Soon. She'd burn away soon. Her foot came down on the shard and the obsidian shattered into pieces. She lowered her eyes, full of blood and yellow, on him. The corona of tentacles undulated.

Something gray and shining fell from the hospital's roof. Annie paused as Argent collided with the ground, making a web of cracks in the concrete. She leaked magic, glowing like a falling star.

"Hungry?" she asked, holding her empty hands open, baiting the spirit with her life.

No.

Adam forced himself to sit upright.

Mad-eyed, howling, Annie darted, propelled forward by impossible speed. Adam heard a bone snap.

Argent dodged and leapt away, leaving Annie at a distance, her leg crooked, her face twisted with rage and pain.

Annie charged again, ignoring the broken leg. Argent dodged again, but it had been close. Adam read the hunger in Annie's jaundiced eyes. It wanted Argent. It wanted her magic.

"Don't let her touch you!" Adam shouted, pulling himself to his feet

"Thank you, Adam!" Argent shouted back, leaping to land atop a parked car. "I got that part."

Annie continued to chase Argent, scrambling with singular focus. Adam would never catch her, not on foot, and the shard lay in pieces, slivers—

Like glass. Like arrowheads.

Bobby reached him as he scooped up the shards.

"What are you doing?" Bobby asked, his voice torn. He looked ragged, wild-eyed as he demanded, "What about Annie?"

"Help me," Adam said. "This is the only thing that can stop her."

Annie blew up another car. Argent, in midleap, landed awkwardly on the ground. She only looked stunned, but it was long enough for Annie to start toward her, slowed by the broken leg, but not enough.

"You want magic?" Adam shouted. He lifted a chunk of broken sidewalk and threw it with all his might. It connected with the center of Annie's back. She swiveled, stared at him. "How about mine, asshole?"

Annie hissed, a screeching inhuman sound. It might have been intended as a roar, but the spirit hadn't seemed to master vocal cords. She lurched in Adam's direction, slowed only by the broken leg.

She was almost to Adam when a voice shouted, "Annie!"

"No, Bobby!"

"Annie, please," Bobby said. Sobbing, he took her by the shoulder before Adam could stop him.

She wrapped her empty hand around Bobby's wrist. His eyes went white. The tendrils lashed, driving into Bobby. They began to swell, to move the spirit from the dying host to the new.

Adam reached Annie. Bobby's lids were fluttering. Adam drove the largest of the shards into Annie's neck.

She roared her raspy screech and batted Adam away with her free hand. The magic swirled around her, wild and pulsating. She dropped Bobby and tore out the sliver. It wasn't enough. She had to be bound.

Annie vanished, fleeing into the spirit realm where Adam could not chase her.

She ran away, heading for downtown and the cover of the debris cloud.

Adam rushed to Bobby. His brother lay on the ground, his eyes closed, but the slight rise and fall of his chest said he was alive.

"What did she do to him?" Vic asked, catching up, a wall of cops behind him.

"She drained the magic from him," Argent said, reaching them at the same time. "However much he had, it's gone now."

*****

Vic stayed to help sort the damage. Adam and Argent watched Bobby be admitted and given a room, and then lie pale in a bed.

They'd made calls. Jesse would bring Adam's mother. He'd stay with Bobby until she came.

"Are you all right?" Argent asked, watching the light of the monitors. Adam had opened the blinds, let the sunset light the room.

It should have been beautiful.

"No," he said.

They said nothing for a long while. In whispers, he conveyed what Death had told them, what she'd planned for the brothers, what she'd done.

That cop with the broken back, the people terrorized and hurt by the explosions, Bobby. Annie. It was all on her, and his father. And Death was Vic's new boss, just to twist the knife in Adam's gut a little harder.

"We keep underestimating its intelligence," Adam said. "It wanted a new host, but you distracted it. It wants magic more."

"Even though it was nearly bursting," Argent said. "Did you see?"

"Yeah," he said. "Healing or not, Annie can't contain it."

"It craves its former stature, and it's quite mad. It will not stop."

Adam chewed his lip. He couldn't say exactly what Argent was to him, a mentor or a friend. He settled on friend. An elf, sure, but he could be friends with elves. He did not want to consider what that made Silver. A friendly ex, maybe?

Neither would talk to him once he did what he had to do. They may even come after him.

She raised an eyebrow at him, as if to watch his thought process churn.

"Be careful, okay?" Adam asked.

"All right, Adam Binder, I shall do my best to not die," she said.

They stood in silence for a while, watching Bobby, watching over him.

"What about the hospital?" Adam asked. "The other people?"

"It's bad," she said. "But not as bad as it could have been. We contained the damage. We're telling the media it was a gas leak."

"Will they buy that?"

She shrugged. "It's worked before. If we must, we will change memories. It is part of the Guardians' duties to keep the mortal world safe."

"You can manipulate minds?" Adam asked.

"There are spells for it, though I hesitate to use them. They dip into the black."

Adam wondered if Bobby woke, would he prefer to not remember any of this. To forget seeing Adam again or his failure to rescue Annie? Maybe he'd prefer to forget Annie herself and just start his perfect life over again. And maybe that would be easier in light of what Adam had to do.

He'd brought the bow and arrows from the car. He took the shards from his jacket pocket, laid them out on the rolling table beside Bobby's bed.

He read the recipe one more time. Sara, Death, hadn't lied. He had everything he needed.

"I'm sorry," he said to his sleeping brother. It was one thing that he hadn't been able to save her. It was quite another that he was planning to kill her.

38

ADAM

At fifteen, Adam Binder sat in yet another pointless class taught by another teacher whose name he could barely remember. He'd picked a desk with a good sunbeam and dozed like a cat, eyes almost shut, letting the sights and sounds of the Other Side ease the press around him.

Who liked who? Who'd had sex? Who hadn't? Who likely never would? The jocks, the posturing, the ambitious, the nervous. It was a daily, eight-hour onslaught relieved only by lunch and the happy grind and clank of auto shop.

The intercom, tinny and antique, broke the spell of his happy drifting, "Adam Binder, please report to the counselor's office."

"Adam!" the teacher snapped.

Clearly the intercom had already sounded once or twice.

"Going," he muttered, scooping up his backpack. He hadn't taken anything out of it.

His grades just weren't something he thought about. He'd drifted through the world, for a year, from school, to the bus home, to his room. All the while, the Other Side called to him. It started with a faint glow, a white nimbus outlining people.

Sometimes, it felt like he was spinning inside his body, that if he could just step sideways, in the right direction, he'd be free.

He floated through school, doing his best to keep his head down, especially in gym class during shirts and skin activities. The only thing worse than being a space case was being gay. Better to drift, half-asleep—than out himself by staring too long at a guy and dealing with the consequences—until he graduated.

"Adam!" the teacher called again.

He focused, found the class on pause, staring at him, some with faces of disgust, more than one with laughter. It stabbed into him, bright and cold at the same time. Cruel, it reminded him of his dad.

He forced himself to stay in his body, in the moment. It took a lot. He was tired, always so tired, from those moments of effort.

"Stoner," someone muttered.

He wasn't, not that it mattered to them. Adam wiped the drool from his mouth and exited. Where—

Right. Counselor's office.

He expected expulsion. He sort of welcomed it. He'd never belonged here, and escaping the teenage turmoil might clear his head.

What he hadn't expected, when he pushed open the door to the office, was Bobby. Adam's brother sat talking to the counselor, Mrs. Pearce, a pleasant black woman who always smiled at Adam like she knew him. Like anyone knew him.

Bobby only half-turned his head when Adam entered. What Adam felt from him, resolution like raw iron and some blue feeling he couldn't name, was a sobering mix.

"It was good to see you again," Bobby said to Mrs. Pearce. "Let's go, Adam."

Bobby carried a paper shopping bag. Adam guessed it held the meager contents of his locker.

"Where?" he asked, looking to the counselor. Her smile, terse today, flattened as she looked down at a stack of papers on her desk.

She wasn't memorable, his counselor. She didn't really even seem to react when he saw her. Her name dropped like a fish into water.

"Where are we going?" Adam asked Bobby, following him out.

Outside, he caught the smell of roses, of blooming flowers, so cloying that he almost gagged. He sneezed, even though the school had little green and the blooming field of toothed snapdragons should have been a parking lot. Another vision, another delusion.

"You haven't been taking your medication," Bobby said. "Have you?"

Adam was distracted by a four winged, two-headed eagle. Pretty. It saw him too.

Bobby sighed and led Adam to his car, something dark, something battered and Japanese.

"I hope you're happy," Bobby said as Adam settled into the passenger seat, his head pressed to the closed window. The tinted glass felt warm against the skin of his face. "I had to drive down from Norman for this."

Bobby went to Oklahoma University in Norman. He said "Norman" like he was proud of it, like it wasn't a football-obsessed enclave for jocks and morons.

"I'll have to make up a test," Bobby said.

"Sorry," Adam said.

Bobby liked taking tests. He liked being right. He liked proving it, having it on paper.

In the distance, in the fields, Adam saw figures. Sometimes they were almost too far to make out their features. Then he'd blink, and they'd be so close he could count their nose hairs. Old men, young women. Children. They wore the timeless clothes of the rural poor. They might be the ghosts of pioneers, the first settlers in Oklahoma during the land rush, which they'd acted out every year in elementary school.

A dragon snatched one up. A second dragon fought the

first for the prize. Adam blinked and the landscape returned to oak-dotted plains. It took him a while, struggling to sort this from that, to discern that they weren't headed for the trailer, for home and another night of Mom working late or locking herself in her room to whisper white, gauzy prayers, her hopes. Once there'd been the red of Dad, his anger and the brighter yellows of his happy or funny moments. Since he'd gone, and Bobby had gone off to college, there had only been blue when it came to Mom.

"Where are we going?" Adam asked . . . the first time? The fifteenth? He wasn't sure.

"It's near the lake," Bobby said, turning off the main road.

Adam didn't have to ask which lake. He didn't have to ask which end. Their end was the poor end, no real dock except the one Dad had built, now fallen apart, and no houses, just scrub oak and snakes. Still, their trailer was a short walk.

The spirit roared back, washing away the real world. Adam saw the fields, the endless grass on both sides, mixing with forests and waves of flood water, though it hadn't rained in weeks.

He'd had too much. He needed to sleep, to reset his sanity before another day.

Then the spirit water receded. Around it, cottonwood trees sprinkled white across the air. It mixed with the fireflies from the spirit realm until the house solidified. It looked like a plantation home out of the Gothic South, like something from *Gone with the Wind*. Only this home had no grandeur.

It was more like a varsity athlete gone to seed. It could have been a contender, once. Time had worn away the paint on the large wooden pillars lining the front. The tall doors stood open at a crack. The wind didn't shift them. They looked too thick and sturdy, designed to keep things inside. The lake water lent everything an odor of sweet dampness tinged with rot.

Gnats swarmed in clouds across the yard, which was filled

with mud puddles and yellowed, uncut grass. The mailbox, a brick column nearly Adam's height, sported a brass plaque that could use a cleaning. Its address, 1212 Seward Road, lay beneath its name: Liberty House.

"What is this?" Adam asked as Bobby pulled into the driveway, which was just bricks pressed into the mud. The car tires ran like a thumb over a washboard.

"Your new school," Bobby said. "They can help you."

"This dump?" Adam demanded, taking in the faded, peeling paint and the curling wooden shingles. The whole place had an air of rot, or age and faded glory.

"It's a modern school. I'm amazed it's out here. And it's close to Mom. She can see you anytime you want. She'll bring your clothes and things later."

Then Adam understood the blue feeling Bobby had hid under that resolution. Guilt.

39

BOBBY

Bobby ran beneath the scrub oak, along sandy paths flecked with bits of their gray-black bark. Some sense told him to hurry, that he had to hurry home. He went from tree shade to sunny clearings. He'd always avoided those bright patches and kept off the rocks. Rattlesnakes liked to sunbathe atop them.

He avoided the tall grass for the same reason, didn't take any shortcuts but stuck to the sandy path. They didn't have a fence, but the former owner had buried old car hoods in the path to tell Bobby when he'd crossed back onto the Binders' property.

The trailer came into sight, a long, shabby box without a skirt. His parents had piled sandstones into rings, cemented them together with concrete and filled them with dirt to make planters. It added some decoration to the mud and weeds, but the flowers his mother planted withered in the shade of the oak trees.

They sprouted from the ground in clumps of three or five, casting shade over the trailer, but not quite so much that they didn't run the window air conditioning units or that his mother didn't tape aluminum foil and black plastic over most of the windows to keep the heat out.

Bobby passed the shed where his dad stored all the fishing gear and the tent they never used since a cow had peed on it. Carried on skinny legs. Bobby heard a sound he knew too well, the slap of leather on skin. Adam wailed.

"I told you not to cry," his dad said. Another slap. "And I'm going to keep going until you stop crying, you little faggot."

Another slap. Another wail from Adam.

Bobby's feet, too slow, carried him up the wooden steps Dad had built for them to reach the trailer door.

Inside, Dad held a squirming Adam across his knees with one arm. His bare bottom, red and welted, lay exposed to the air. Dad didn't see Bobby. He had his back to the door. How did he not hear him, with his heart beating so hard in his chest?

"I told you," Dad repeated.

The belt slapped again. Adam sobbed.

Mom cowered in the kitchen, her eyes warning Bobby not to interrupt.

Last time, Dad had put him in a sleeper hold until he'd passed out. Then he'd gone back to beating Adam.

Their father had wrestled in high school. He'd always been proud of that, liked to brag that he could have gone professional if not for Bobby, if not for getting Tilla Mae pregnant in their senior year.

Bobby remembered the feel of Dad's hairy, sweaty arm around his neck, and the words before he slipped into darkness, "Next time you won't wake up."

Mom's eyes flicked to the windowsill. A hammer and a box of nails sat there, dusty, waiting for Dad to fix the loose curtain rod like she'd asked him to a dozen times.

Bobby stood frozen in the doorway, the windowsill, the hammer a few feet away.

Do it. Her voice, silent, was as clear as if she'd spoken aloud.

His eyes met hers.

Do it.

Dad had his back to Bobby. He sat on the couch, Adam stretched across his knees. Bobby didn't think Dad even knew he'd come in.

The belt came down again, and again, slapping against Adam's ass. He wailed, weeping and begging Dad to stop.

Bobby stopped thinking. He grabbed the hammer. He swung. The impact with Dad's skull made a dull, almost squishy sound. Another swing, harder, and a crunch, against something that gave way.

Dad stood. He staggered. He fell to the floor and did not move again. Adam rolled to the floor. He fell silent. The world fell silent.

Bobby exhaled. It was like there was air again, like he'd been drowning and reached the surface.

"Bobby," his mother said from what felt like somewhere far away. He didn't answer. He didn't move.

"Bobby Jack," she repeated. "Give me that."

Numb, slow, like he'd been the one struck, Bobby passed her the hammer.

"Take your brother to your room," she said. "Then come help me."

Bobby remembered how to make his legs work. He found Adam, still crying and curled up in front of the couch. He made no sound, didn't fight when Bobby scooped him into his arms.

Walking stiffly, awkward with his brother's weight, Bobby took Adam to their room, tucked him into the lower bunk.

He was so small, like a miniature person.

"Stay here," Bobby whispered. "It's going to be all right."

He didn't know why he said it, only that it was the sort of thing you were supposed to say, but Adam nodded.

Outside, his mother had taken her husband by his feet.

"Get his arms," she said.

Together, they dragged him outside, over the hard ground, rocks and soil digging at him.

"Where are we going?" Bobby asked, gulping air from the exertion. They'd made it about ten feet. Dad, the body, weighed too much.

"Out back," she said. "To the pond."

He knew where she meant. A little gulley led to a hollow, a dip in the land that lay dry most of the year. When it wasn't, they caught tadpoles there, came back to see them become frogs.

"Wait here," Bobby said.

He hadn't touched the ATV since Dad had bought it. It sat in the shed, beneath an old tarp. Dad would start it from time to time, to keep it working, but he never rode it.

Together, Bobby and Tilla wrapped the body in the tarp. Bobby wound it in ropes and hitched it to the back of the four-wheeler. All of it, every bit of the work, went sluggish and hard.

Bobby drove into the woods. Mom walked behind. No one would think of the noise as out of place, not in the country.

He kept thinking of Adam, alone in the trailer, hopefully asleep after crying himself out. Hopefully he did not awake alone. Hopefully, he wouldn't remember what Bobby had done.

The tarp was mud- and grass-covered when they reached the pond. Bobby tried to ignore the shape when they had him placed in the dry bottom. There were granite stones there, all different sizes. Without a word, Tilla shifted them. Lead-limbed, Bobby helped.

They kept it up long after he was buried, long after the tarp and its contents were gone from view. Then they hauled dead wood, the fallen oaks Dad always said he'd cut and sell as firewood.

It was dark when they went back to the trailer. Bobby drove slowly, not wanting to leave his mother behind. He watched for drag marks, but the grass had already started to spring back from where they'd crushed it. A few good rains and the mud would swallow any trace. It would fill the hollow. There'd be animals, the feral dogs that roamed the woods, and maybe coyotes, but they wouldn't easily shift the cairn Bobby and Tilla had piled.

"What do we do now?" Bobby asked her, as they climbed the little porch.

"We go on," she said. "You're the man of the house now, Bobby Jack."

In the little room he shared with Adam, the tears came. The afternoon had already faded. He thought the sheriff would come, that someone would call, yelling, "Murderer. Murderer."

But they did not come. Not that night, not in the week that followed. They didn't speak of it, and slowly, Mom burned his papers and his things along with their other garbage, in the cinder block furnace behind the trailer. Still no one came.

When Bobby came home at twilight, he'd spy the orange starburst of his mother's lit cigarette. She always seemed to be out there, smoking on the steps, staring into the dark. Maybe she was waiting for someone to come too.

No one did. No one cared that a white trash man lay buried in a dry pond beneath a pile of stones. Bobby skirted it, did his best to forget it existed. Adam did not ask to go see if the August rains had started to fill it up.

He would not leave Bobby's side. At night he insisted on sleeping in Bobby's bunk, curled against his older brother, too hot, like he ran a fever. Though it made Bobby sweat, he didn't make Adam move, let him stay put. When Adam stirred, restless, Bobby would hold him closer and whisper into his sandy hair.

By day, Adam often asked when Dad would come home.

Mom would shush him, but Bobby would say, "It's just us now, Adam Lee."

40

ROBERT

He'd always known he'd never get to escape. Not really, not after he'd killed his father.

He sat in darkness. It smelled of antiseptic, too sweet, like candy mixed with bleach.

It never lightened. His eyes did not adjust. He didn't know how many hours he'd listened to his own heartbeat, listening to his own breathing. He felt the floor beneath him, found thin, almost imperceptible lines. The slick, waxy feel of Formica or vinyl, something synthetic, not wood or stone.

He crawled, cautious, until he found a wall. Cinder blocks, by the cold feel and rough, gritty texture. Hands lifted to make sure he didn't bang his head, Robert stood. He stretched, but felt no ceiling.

He wanted to call out, shout for help, but every instinct told him not to, that there were *things* listening, watching for something just like him. So he kept quiet, and circled the room. He bumped into no furniture, felt no window. He exhaled, too loudly for comfort, when his hands found a door. The knob, cold aluminum or some other metal, surprised him by turning. It was unlocked.

Robert swung the door open and stepped into a hallway.

Finally, some light. Incandescent bulbs hung at intervals above him. Some were out. The rest were yellow. They buzzed as they cast a sallow, flickering glow over the hallway. Painted green halfway up and white above, the place tugged at Bobby's memory, but he did not recognize it. The floor, gray flecked with white, was old, cracked and gouged.

There were doors to other rooms, but he did not open them, felt he *must* not open them. He didn't feel thirsty or hungry. Ahead, double swinging doors, like at the hospital, stood closed. More and more this place felt familiar, and yet he did not know it.

No light peeked from beyond the doors ahead. Robert straightened at the sight of them, at the chill running down his spine at the perfect black beyond their round glass windows.

"Not that way then," he muttered.

He turned to reverse course, and the doors creaked open.

"Hello, Robert," a voice said. A petite black woman stepped out of the darkness beyond.

"Mrs. Pearce?"

His high school counselor, who'd set him on the road to college, to freedom, who'd helped him get Adam into Liberty House.

"Yes, Bobby," she said. "That's the name you knew me by."

His skin crawled. He felt the need to run, to scurry back into the dark. He took a backward step.

"What are you?" he asked.

"I am inevitable," she said. Smiling, she extended a hand.

He did not take it. She shrugged, didn't seem offended.

"You haven't aged." He said, scanning her eyes for circles, or crow's feet. Her hair no more gray now than it had when he'd been in high school.

"Well, ain't you sweet," she said.

"Why am I here?" he asked.

"The long version is that a long time ago, something tried to escape me. In its defense, it predated the natural rules, so it was grandfathered in and allowed to linger. That needled me. So I engineered a solution, maneuvering this witch and that, letting you all do what's predictable when you put horny mortals together, until I had the results I needed." Pausing, she removed her glasses, polished them on her shirt, and took a long breath. "The short version is that you sort of died."

"Sort of?" he asked. "I'm in a coma."

"That is astute, Doctor Binder." She put her glasses back. "The spirit took quite a bite out of you. Specifically, it took the magic out of you. As I'm certain you're tired of your family's witches saying, magic is life."

He nodded. Sue and Adam had muttered the expression from time to time. He'd always thought it sounded a little cultish, hadn't known they'd meant it literally.

"Am I going to recover?"

"The prognosis isn't great," she said. "Normally I wouldn't drop by personally, but I feel I owe you, after the whole thing with your wife and your brother."

"You talked me into sending Adam to Liberty House," Bobby said, his chest tightening. He clenched his fists. He hadn't felt this angry since—since his dad. Bobby relaxed his grip.

"He hates me for it," he said, almost quietly, almost a whisper.

"Oh, I did far worse than that," she said. She sighed. "I made him hate you."

"Why are you telling me all of this?" Robert asked.

"I felt I owed you an explanation," she said. "You've been

a good tool, you and your family. I like to see my tools put to proper rest when their use is done."

"What does that mean?" he asked as she pushed the door into the blackness open. "What happens to me?"

"Just wait here," she said, smiling over her shoulder. "Someone will be along for you shortly."

41

ADAM

Adam pulled the string and fired. The arrow lodged into the paper target.

"Nice shot," Vic said.

"Thanks," Adam said, still feeling the stretch in his arms. "We grew up with these."

"You're really going to do this?" Vic asked.

Adam plucked another arrow from the quiver. He'd picked up a few normal ones to practice with.

"Do I have a choice?" he asked before turning and firing again.

And it was so much worse than Vic knew.

The hardware store had had what he needed: caulk and a heavy hammer. He'd taken the bog iron from Bobby's mantel, pounded it to bits with the hammer, and ground it together with the shards, obsidian, black glass. He'd added the caulk and his own blood, his fingertips bleeding as he shaped the arrowheads. Because it took blood. Of course it did. He had the shard from the hospital, the one he'd stabbed Annie with. It had her blood on it, but he would not use that.

Now they lay drying while he practiced.

His hands shook, sending the second arrow wide. It bounced off Bobby's privacy fence. He'd probably complain, though Adam was using harmless practice arrows. They barely left a divot in the pine.

Just the thought of his brother gripped Adam's heart in black. Sara had set this all in motion. She'd left him no choice, steered him to a point of no return. And Sue. He thought back on all her comments about his dad, all his attempts to learn from her.

His heart ached to think she could have known, could have offered him up, had any part in Death's long game. Adam's sight was shiny with welling tears.

"He's not dead," Vic said, sensing Adam's grief but misreading its target. He stepped closer, wrapped his arms around Adam and pulled the bow out of his hands.

"But he won't wake up," Adam said. He considered jerking away. Sensing that, too, Vic tightened his grip.

"I woke up," he said into Adam's hair. "You woke up."

Adam pulled again, but Vic tightened his arms, even though Adam felt it hurt his stitches.

"Stay," Vic said.

"I'm not a puppy," Adam whispered.

"No, you're not," Vic said. "And I can't let you kill a woman, even if she is possessed."

"You heard her," Adam said. "Death."

"I'm still a cop," Vic said. "I'm still a law enforcement officer."

"So, what, we're supposed to cuff her?" Adam asked.

There's still time to save her.

Had Dad's note lied?

"No," Vic said. "But there has to be another way."

"I don't see one," Adam said, twisting in Vic's arms so he could look him in the eyes. "I don't see another way, and she won't stop. She'll keep coming, and killing, and consuming."

He felt Vic work his way through the problem, come to the same terrible conclusion. Natural law had to supersede the laws of man, and the laws of magic.

First, do no harm.

Sue had told him that a hundred times, maybe a thousand.

"Dammit," Vic said, accent thick.

Adam hated that it had come to this. Vic had accepted so much about the situation, about Adam and magic and even becoming a Reaper, but this, this might be the thing that changed his mind, made him look away from Adam forever—when he found out Adam was about to turn warlock.

Light shimmered. Argent's white van appeared in the yard. The elf who'd driven them to the clock tower sat behind the wheel. She shot them an impatient glance.

"It's time," Adam said, gathering up the bow and arrows. "You don't have to come."

And he so wished Vic wouldn't. Adam didn't want him to see, didn't want Vic to be there. Because he had to do it. To save his brother, he'd do it, even though it would cost him everything.

In the end, Bobby was family, and Adam loved him.

"Let's go," he said.

*****

Silver had abandoned the ballroom for the fun house, a structure that no longer stood in the real world. Full of large wooden barrels and a sort of people-sized roulette wheel, Adam couldn't imagine how anyone had ever found such a place fun. To enter, they walked past a creepy, laughing marionette in a cage.

Seamus was there with a few of his fellow leprechauns. A few dwarves kept to the shadows. Adam hadn't seen them before, and they lived up to every stereotype he'd had. His heart lifted to see a pair of gnomes, though the aura of magic around them was dim.

And there were Saurians, a trio. The leader tipped his head and Adam smiled.

"Bill?" he asked.

"Yep," the big lizard replied, the Oklahoma drawl sounding odd coming from his toothy mouth.

"Why are you here?" Adam asked. The Saurians weren't among the Guardian races, at least not currently.

"Consider us character witnesses, if anyone doubts you."

"Thanks," Adam said, head dipping. "And thank you, for what you did."

He almost asked what Seamus had demanded to deliver the package, but he wasn't certain he could bear knowing. Nor did he want to know how Bill would react if he knew that the source of the charms, the source of the pain inflicted on one of the Saurians was likely Adam's own father.

"It was the right thing to do," Bill said. "After what you did for us."

"See?" Vic whispered as they walked on. "You do good, people do good for you."

Adam wasn't certain that was always true, but his steps lightened that Vic was there. Argent and Silver stood at the center of things, the light around them harsh, reflecting the tension in their stance.

"This place is a health and safety nightmare," Vic muttered, looking at the archaic amusements.

"We thought the bumper cars would be too distracting," Silver said.

Vic smiled, and Silver inclined his head in a friendly way.

At least they weren't fighting over him.

"You have a plan, Adam Binder?" Argent asked.

"We need bait," he said. "Get her to come after us."

"What do we use?" Seamus asked.

"Magic," Adam said. "Your magic. As bad as it wants me, it wants its power back more."

"So then it dies," Silver said. "What keeps it from escaping again, just going back to what it was?"

"I have to bind it," Adam said. He held up an arrow in his bandaged fingertips.

No one gasped. No one shouted "Warlock!" and tried to haul him to a dungeon. They fell perfectly silent, which felt so much worse.

"That binding takes a sacrifice," Argent said. "It takes the pain of a living thing."

"Which is why I used my own blood," Adam said.

"Adam . . ." Silver said, quietly, his sadness a blue cloud filling Adam like rain.

"What?" Vic asked. "What do they mean?"

"Adam will maim his soul," Argent said. "He'll be in pain if he makes the binding. Forever."

"I can take it," he said, looking around the room. "It was me or one of you. I may have to become a warlock, but I won't do that."

No one spoke then. The room stayed quiet until Argent asked, "When?"

"Now," Adam said. "Let's get this over with."

"I'll drive you," she said.

"Nothing too nice, please," Adam said, thinking of the Cutlass and trying to lighten the room's heavy air. "I don't want it to get crunched."

"Something domestic, then," Argent said. "If I must. But I'm not a taxi service."

"Yeah, you're not," Vic said. Adam felt him pick up on what Adam needed and chime in. "Your car is nicer."

"Cars, Vicente," Argent stressed. "Cars."

"No," Silver said, interrupting the banter. "This is my duty, sister."

They only clashed for a moment this time, and Adam was certain it was Argent who relented, yielding to her brother for once, because he needed it.

"Fine," she said.

42

ADAM

Dusk settled over downtown. The lights still shown in the theater district, but the debris and dust from the explosion still fogged the air. Adam could feel the remnants of the Gaoler's magic, his attempt to stop time, or at least slow it so others could escape.

Spirits no longer strolled or partied here. The clock tower's destruction had burned away the carnival feeling. The things he spied scurried or hid.

Silver stopped the Audi at the edge of downtown.

Something roared, loud and vibrating.

"What was that?" Vic asked.

"Manticore," Adam and Silver said together.

Adam was torn about his presence. He did not want the prince to come to harm, but without him, they had no way back to the mortal plane.

"Where should we make our stand?" Silver asked, unbuckling his seatbelt.

Adam had searched the internet, looking for the right spot. The open field among the classical structures would serve. He wished he'd called Aunt Sue again. If this was it, he'd had no chance to say goodbye.

"Civic Center Park," he said. "Lots of room to use a bow there."

"And to maneuver if anything big happens along," Vic said as the manticore roared again. He had his gun and baton. They weren't going to stop Annie, but he could slow anything else that might take an interest in them.

Silver parked, and they climbed out.

Dust flecked their hair and shoulders as they walked on. They reached the park, Silver, seeing better than them, stiffened. He threw out an arm to block their progress.

"Careful," he whispered.

Bones, massive and bare, filled the space. Crows, who seemed to have no trouble crossing worlds, had done their work, stripping the bones of flesh.

"What is this?" Vic asked, gaping at a rib cage that could have belonged to a whale. Several red-eyed crows sat atop it, silently watching.

"I think the spirit has been feeding," Silver said.

Vic drew his pistol, chambered a bullet. Adam slung the bow's case off his shoulder, biting down a comment. Vic was a cop, an expert. That didn't lessen Adam's feelings on the matter of firearms.

Shadows flew through the cloud, blotting out the gas street lamps and marquis signs.

"This is creepy," Vic said.

"Says the baby Reaper," Adam said.

"Rookie," Vic stressed.

"Are you ready, Silver?" Adam asked.

"Look away," he said. Adam obeyed and heard the ring as the knight unsheathed his sword.

White light burned through the dust and dusk. The former

prisoners of the clock tower, the flying things concealed in the cloud, fled the light with shrieks and hisses.

The raw magic was like a lighthouse beacon, shining into the sky.

The manticore roared.

"We have someone's attention," Vic said, pistol raised. "But do we have hers?"

Adam extended his senses, knowing the spirit may feel it, that he may add bait to the trap.

Silver had put away his aspect, but he still held a sword, long and willowy. They waited, listening, scanning the shadows between the shifts in the cloud that obscured the spirit moon.

Adam felt a tendril of cold hunger.

"She's here," he said.

Annie stepped into the arch at the park's end, about a hundred feet away. The spirit flickered around her like living fire, illuminating her in red and yellow. She still wore the clothes she'd on when they'd taken her to the clock tower. Filthy, burned, and blood covered, she moved with grace. The spirit had mastered the body, though still Annie could not contain it. Her hair had fallen out.

Adam nocked an arrow, drew the bow.

"You sure about this?" Vic asked.

"No," Adam said. He loosed the arrow.

The arrow struck her shoulder. Annie and the spirit, fully bound together, screeched, like a bird of prey or a cat in pain.

His dad had taught him this, to use a bow, expecting to take him hunting, that they could supplement the grocery bill with squirrels and rabbits. After the BB gun, after Dad left, Bobby had never made Adam shoot a living thing, but he'd enjoyed the practice, and the time spent with Bobby.

Adam could feel the arrowhead stuck in Annie's body. Part of the seal, the binding circle that had imprisoned the spirit for so long mixed with his iron and set in iron. Pain flared through him. He and Vic gasped together. Adam forced his sight to clear, to keep the pain and tears away. He scrambled to nock another arrow as Annie rushed them, using that impossible speed like she had at the hospital. Vic took aim at her. Silver lifted his sword.

Annie, the spirit, roared again, but this time a roar answered her.

The manticore dove out of the fog. It landed on the arch behind Annie with force enough to shake the piles of bones. A lion with a scorpion tale, it had leathery bat wings.

The manticore dove for Annie, its wings, blotting the haze-filtered moon.

The lion's mouth opened wide, ready to swallow her whole. Annie sidestepped the blow, and Adam shot her in the back. She roared again as the manticore sank its teeth into her shoulder. It should have killed her, but it was the beast that withered. Aging, it folded in on itself, until a skeleton of ancient bones collapsed around Annie as she drank its magic, its life. Annie straightened.

"Dammit, what good is it?" Adam asked. She'd just healed herself.

"Look," Silver said. "See."

The binding remained. The magic no longer exploded from her. It was contained, roiling, too hot, too much.

Adam shot her again, and the magic compressed even as he felt like he'd cut off a limb. The arrows weren't killing her, but they were sealing the power inside Annie, tightening the lid on the pressure cooker. They had to bring it to a boil.

She straightened, looked Adam in the eye.

"We have to get to the car!" Adam said, taking off at a run.

"Why?" Vic demanded.

"We need more magic," Adam said.

"Isn't that what she wants?" Vic asked.

"We have to push her over the edge."

"I can—" Silver started.

"That's not an option, your majesty," Adam said.

"It's my duty," Silver said, though he kept running with them, back toward the Audi.

"Yeah, I'm not big on that," Adam said. "Just ask the Reapers."

Annie had nearly caught up.

Vic turned, fired twice.

She went down.

"Keep moving!" he said, springing back into motion.

They piled into the car, Silver behind the wheel. Adam felt Annie before he saw her. She rose into the air, leaping in a great arc.

Silver floored it, racing down streets built for carriages. Annie crashed to the ground where they'd been parked, making a divot in the earth. Sealed or no, the spirit still had a lot of power.

"Where are we going?" Silver asked.

"Lookout Mountain!" Adam shouted.

"Why?" Vic demanded.

"Don't go too fast," Adam told Silver. "We don't want to lose her."

"I don't think that's going to be a problem," Vic said. In the mirror, she came on, running at that impossible speed.

Silver kept it floored. Adam took gulping breaths as a bat, then a larger flying beast, bounced off the windshield.

The pain in his chest was heaving.

"Are you all right?" Vic asked. Leaning forward, he set his hand on Adam's shoulder. Adam reached to lay his palm atop Vic's.

"I can manage it," he said. And he could.

They were out of the city. Silver crossed lanes, avoiding ghostly bison and a caravan of dinosaurs.

"What the . . ." Vic trailed off.

The signs to I-70 were like tiny moons. They glowed and burst into flame, burned out, and formed again. The mountain, a dwarf compared to the pine covered peaks behind it, rose ahead. Adam didn't look at the mortal side. He stayed focused on what lay ahead and what chased from behind.

Anticipating Silver's driving, Annie leapt again. She crashed atop the short trunk and ripped the top off the Audi. It wasn't Bobby's car anymore, but Adam still cringed. She cast the top aside with one hand, the other clawed into the trunk's hood. Vic shot her again, point blank, but she batted him aside, climbed over him, heading for Silver. Adam, seatbelt unbuckled, wrapped his fist around a third arrow and drove it into her chest. She screamed again, and tumbled off the car.

"Vic!" Adam shouted.

"Put your seatbelt on," Vic said, scrambling to retrieve his gun. "Your ex drives worse than his sister."

Lips a tight line, Silver cocked his head, but he kept his eyes on the road.

Adam obeyed as Vic sat up. He had a scratch across his face, but he seemed okay.

"Almost there," Silver said, turning off the highway into the hills.

The roar was like a city sinking into the ocean, like a volcanic eruption.

"We're here for your hoard!" Adam shouted, broadcasting it as loud as he could, as loud as he'd ever sent his timid just passing through.

The dragon bloated the emerald moon. Its skin was like footage of running lava, all molten and charred, but with cracks of fire shining where its scales joined. It was colossal, raw magic. It was the most beautiful, most terrifying thing Adam had ever seen.

"She's almost here!" Vic shouted.

Annie saw her leap in the mirror. At the same time, the dragon dove.

"Now, Silver!" Adam shouted.

The elf slammed on the brakes, so hard, Adam was certain his spirit would have whiplash.

Possessed woman and dragon met midair. Annie dug a hand into the dragon's scales. The dragon's roar deafened. Silver slammed the car into reverse and floored it again.

Adam and Vic twisted to see.

The dragon's fire, the light running between its scales, dimmed a little.

Annie glowed. The pain in the seal grew. Adam burned with her.

Too much. Too much.

He wasn't sure which of them thought it as Silver stopped the car.

The dragon, wounded, but not fatally, retreated.

She'd taken a small measure of its magic, but still it was—

Annie exploded into light.

The wave of force tore over Adam's defenses. He felt Silver's ward wrap the car, buffering the magic. The wave passed. Annie lay on the road.

The passenger door opened. Vic stepped out.

Blackness gathered around him, inky and creeping.

He didn't look like the other Reapers, not exactly. White-dotted lines made patterns, flowers and geometric shapes, on his robe.

Vic drew his baton, extended it, and it kept growing. The scythe blade swept open, cold and pale like true moonlight.

Adam watched Vic kneel over Annie, rise, and sweep her with the scythe.

Something fluttering, made of light, like a bird or butterfly, rose. It landed on Vic's open palm. He closed it, and he was himself again.

Annie.

She was gone.

43

BOBBY

Ten of the bulbs remained lit. Then nine. One by one, they dimmed and died. Bobby knew where he was now. This was Liberty House, the real Liberty House, as Adam had seen it. He followed echoes of laughter, avoided the shouts of madness. Above all, he kept his distance from the double doors and the darkness that lay beyond them. He still wasn't hungry. Hadn't needed to pee. He had some tenuous awareness of his body, but it felt faint. Occasionally there were small jabs of pain, needles, he suspected. That was his only real sense of time changing, of the world outside his prison.

He'd tried praying, something he hadn't done since he was little. He'd called to Adam, closed his eyes and said his brother's name, over and over. The one time he'd had magic, the ability to speak silently with his mother, he'd done something horrible with it and lost it forever.

Adam did not come. His mother did not come.

As alone as he felt, he did not want Mrs. Pearce, whatever she really was, to return.

Robert turned another corner and found Annie standing

there. She glowed. She wore jeans, a T-shirt, and looked so much more like herself than she had in a long time.

"Robert," she said with a beaming smile.

"Is it really you?" he asked. "Are you dead too?"

"You're not dead," she said. "Just sleeping."

She examined the water-stained walls, made a disgusted face. He couldn't really blame her.

"But I can't wake up," he said. "I've been trying. And the lights are going out."

"It's okay," she said, offering him a hand. "I brought what you need."

She stretched out a palm full of cotton candy. Well it looked like cotton candy, but it glowed, clung to her fingertips in wisps.

Bobby reached for it, for her, but paused just shy of taking her hand.

"It's magic," he said.

"It's life," she stressed, pressing it toward him.

"Whose?" he asked, reaching, tentatively, but not touching.

So many dreams, of their future together, their children. It had all gone wrong.

"I can't give it back," she said, bright eyes watery. "But I can at least do some good with it."

Robert chewed his lip. He'd chosen normal. He'd denied this part of himself his entire adult life. He'd wanted nothing to do with the shadows and magic since he'd killed his father at his mother's silent urging. The light flickered at her fingertips, curling away in wisps, a dimming warmth he did not have long to seize.

"I can't hold it forever," she said. "You have to decide."

"If I take that, I'll be like Adam," he said. The door to that world might never close.

"Would that be so bad?" she asked. "He loves you, your brother. And you love him."

"I . . ."

"And he needs you. I need you. Come back to us. Come home."

She was right. He had to live. The lights were going out. This was his chance. He could still make things right with Adam, show Annie how much he loved her.

Tears welling in his eyes, Robert—Bobby—took her hand.

He felt it, the moment the light poured into him. She had lied.

"Annie?" he asked, looking into her bright eyes.

"Live," she said, smiling as the lights winked out. "Live for me."

He woke, choking, gasping. Everything felt so stiff, his limbs and head were so heavy, but he felt—the catheter, the leads for the monitors. He was alive.

"Bobby?" a voice asked.

Robert opened his eyes.

Adam sat beside him. His eyes were sunken. He looked rough, beaten.

"You look like a raccoon," Bobby said.

"And you look like thirty miles of bad road," Adam snipped, but he smiled.

"Where's Mom?"

"Getting a smoke. Not happy she has to cross the street from the hospital to do it." Adam opened his mouth to speak, but he choked on the words, finally managed to say, "Annie . . ."

"I know," Bobby said. "I saw her."

Adam squeezed his eyes shut.

"So much happened," Adam said. "I have so much I have to tell you."

"Me too," Bobby said. "I need to tell you that I'm sorry, and I need to tell you about Dad."

44

ADAM

Adam would get answers. Sue still wasn't taking his calls. The need to know why she hadn't told him made him put in very long days at Jesse's shop.

His brother and mother circled the Cutlass now. Bobby didn't smile. He hadn't smiled since he'd woken up. He wore black grief like a shroud of tar slow and clinging. Perhaps Adam's brother hadn't loved his wife the way that Adam loved Vic, not that he'd drop the L-word into conversation anytime soon, but Adam knew he'd been wrong to doubt Bobby's feelings.

They'd buried her body on the Other Side, on Lookout Mountain. She'd have a dragon to watch over there, and no one would ever be fool enough to disturb her. It was easier than the questions. No one would blame Bobby. The elves had constructed a tidy paper trail of her leaving him.

"Well?" Adam asked, resisting the urge to wring his hands. "How'd I do?"

"It looks a lot better than before," Bobby admitted, drawing Adam back to the driveway. "You did all this yourself?"

Adam scratched the back of his head.

"Jesse helped me, especially with the body and the paint."

When he wasn't on the clock, he'd replaced the smashed panels and the hood. He'd scrounged for parts across three states, calling salvage yards and searching for them online.

Vic had ridden out with Adam, borrowing Jesse's old truck, to fetch pieces from Kansas and New Mexico. Cleared for the streets, he'd go back to his day job soon. So far he hadn't taken another soul. And he'd gone home, back to his apartment in Capitol Hill. It was small and sparse. Adam visited him there, though he had yet to stay the night.

Things between them were cool since Annie, and Adam did not blame Vic for that. He had no one to blame for anything except Death herself.

The car looked good, better even, but it wouldn't win any awards for accurate restoration.

"We couldn't match the paint," Adam said. "They don't make that color anymore."

"I like the black better," Bobby said.

Adam had to agree. The new paint had an inky shine.

"Mom, what do you think?"

Tilla circled the car at distance, nibbling her lip. She'd been quiet since Bobby had woken.

Adam knew he'd never bridge the distance between them. They'd each come as far as they could. But she liked Vic, and she took care of Bobby.

She'd go home soon, to guard Dad's secret grave. Adam would go with her. He had to know, though he worried that what he had with Vic wouldn't survive the distance. He hoped it would. He hoped he'd learn what he had to, make his peace with Sue, and find the warlock, the other warlock, for Seamus and for Annie. Because the note had lied.

There's still time to save her.

Adam pressed a hand to his chest. The pain felt like a ring around his heart, a tension. He would live it. It would remind him that magic had a cost.

He'd come all this way, hoped to solve a mystery. Now he only had a new one. His dad could not be the warlock, the dark druid. His dad had died.

Bobby had killed him, to save Adam, and the ache that put in his heart was almost as bad, sometimes, as the wound he'd inflicted on himself. Bobby—Robert—had saved his life.

His mother and brother's secret was laid bare, to Adam at least. Maybe, just maybe, the three of them could start to heal some of the space between them.

"Say something, Mom," Bobby prompted, pulling Adam back to the moment.

"I was just thinking that I always found it strange how much you loved this car," she said to Adam.

"Why?" he asked.

"Well you were conceived in it," she said, her face cracking with a faint, wistful smile.   *LoL*

Adam made a sound between "yuck" and "yeargh."

Maybe he didn't need their family to be as open and talkative as Vic's after all.

"Maybe you can find new seats," Bobby said, a little smile of his own dawning.

Adam thought that maybe, just maybe, they would be all right. In time. When the grief lessened.

The sense of it, the strange feeling of almost peace, followed Adam downstairs. It was over. For now.

With the Cutlass rebuilt, he'd put as much to bed as he could before he talked to Sue. He felt like sleeping for a week. Vic had the day off tomorrow. They could spend some time before Adam left.

Adam reached the basement, started unbuttoning his blue

coveralls from the shop, when he spied a shadow, something dark, curled at the foot of the bed.

"Spider?" he asked.

The black cat opened its green eyes and lifted its head.

All the weariness rushed out of him.

"Is Sue okay?" he asked.

The cat meowed, long and sad, then vanished.

Cold dread pulsed through Adam as he dialed the trailer. No answer.

He started throwing his clothes into his backpack.

If he drove straight through, he'd be there in twelve hours, ten if he drove like an elf. He'd call again and again until he heard her say she was all right.

Adam knew she wasn't.

ACKNOWLEDGMENTS

The list of people who helped bring Adam's story to you is long. Some of the biggest thanks go to the following people. I owe them so much for bringing a lifelong dream into reality.

My incredible agents, Lesley Sabga and Nicole Resciniti. To everyone at Blackstone, especially Rick Bleiweiss, who saw what I was trying to do with this book. To Marco Palmieri and Deirdre Curley for edits. To Mandy Earles and everyone in marketing. To Sean Thomas for the incredible cover. To James Persichetti, who leveled me up.

My partner, Brian McNees, who baked phrases from this book into fortune cookies for Valentine's Day.

To the friends and family who stood by me and believed in this bloody little windup toy of a book: Sara Albert, Mary Block, Marnie Christenson, Stephen Chubb, Nikki Cimino, Angela Del Ponte, Carisa Goho, Debby Haude, Adrian Hellberg, Suzanne Johnson, Lisa Manglass, Lynn McCormick, Bob McNees, Barbara Middleton, Neva Murphy, Richard Patrick, Lauren Piner, Bonner Slayton, Kaleb Slayton, Brian Staley, Alfred Utton, and Aaron Wood.

My aunt, Bonita Dyess, who first sparked my love of writing.

The amazing soon-to-be published writers, critique partners, and editors in my life: Elly, Amanda Barrentine, Cat Clyne, Katie Day, B. D. Ervin, Liz Freed, S. J. Kemsley, Erin Kennemer, Kim Klimek, Kim Lajevardi, Chad Mathine, David Myer, Amanda O'Connell, M. B. Partlow, Lee Sandwina, Anitra Van Prooyen, and Nikki VanRy.

Everyone at Pikes Peak Writers and Rocky Mountain Fiction Writers.

My rock stars, whose books I love: Rena Barron, Carol Berg, Lisa Brown Roberts, Veronica R. Calisto, Gail Carriger, Kat Cho, Kameron Claire, Helen Corcoran, Hilary Davidson, Alex Harrow, Sara J. Henry, Angie Hodapp, Josi Kilpack, Shannon Lawrence, Jenna Lincoln, Heather McCorkle, Axie Oh, Cecy Robson, M. R. Rutter, Angela Sylvaine, Mason J. Torall, Aimie Trumbly Runyan, Danica Winters, and Barbara Ann Wright.

And finally, those I've lost. I miss you every day: My grandmothers—Tilla Slayton, who read everything, and Juanita Dyess, who let me build worlds. Summit, the paw-shaped scar on my heart.

THE ADAM BINDER NOVELS,
BOOK 1